Counting Down

Counting Down

GERARD STEMBRIDGE

PENGUIN
IRELAND

PENGUIN IRELAND

Published by the Penguin Group
Penguin Ireland, 25 St Stephen's Green, Dublin 2, Ireland
(a division of Penguin Books Ltd)
Penguin Books Ltd, 80 Strand, London WC2R ORL, England
Penguin Group (USA) Inc., 375 Hudson Street, New York, New York 10014, USA
Penguin Group (Australia), 250 Camberwell Road, Camberwell, Victoria 3124, Australia
(a division of Pearson Australia Group Pty Ltd)
Penguin Group (Canada), 90 Eglinton Avenue East, Suite 700, Toronto, Ontario, Canada M4P 2Y3
(a division of Pearson Penguin Canada Inc.)
Penguin Books India Pvt Ltd, 11 Community Centre, Panchsheel Park, New Delhi – 110 017, India
Penguin Group (NZ), 67 Apollo Drive, Rosedale, North Shore 0632, New Zealand
(a division of Pearson New Zealand Ltd)
Penguin Books (South Africa) (Pty) Ltd, 24 Sturdee Avenue, Rosebank, Johannesburg 2196, South Africa

Penguin Books Ltd, Registered Offices: 80 Strand, London WC2R ORL, England

www.penguin.com

First published 2009
1

Copyright © Gerard Stembridge, 2009

The moral right of the author has been asserted

Grateful acknowledgement is made to reprint lyrics from 'Psycho Killer'.
Words by David Byrne, Chris Frantz and Tina Weymouth.
Music by David Byrne © 1976 (Renewed) Index Music, Inc. & Bleu
Disque Music Co., Inc. All rights administered by WB Music Corp.
Used by permission of Alfred Publishing Co., Inc.

Set in 13.5/16 pt Postscript Monotype Garamond
Typeset by Rowland Phototypesetting Ltd, Bury St Edmunds, Suffolk
Printed in Great Britain by Clays Ltd, St Ives plc

A CIP catalogue record for this book is available from the British Library

ISBN 978-1-844-88113-0

www.greenpenguin.co.uk

For Donal

Acknowledgements

Thanks to Neal Shanahan, Trevor White, Alan Maher, Ann Callanan, Seán Holmes, Anna Devlin, Patrick Gannon, Vincent Kelly and especially my editor, Patricia Deevy.

Transcript from a television news report, 20 November 2006

. . . This exclusive apartment block overlooking Dublin Bay was the unlikely setting for the grisly scene that unfolded this chilly winter morning. Gardaí were alerted by neighbours, concerned about an increasingly unpleasant odour coming from behind the door of the third-floor apartment. On gaining entry, what they discovered was shocking and tragic. Inside the luxury apartment, on a sofa, were the decomposing remains of a man. He may have been dead for two weeks or more.

The assistant state pathologist is at the scene right now, but because of the condition of the body it won't be possible to establish cause of death for some time. A Garda spokesperson refused to confirm or rule out any possibility, including foul play or suicide. The man cannot yet be identified, and even if, as seems most likely, he was the occupier of the apartment, very little seems to be known about him. The mailbox in the main hallway has no name on it, just the apartment number, and only one of his neighbours appears to have spoken to him. The young woman didn't wish to go on camera, but she told me he was a quiet, good-looking man in his mid-thirties, always rather distant. As if, she said, and I'm quoting here, 'nothing you might say would ever be of interest to him. He never even told me his name.'

25

Joe Power, realizing he had an hour to kill, stopped in Ballinalee. He knew there was no point in arriving early. Juliet wouldn't like that, and he didn't want any vibe whatsoever on the first access visit. It ought to be – had to be – civilized. Just as their last meeting had been, when they met to sign the papers; a bit stiff of course, but with no pugnacity; voices calm, with at least an attempt at warmth, which was conscious on his side, but he thought he detected it from her too. Their eyes had managed to meet. And why not, after all? She was getting everything she wanted. Willingly. She looked a little fatter that day.

Time passed in slow seconds. Joe sat in the car considering what to do. Farrell's across the road had a freshly painted black frontage, and new old-fashioned lettering on the windows. Wines and Spirits on the left and Undertakers on the right. Ho ho ho. He wondered if it had ever been true. Probably, way back in the dismal thirties and forties, that other Ireland. It might be pleasant to pass the hour in there with a Jameson and the morning paper? No. No. Definitely no. Joe turned his face from Farrell's bar and lounge and switched the radio on. The levees in New Orleans had been breached during Hurricane Katrina. It was a real live horror tale and a godsend to talk radio. A young-sounding male, with an authentic Southern American voice, was talking down a phone line.

'. . . And I guess what is really most tragic, is that it seems to be primarily folk from the poorest sections of town, mostly from the African-American community, who are worst affected . . .'

Big fucking shock horror surprise.

'. . . And I tell you something, these scenes unfolding now before the eyes of Americans are nothing less than apocalyptic. People are asking could this really be happening in their country? —'

Joe switched off. Was apocalyptic the most overused word of the new century? Every fucking chunk of ice that broke off and fell into the fucking foamy deep was a fucking apocalypse. He needed to get out of the car and do something to fill this lump of time. It would have been amusing if some locals had passed at that moment, so that he could have enjoyed their reaction to his Maserati, his recent 'single-again' gift to himself. But no one passed. Stepping away from the car, he stood alone at an empty crossroads. In the mild calm of mid-morning in Ballinalee, Joe Power listened, automatically sorting the soundscape into its individual elements. There was a car somewhere in the distance to his left, a tractor too, nearer but not approaching; birds all round of course, a cackling magpie and something sweeter he couldn't put a name to; his right ear caught a cow howling somewhere as if in agony or dread. In the village itself the only sound was the rattle of bottles in a crate somewhere, probably from the back of the pub. Further away, a heavy door slammed. Strangely, there was no human chatter or movement. There was literally no one on the street. What options were there? He could walk to the old Protestant church at the far end of the village. Juliet used always remark on it when they drove by. They always agreed that they must have a look inside, but never had. In fairness it never looked open.

And that was enough about the past.

Focusing on the slow present at not very long after eleven in the morning, Joe realized his choices were either to pay a pointless visit to Farrell's hardware shop thirty yards down the road to his left, or cross to the other side and buy a 99 or a Dairy Milk in Farrell's mini market. Joe suddenly noticed a little Garda station on the corner. How many times had he driven through Ballinalee in the last five years and never realized it was there? It just showed how little . . . stuck sometimes. It was, however, of no particular use to him now. Why the fuck did a dead village like this have a Garda station to itself in this day and age anyway? Joe stood gazing, listening, becalmed, resentful. He began to hear, deep inside himself, a rumble of blame directed at Juliet for putting him here at this moment. He was snared, unable to fill this oppressive hole in the day. The last day of summer. Literally nothing was moving around him. It was as if time had paused, and was just hanging around, waiting for him to do something? How long would this fucking hour last?

A car approached the corner from the Longford road, an old Opel Kadett station-wagon. Joe didn't hear it until he saw it, which was amazing given the clack of its old engine. It slowed as it turned the corner. The old driver had time to nod a country nod at Joe. There was something odd about the way he sat in the car, but Joe couldn't put his finger on what it was. Was he a dwarf or something? Forty or so yards further on, he turned into a small open area in front of the ugly Catholic church, parked boot out, opened the door, and struggled from his seat. Had he a hump on his back, was that it? He opened the boot. Joe saw that it was absolutely jammers. The old man took a piece of card-board from the car and went to the nearest streetlight pole. Suddenly, Joe knew not from where, he had a little hammer and some tacks in his hand. He tap-tapped quickly until the cardboard was fixed to the pole. Joe could read the hand-printed message clearly from where he stood.

CAR BOOT SALE – ALL DAY

The old man went back to the car. He started to unpack. Joe could see now that he wasn't a dwarf, and he didn't have a hump. He just carried himself strangely, his neck sunk into his shoulders. It was obvious he was no first-timer at the car boot sale game. He had a little system going. First, a series of small folding tables were arranged in what he probably thought was an elegant little arc. Then he started to create his display. Joe checked his watch: 11.11. It took about ten minutes to drive from Ballinalee to the cottage. The choice was to leave now and fill the time elsewhere or hang around for another forty minutes. The old man's car boot sale might be his salvation. More vendors might arrive soon, a whole relieving cavalry of them. There was room for at least a half-dozen cars on this patch. It might be a great kitsch-fest, fingers crossed. Would there be, maybe, a Sacred Heart lamp? He and Juliet had always wanted a proper old Sacred Heart lamp for the cottage . . . Enough of that. Stop. Now. Still, if he found one Joe decided he would buy it for her. It could be an amusingly appropriate peace offering.

Joe felt his mood lighten. Fuck it, he thought, the whole mess might work itself out in time. He and Juliet could even become pals or something, easy with each other. Milo would grow up absolutely cool with the whole situation. By the time he got to secondary school, half his class would be from separated homes anyway, more would be kids of single parents, and most of the rest would be from marriages that were, in reality, fucked up only the parties concerned wouldn't admit it. If Juliet persisted with her lunatic scheme of living in the Longford cottage, and renting out Brighton Vale – Joe couldn't believe it when he first heard that, but he was hardly in a position to say anything – it might actually work out well for him in the long run. The cottage was mickey mouse, only ever intended as a bolt-hole, for time out. By the time Milo was thirteen or fourteen, he would definitely think it so much cooler to spend time in his dad's high-end Dublin pad than in the arsehole of nowhere with his fat and bitter mother. In time, Joe would win. Just how attractive this grand prize would be was less certain. Would he want a teenage male suddenly in his space, dependent on him, as he reached his mid-forties? Well, who knew the future? Feeling a certain amused anticipation, Joe approached the tables, which were now pretty well groaning. The old man had managed to squeeze an astonishing amount of stuff into his car. Looking at it laid out now, Joe wouldn't have believed it all came out of one boot if he hadn't actually seen it himself. No sign of a Sacred Heart lamp. The old man clocked him. He nodded hello, but made no sound. Was that a smirk or just a naturally weird expression? The eyes shone bright from spiralled skin. Joe heard himself use a bantering tone.

'You've a nice day for it anyway.'

Again a nod rather than words as the old man continued some tasteful rearranging. Joe looked along the tables: plates, bowls, old cutlery, a battered wall clock, a sixties transistor radio, picture frames, assorted ashtrays, candlesticks. Crap really, and not even interesting crap. He began to rattle through a pile of plates. One design, which he guessed was from the 1940s, caught his eye; white with a simple green line round the edge; the kind of thing Juliet would say was just right for the cottage. He searched and found three such plates in all. He might as well buy something.

7

'How much?'

'A pound. Everything's a pound.'

Joe smiled.

'As in, a euro?'

'No. A pound.'

The old man made a little sighing noise and went to the car. He came back with a cardboard disk. He spun it slowly, concentrating. Joe recognized the cardboard euro conversion disk that every household had received from the government, way back when the currency changeover was happening. Was this old guy having him on?

'That's one euro twenty-seven cents.'

There was no flicker of a smile. Joe decided to play the game.

'Fair enough. I'll take these three. But hold on for a minute. I might buy more.'

The old man nodded. He took the three plates and put them in a little cardboard box. At the bottom of another pile Joe found real treasure. Fantastic! A plate with JFK and Jackie on it, hand-painted style, cheek to cheek; a golden, almost saintly couple. This was nearly as good as a Sacred Heart lamp. This was classic.

'Is this a pound as well?'

'Everything's a pound.'

Fair enough. A real bargain. Joe moved along the arc, re-energized, convinced he would turn up some other little treasure. His eyes almost passed over a small wooden box filled with assorted tennis balls, golf balls, and a couple of well-worn sliotars, but he noticed something odd. It was a moulded white plastic sphere, clean and bright amid the shabby used balls surrounding it. Looking at it more closely Joe saw it was not all white. It had a narrow rectangular black face, plastic, reflective. He picked it up. The sphere was perfectly smooth and round, with a matt finish, scratched from the passage of years; a mini space helmet on a plinth. A curious thing was, there seemed to be no buttons or switches. What did it do? How did it work? Joe turned it upside down, and saw a sliding piece set into the underside of the plinth. Even before he opened it, he knew it was a battery chamber. Of course there were none inside. What the hell was it? Turning it right side up again, he looked closely at the black plastic rectangle. It merely reflected his ballooned face, but if the thing was working presumably that would show a digital readout of some kind. On the bottom corner of the plinth a trademark name was impressed on the white plastic.

Millennium©.

Something about it reeked of the seventies; just had to be. Joe just about remembered the digital watch fad, but he had never owned one. This thing was clearly from the same period. It had the feel of a clock of some kind. Even if it wasn't the kind of kitsch he had been expecting, it was tempting. He held it up.

'Does this work?'

The old man looked up. The pause before his reply seemed long to Joe. Did something change in his eyes? He definitely heard something different in his voice when finally he spoke; a shift in tone, the slightest hesitancy. All the more surprising given that he spoke just three words.

'I don't know.'

Clearly the old man wasn't going to say any more.

'Well, do you know what it is?'

'Some class of a clock.'

Keep it a secret why don't you, Joe thought, but held his patience.

'Right. What kind of a clock?'

'You've never seen one before?'

So, Joe thought, it's the old 'answer a question with another question' technique.

'Like this? No.'

A shrug was the only response. Joe wondered what form of question would get him the information he wanted.

'So, is it just an ordinary digital clock?'

'No. Not as far as I know.'

This old fucker was obviously just taking the piss. The thing now, Joe thought, would be to say nothing more, and put the thing back where he got it. Let him go fuck himself. Joe placed it back in the box. It now seemed completely out of place there. He couldn't resist one last question.

'So if it's not a normal clock, what's it supposed to do?'

Suddenly, surprisingly, a relatively straight answer.

'Ah, it was one of those fad things. It was supposed to count down to the millennium.'

Joe leaned in and stared again into the narrow rectangular face, trying to see something beyond his own fat reflection. A countdown to the millennium? So. Not much use now then. A definite case of built-in obsolescence. He picked it up again and brought it to the old man, holding it towards him.

'Sorry if I'm being stupid, but could you explain how it worked, like without any dials or switches?'

The old man didn't take it from him. His eyes looked elsewhere.

'I never saw it working myself. Like I say, they were only a fad. Never took off. As far as I know, you put in the batteries, and a number came up on the thing there, the face, and that was supposed to be the exact number of seconds to the millennium.'

'Seconds?'

'Yeah. That's what I was told anyway. As I say, never saw it working.'

A memory stirred in Joe: a school tour to Paris in the early eighties? The Pompidou Centre? Hadn't he seen something like this on a giant digital readout?

'But back in the seventies, it would have been millions of seconds to the millennium.'

The old man shrugged. Joe felt a little buzz. He put down the clock, and took out his mobile. He searched for the calculator. Sixty by sixty . . . 3,600 . . . by 24 . . . 86,400 . . . by 365 . . . 31,536,000.

'Thirty-one million, five hundred and thirty-six thousand seconds is one year. So say . . . to make it easy . . . 1975, thirty years ago. By thirty that's . . . nine hundred and forty-six million and eighty thousand seconds. What about that?'

He picked up the clock again. Could the long narrow black plastic face fit that many digits? A thought occurred to him.

'Hold on. What about batteries? They'd never last that long. So what happened when they ran out?'

The old man shrugged.

'You haven't any, I suppose?'

'No.'

Joe wondered if Farrell's would have the right batteries. Suddenly he got impatient with himself. What was he hesitating for? It was a measly pound, one euro twenty-seven. That was all it would cost him to find out.

'A pound, yeah?'

It was hard to be sure with such a riddled face, but Joe thought the old man showed some surprise.

'You want it?'

'Yes.'

'Even though you don't know if it works any more or not?'

'I'm feeling reckless. I'll take a chance. So what's it altogether? Five pounds? Call it seven euro.'

'I've had that there for five years. No one ever offered to buy it before.'

'There you go, today's your lucky day.'

Joe wondered what was going on. Was the sly old fuck going to raise the price now?

'Are you going to try and get it working?'

'Well . . . yeah, if I can find the right batteries for it.'

'Well then . . .'

In the pause, Joe thought, here we go, rip-off time. Oh, I couldn't let this go for a pound. This is a seventies design classic. You'll have to make me a better offer. Fuck you old man.

'. . . Before I sell it to you, I'd better tell you how I got it.'

Joe noticed the time on the old man's watch. Jesus! 11.28 already.

'Look, I haven't much time I'm afraid. I'll pay you a pound for it. No more.'

'That's all it is. I told you everything was a pound.'

No rip-off? So what was the story?

'Fine, well let's do this then.'

The old man handed him the little box of purchases. He picked up his cardboard currency converter. Joe interrupted.

'Seven euro is more than enough, I promise.'

The old man reached for the money. As he did so, he caught hold of Joe's wrist.

'Please, let me tell you about the clock. For the sake of my conscience.'

Feeling his grip and seeing the brightness in the old man's eyes become a hard stare, it occurred to Joe that he was a bit loohla. Maybe that was what he had sensed about him from the start. Thankfully he was too frail to do any harm.

His conscience? Jesus Christ, what next? Joe had paid up and the cardboard box was in his hands. He should just go. He heard the church bell ring. 11.30. Why not give him three or four minutes? He could always cut him off if he started rambling.

'I'm in a bit of a hurry, but yeah, go on. What's the story?'

The old man began.

'When an old house is being sold off around the area, local auctioneers usually give me a shout to see if I want to buy the contents. Not the furniture now, I don't deal in the big items, just the bric-a-brac. Usually an all-in price for the lot. Early in 2000 I was asked to go to this house near Lanesborough. Taylor, the auctioneer, told me it was a bit of a tragic case. The owner was a Dublin barrister with plenty of money and time on his hands. The house was his hideaway. He wasn't married or anything. Do you see what I mean?'

The old man's inference was obvious. Joe allowed his impatience to be heard clearly.

'What? He was gay?'

'Yeah, a bit lavender right enough. Anyway, what happened was, he had a crowd down from Dublin for a big party he was having on the night of the millennium, and whatever state he got himself in, he had gone out on the road and got himself knocked down. Killed instantly. I'd heard something about it all right, it was in the papers an' all, I suppose happening on the night it did. Anyway, the place was being sold up, and they wanted to get rid of the contents. Taylor tipped me the wink that they'd accept any kind of a reasonable offer, if I took everything away there and then. Whoever was handling the estate just wanted to get shut of it. Grand so, I went down for a look. Straight away I could see plenty of good stuff. He had any God's amount of nice little knick-knacks; very sellable. I mentioned a meagre enough sum, and the Dublin fellah said fine, take it away. No argument. I won't go through all the items he had –'

'No, don't, look, I have to be going –'

'Wait! Listen now.'

Joe heard insistence in his voice. His eyes had lost their smirk. It seemed almost as if he was frightened that he wouldn't get to say his piece. He spoke faster.

'When I noticed that thing –'

He pointed at the white plastic sphere.

'I said, what in God's name is that, the same as you did earlier. The same as hundreds of people since, who had a notion to buy it off me, but never did in the end. What is it? I could tell straight away they weren't too happy at me asking, Taylor and especially the fellah from Dublin, the friend of the deceased, or whatever he was if you see what I mean. What is it? I asked them again. What's the big mystery? Taylor dived in first, trying to pass it off. Some kind of an old clock, he said, it's worthless, you'll probably end up throwing it away, but you know yourself, he said, that's how it goes, you take all or nothing. Do you know what the pair of them were like? They were like two school-boys caught smoking behind the toilets. I'd only asked out of normal curiosity because I'd never seen a thing like it before, but now I was . . . well, I was a bit suspicious. I looked at the thing a bit more closely. I thought the same as yourself. How did it work? I found where the batteries went. They were still in there. Dead of course. All that only took a few seconds I'd say, but the silence was pure deadly. You'd swear it was a bomb I had in my hand.'

Joe Power had now forgotten about time passing. He was trying to figure out what was coming. The old man paused, confident his listener was hooked. Then he resumed more slowly, pointedly.

'Your man from Dublin decided he'd better give me a proper answer. He told me what had happened. Maurice he called him, the dead man, had bought that thing in Paris in 1976. He was told the same as I told you, that it would count down second by second to the millennium. He thought it was the best thing out. He loved all that kind of stuff, your man said. He called it something, can't think of the word . . .'

Kitsch. Joe guessed silently.

'. . . Gave it pride of place on his shelf, loved showing it to people. "Look," he'd say, "stand looking at that for a while, see your life disappear second by second by second. It's a terrifying thing." Anyway . . . he bought the place in Lanesborough back in 1993 –'

Coincidence. Joe had bought Brighton Vale the same year.

'A few months before the millennium he started inviting all his special friends down for a big do. From what your man said, once Maurice invited you, that was it, you had to go.'

Joe knew the kind of people the old man was talking about. College had been full of them. He could hear them in his head. VSF only. Very special friends. 'It'll be fabulous. Maurice's hospitality is legendary.'

'Everyone was told that they were welcome from the middle of the morning for champagne and a bit of grub. By the afternoon people were fairly well-on already. Your man Maurice was making a big thing out of the clock. He'd put it on the mantelpiece so that everyone could see the countdown all the time. People were knocking crack out of it, you know, shouting out how many seconds were left and clinking their glasses. Of course none of them did the sums. They had better things to be doing. By the time it got dark sure most of them were in no condition to count to ten without tripping over themselves . . .'

Joe could imagine the scene very well; all over the world the same story. Like their own millennium madness in Dromoland Castle with Shane and Orla, Rory and Lisa, Steve and Karen. What a night. When Milo was conceived.

'. . . But there was this one fellah, another barrister. He was staring at the clock for ages, like he was hypnotized. He started working it out. Next thing he's over to Maurice, having a sneer. The clock is wrong, he says. There's too many seconds.'

Joe could hear the smug stretched vowels braying above the drunken hubbub. 'Too many seconds I'm afraid, Mo darling. Too many ticks and too many tocks.' Then rummaging for what he imagined was a bon mot: 'Seems you may have some time on your hands.'

'. . . Tried to shut him up, but of course people start taking notice. Next thing a few more are trying to work it out, to see if he's right. People are getting pens and bits of paper. It's just coming up to eleven, so it's easy enough to work it out. Your man told me he could tell from looking at Maurice that he was starting to worry that the clock might be wrong . . .'

A man who hated being wrong, Joe suspected.

'. . . Because he'd gone on and on about this clock for years. It takes a while to figure it out because everyone is pie-eyed at this stage. No one is listening to anyone else. They all have a different estimate. Next thing Maurice tries to take the clock away, to stop them, but someone grabs it off him and runs away with it up the stairs. From the way your man told me the story he had this bozo down as the real troublemaker. He shouldn't even have been at the party, according to your man. It was like he blamed him for everything. Anyway, a few go after him, but Maurice doesn't.

It's getting very near midnight and the millennium. Next thing the young fellah comes back down, holding up the clock and saying he's worked it out for sure. He makes everyone shut up and tells them that it's out by twelve minutes and twenty-four seconds –'

Joe interrupted.

'You mean that at midnight the clock would still have that much to run?'

'Yes. Seven hundred and forty-four seconds. The young fellah gets a kind of a chant going: "Seven-hundred-and-forty-four, seven-hundred-and-forty-four," and that's when, your man told me, that's when Maurice goes for him and the two of them wrestle on the ground, and he finally gets the clock away from him, and goes off into a corner. Won't talk to anyone. Next thing someone shouts out there's only a minute to go, so the real countdown starts and everyone is gathering round in a big circle. Maurice won't join in. Some people go over and try to drag him back but he won't be budged. Your man said it was as if just by staring at the clock he could somehow work out what had gone wrong with the thing. So now it's only ten seconds to midnight, and people just let him be. They look at the telly and count down the last few seconds. Everyone starts jumping and hugging and singing Aul' Lang Syne, no one is taking any notice of the poor fellah any more. After a few minutes your man said he went over to try and talk to him, but Maurice suddenly jumps up and says, "I'm throwing it in the river, that'll be the end of it," and he ran out of the house.'

The old man stopped talking. He seemed to need a break. Joe felt certain he knew what was coming next and asked.

'How long after midnight was it at this stage?'

The old man acknowledged what Joe was thinking with a nod.

'I should tell you this fellah's house was set up high, with a clear view of the Shannon just across the road. He even owned a lump of land at the river itself. He had a boat moored there. Very nice. That day I was there I was able to look out the window and see exactly where the thing had happened, at the same time as his friend from Dublin was describing it to me. It was freezing out on the night. No one went chasing after him. A few smoking outside saw him open the gate and go across the road, but no one remembered hearing the car, and the headlights seemed to come out of nowhere. They heard the brakes and then a bump. They ran down straight away. Some said they saw him die just as they arrived. Then someone noticed the clock lying next to his hand . . .'

The old man paused and shrugged at Joe.

'Well now, you see, no one can say for certain that he died at the exact second that the clock got to zero, but from the way your man told me the story, everyone who was there believes that that is what happened. That clock was counting down his life for twenty-four years.'

Joe Power waited, afraid there was going to be a bad joke now, a shaggy-dog punchline. He was relieved when the old man said, 'That's exactly the story as I heard it. Your man was there himself that night. He was giving me fair warning. He told me if I didn't take the clock I couldn't have the rest of the stuff. What I did with it after that, he said, was my own business. But he wasn't going to touch it.'

Joe felt the plastic hard and cool in his hand as he held it up.

'So do you believe this thing somehow foretold how long this barrister was going to live?'

'What I'm telling you is, I never tried to find out. I haven't as much as opened that battery thing there since the day I

18

got it. That's why I don't even know if it works or not. So anyway. As long as you know.'

Quite suddenly Joe became aware of sounds left and right. Clatter. Chat. A car pulling up. He looked around. Four more cars had joined the car boot sale. The owners had set up their stalls. Locals were arriving for a gawk. There was a cheerful hum. How much time had passed? Joe picked up his box of goodies.

'Buyer beware, ha?'

'That's right.'

People of this old lad's generation didn't understand how for Joe's generation a warning of the possibility of something 'other' was enticing; the combination of kitsch and the supernatural, pretty well irresistible.

'Well . . . I've paid for it now. I'll take my chances.'

He foresaw the scene: a few of the guys round the table at his place; booze, a deck of cards and in the centre, the countdown clock. Batteries. Joe would retell the story he had just heard, with suitable flourishes. Which of them would then be drunk enough or cool enough to tempt his fate on the turn of a card or some other game, and set the clock in motion? Just for a laugh.

24

When Joe sat into the Maserati he decided it was sunny
enough to put the top down. His pleasure as the roof slid
back was interrupted when he noticed the dashboard clock.
It was 11.58. Now he would be ten minutes late to pick up
Milo. Fuck. There would be tension after all. He pulled away
fast to make up time. More ammunition for Juliet. At least
he had the plates as proof of good intentions. Anyway, ten
minutes or so, she couldn't make any trouble about that,
not when he had to travel ninety miles from Dublin to visit
his son. The road from Ballinalee was narrow and twisting.
Joe liked speeding on roads like this, but he was annoyed
that it was the threat of Juliet's disapproval caused him to
go so fast this time. Well, fuck her. Juliet had nothing to do
with this day at all, in actuality. He was going to spend his
rightful access time with his son. Things should get simpler
from here on in. He certainly wouldn't be making trouble.
Both sides seemed to be happy that it was a fair deal all
round. Certainly she had no cause for complaint. Joe was
cool about everything, apart maybe from Juliet's loony-tunes
decision to live in Longford. Joe couldn't believe she was
going ahead with her bullshit plan to start Milo in a local
school in a couple of days. What would it be, some grey
one-room job, with a turf fire, all the local kids talking in
that really aggressive accent? He hoped she wasn't doing
this just to piss him off, to make life hard for him travelling
up and down for visits. Joe suddenly thought of millennium
night, and the weird coincidence of the gay barrister bowing

out more or less as their little boy was springing to life. Juliet and Joe rocking the four-poster in Dromoland Castle, almost sober again by four o'clock. The best New Year ever maybe. Without doubt the best New Year fuck ever. How about that; their millennium baby, starting school in a couple of days. Rounding the dogleg near Black Horse Lane at 100 kph would have not been a problem if the old banger coming towards him wasn't taking the bend on the wrong side of the road. There was no more than fifty yards between them and closing fast, so Joe's instinctive wrench left would have been of no value if the stupid fucking bollocks coming at him hadn't got his act together at the last second and pulled equally fast towards his proper side. The relief that they had passed each other without even a scrape caused Joe to brake hard before the approaching hedge did any damage, and jump out of the car screaming.

'You fucking stupid fucking thick fucking –'

On and on he let it all out, punching at the disappearing old banger.

Joe, calmer, got to the cottage eleven and a half minutes late. He noticed with a smirk that the hedge at the entrance had not been cut back. Juliet had nagged and nagged about that hedge. It was too big. It concealed the entrance. Get it cut. There were many little niggles that wore him down in the end, that made him rage. Now that Juliet was living there full-time, she had done nothing about the hedge herself. Such bullshit. He figured a little extra roar from the engine as he swung in the entrance would bring Milo to the window. He hadn't seen the Maserati yet. Joe had described it in detail over the phone. Milo appeared, smiled, and disappeared again. The question that had been on Joe's mind, about whether or not he should use the front door key still in his possession, did not arise. As he stepped from the car, Juliet opened the door, and let Milo run to his dad. She smiled; not a particularly warm smile as far as Joe could see, but he understood what it meant. There would be no comment on his late arrival. Fortunately, given what he had just been through, she seemed to have decided to avoid tension on this first visit.

'Hey! Milo the lad. How are you?'

Milo's excited run, the lift, the hug, eased Joe through the first moments. A turn to the Maserati would buy a little more time, but as he did so Milo grabbed his daddy's hair.

'Why is your hair so long?'

Joe laughed but couldn't think of anything to say to that. Instead he spoke to Juliet.

'I stopped at a car boot sale. Saw some things I thought you might like.'

Which allowed him to turn away after all, to retrieve the box. They met again closer to the car.

'Thanks. Oh. Very nice.'

Juliet's tone suggested she really did like the old plates. Good. That was good then. Joe realized the millennium clock was still in the box. He reached out and took it back.

'Except that. That's for me.'

'What is it?'

It would have been odd to start into the long story. Somehow inappropriate.

'A bit of seventies rubbish. Some kind of a digital clock.'

'It looks so seventies.'

'I'm not even sure if it works. I have to get batteries for it.'

He showed her the battery chamber.

'Anyway, times-a-moving. We'd better go, Milo the lad.'

'So where are you taking him? Or is it a secret?'

It was spoken lightly but Joe heard scepticism underneath. He attempted the same tone in reply.

'Well, we're so spoilt for choice around here, you know.'
She spoke quietly as Milo ran to the car.

'Joe.'

'Yeah?'

'Just . . . well, just try and listen to what Milo wants.'

Smothering his anger, he smiled and nodded like he was saying, good idea thanks, but as he joined Milo in the car, he thought, fuck you, fuck you, you had to try and tell me what to do and how to do it didn't you, fuck you! You couldn't let it alone could you, with your mature understanding nod, fuck you! And of course she hadn't even acknowledged the car, pretending not to notice it. Now in a really foul temper, he flung the millennium clock into the back and fastened Milo in. They waved and smiled and called 'Byeeee' to Juliet as Joe reversed back on to the road. Don't fucking tell me how to spend my time with my son. Juliet, still smiling, mouthed, 'Six o'clock.' As if Joe didn't know how much access time had been agreed with a review after two years. How many seconds would that be on the clock? Three thousand, six hundred in an hour, so . . . six sixes thirty-six . . . six threes is eighteen and three is twenty-one . . . twenty-one thousand, six hundred seconds to fill. Less nearly twenty-two minutes already. Time flies. Joe knew he took off too fast. He'd slow down in a moment after he had explained to Milo about how powerful the Maserati was.

'It's fast, isn't it?'

'Yes. Mummy can't come today. She has to clean the house.'

Milo sounded reasonably convinced as he said it. Fair dues Mummy, for reassuring him like that, instead of saying Daddy is so mean, he won't let me come with you today my darling. Was Juliet intending to do a lot of house-cleaning once a month for the next few years? Maybe when she settled into rural life she'd be able to expand her range of excuses. Mummy can't come with us today, she's milking the cows, she's cleaning out the pigsty, the donkey has the flu. Joe slowed down.

'Hear the sound of the engine. Isn't that cool, huh?'

Milo nodded.

'Are you comfy back there? Listen, there's a special speaker just for you.'

He turned on *Sign O' The Times* and shifted the sound to the back speakers.

'How's that. Isn't that brilliant?'

Milo smiled and nodded. Joe allowed Prince to fill the silence for a while, giving himself time to consider what activities might be available in Longford town for separated fathers hoping to entertain their sons. Was there a McDonald's? Surely. A toy shop maybe? There was definitely a cinema; Joe remembered he and Juliet going to something on a freezing wet night a couple of winters ago. The restaurant that once got the nod from the Bridgestone guide probably wasn't the kind of thing Milo would appreciate, and he had to remember to listen to what Milo wanted, didn't he? Wasn't he lucky that Juliet was around to remind him of stuff like that. McDonald's was the best bet. Milo would love it, and it would probably annoy Juliet. Two birds with one stone. As they approached the town centre, he tried to think where it might be located. He had no picture of it in his head.

They stopped at a red light near St Mel's cathedral.

'Milo, guess where we're going to now?'

'I don't know.'

'Take one guess.'

'The car park?'

Joe laughed, but he couldn't help being a little disappointed that he was failing to raise Milo to a pitch of excitement about his special day out. He had always been a very placid child, which had been a total relief when he was a baby. It would be a bit worrying, though, if this rural existence made him more introverted and dull. It would be a long six hours – well, more like five hours now – if Joe had to work constantly to keep the happy sappy levels pumped up all the time.

'Well, you like burgers, don't you?'

'Yeah.'

'And you like fries?'

'Yeah.'

'And you lo-ove milkshakes.'

'Yeah.'

'So, guess where we're going for lunch?'

Milo didn't seem to know what the answer was. This was harder than expected. What was up with the kid? Back in Dublin he had often pestered Daddy and Mummy to go to McDonald's.

'Oh, come on. It's not that hard to guess. I thought it was your favourite place in the whole universe.'

'McDonald's?'

Thank Christ.

'Yeah, got it in one.'

'Mummy says there's no McDonald's in Longford.'

Oh, fuck you, Juliet, Joe thought. What did you say that for? How selfish can you get? He smiled and winked.

'Maybe Mummy didn't know where to look. But maybe we're smarter. We're going to find it together, yeah?'

After half an hour of scouring the town, Joe was silently enraged to discover that Mummy seemed to be right. Reluctant to give up, he decided he would have to approach a local to find out one way or the other. The best bet was some lumpy fifteen-to-seventeen-year-old, the type who probably frequented McDonald's. Two hefty girls in school uniform crossed the road towards him. Perfect. They had a bit of a strut about them. Bold straps as his mother would have said. They wouldn't be fazed by a strange older man approaching them, especially with a sweet little kid holding his hand. Jesus, their skirts were short. What kind of nuns were running this school? Did the little sluts hitch them up? The little sluts seemed happy to help.

'Ah yeah, it's below at the roundabout.'

Joe had driven through a roundabout on his way into town.

'Which roundabout?'

'Down by B & Q.'

There was a B & Q in Longford?

'What direction?'

The girls pointed.

'Out the Newtownforbes road.'

'Is it far?'

'Have you a car like? It's a bit far to walk.'

Back to the car park, get the car, go to McDonald's and return in time for the movie? Not possible. One of the girls looked down and smiled at Milo.

'Is it chips you want? Luigi's is brilliant. Much better than stupid old McDonald's, I swear.'

Joe, deflated, thanked them. He sank down on one knee, eye-level with Milo; a big smile.

'Well now. Mummy was right after all. There is no McDonald's *in* Longford. It's *outside* the town, way too far away to go there today. But next time, I promise, we'll definitely go. OK?'

Milo nodded placidly. Joe had to think of something fast

to get things back on track again. He suddenly spotted a possible solution far down the street.

'But we have just enough time before the movies for an even better special treat.'

The girl in Torc Café put a mug of creamy hot chocolate and a fat slice of home-made chocolate cake in front of Milo. She smiled.

'Mmm . . . how 'bout that now, chubby cheeks?'

Joe nodded thank you to the girl, and grinned at his boy, who already had a choccie ring around his mouth.

'How about that? Yummy, huh?'

Milo agreed it was yummy. Joe was fairly sure he wasn't just being nice to his dad. Let him burrow his way through that feast. For the first time since he had left the car boot sale man, Joe felt himself relax a little. Crisis over; the easing dark of the cinema to come. Joe's espresso was pretty good, there was no shriek and whine of other children, just women talking quietly amid a pleasant hiss of coffee machines and clatter of mugs. It was nearly two o'clock; two hours down, four to go.

There was better luck at the cinema. The kids' movie was *Madagascar* and they got there in time for the start. Milo definitely seemed happy now. The day was back on track. Fifteen minutes in, Joe could tell that Milo's favourite character was Melman the hypochondriac giraffe. As far as Joe was concerned, he just sounded like Ross from *Friends* but Milo wouldn't know that. At least not yet. No doubt he would grow up watching the endless repeats, thinking, 'Ross sounds just like Melman, the giraffe in *Madagascar*?' If he still remembered. And hey, maybe he would. Wouldn't it be fantastic if this trip to the cinema turned out to be one of those special childhood moments? Even though, as cartoons went, this one seemed very average to Joe, he still liked

27

the romantic idea that Milo might treasure this time, and *Madagascar* would always have a special resonance for him.

Two years before, Joe had voted for *Star Wars* in an online Channel 4 poll of the greatest film of all time. He had suddenly decided to vote out of some sentimental bullshit memory of his mother bringing him and Denis Crowley to see, what at nine years old, living in Ballyphehane, was the most brilliant movie ever. Had his mother found *Star Wars* as tiresome as he was beginning to find *Madagascar*? If so, he never knew. Just like Milo would never know. Joe promised himself that he would try not to say, 'Yeah, but it wasn't really as good as . . .' Instead he would say, 'Wasn't it fantastic, and who was your favourite character?' The giraffe, he was sure, which was a pity because actually Skipper the penguin was easily the funniest of a not very funny lot, but Joe promised himself that under no circumstances would he impose his opinion on the boy. It was at that moment it occurred to him to try out his favourite animal joke, the snail joke. He noticed Milo laughing at some of the smarter references in the movie, so maybe he was already bright enough to get the snail joke.

It was almost twenty-past four when they left the cinema. An hour and forty minutes to go. For the life of him, Joe couldn't think of a reason to hang around Longford any longer. What to do? He didn't want to give Juliet the satisfaction of bringing Milo home early. He could take the long way round and stop at the lake. That would be something. Walking back to the car, Joe asked Milo who his favourite character was.

'Melman, he was funny.'

Even though he totally disagreed with him, Joe was pleased that he understood his son so well. As soon as they were back in the car, he decided to try out the snail joke.

28

'I have a great joke for you, Milo. Ready? Belt up first. This man is all alone in his house late one night, it's a really warm summer night.' Joe made a sound like cicadas. 'Suddenly he sees a disgusting slimy sluggy snail crawling across his kitchen floor. Ugh! So, what does he do?'

'He squashes him.'

'No, he wouldn't ever do that to a snail, even if it was slimy and sluggy and disgusting. No, what he does is, he picks him up, opens the back door, and throws him out on to the nice soft wet grass. Problem solved. Now. It's six months later. OK? Six months. Now it's a winter night, and it's freezing and the winds are blowing.' Joe whistled a storm. 'The guy is all alone in his kitchen again, making himself some kind of sandwich, what do you think?'

'Banana.'

'OK, a banana sandwich.'

This was going well. Milo was smiling. Joe tapped the dashboard.

'Suddenly! He hears someone at the door. Who is that at this hour of the night? he thinks. Taptaptap. So he goes to the door to find out what's going on. He opens the door. He can't see anyone. He looks left and right and up and down, and then he sees right at his feet . . . guess what? The same snail looking up at him. The same snail he threw out six months before. And the snail looks really annoyed and he says to the guy. "Hey you, wha-wha-what did you do that for?"'

Milo laughed. Joe was delighted. He wasn't sure if Milo really got it, or if he was laughing because Joe made the snail speak in Melman's whiney giraffe voice. What the hell. He laughed. What concept of Time could an almost-five-year-old have, anyway?

The long way home took them through Ballinalee. It wasn't until they approached the village that Joe remembered

29

the millennium clock in the back seat. He had forgotten to buy batteries in Longford. As he drove through the crossroads he looked left. There was no sign of the old man or his car boot sale colleagues. Show over. Just before they reached Dring shore, it started to rain. Joe stopped suddenly and spoke as if in a panic.

'Ohmygosh it's raining. We're going to get so wet! No, I've an idea! Maybe . . .'

His finger hovered over a selection of buttons. He pressed one.

'This one. Shh! Listen.'

A noise came from behind as the roof began to rise up from the boot.

Milo looked up delightedly as the roof passed over his head. Joe wiped his forehead.

'Whew! We're going to be dry after all. Snug as bugs in a rug.'

At seven minutes after five, they turned into Dring shore car park; still more than fifty minutes to fill. Milo was puzzled.

'What are we doing, Daddy?'

'Well, I was thinking it would be nice to take a little walk by the lake, but now it's raining. Let's wait and see if it stops.'

'OK.'

They sat for a few seconds. The sound of the rain on the soft top was slightly agitating Joe. He knew the rhythmic whirr of the windscreen wiper would get to him even more. He racked his brain for distraction. Milo spoke first.

'Are you staying with us tonight?'

Joe noticed how even an almost-five-year-old can pretend to make an important question sound casual.

'No, I can't. I have to be up for work early tomorrow.'

Now Joe heard a sadder shade in the child's tone.

'Will you have your dinner with Mummy and me before you go back?'

'No, I'm sorry, Milo. You see, I have some work to do tonight as well. So I have to hurry back to Dublin.'

Milo said nothing more. Joe could sense him thinking this out. Being a smart kid, he was probably wondering why they were sitting in a car watching the rain, if Daddy was in such a hurry. Joe thought of a distraction.

'Hey, Milo the lad, you want to sit in the driver seat?'

'Can I?'

'Sure.'

Joe unstrapped the boy, who clambered forward as Joe got out and ran through the now heavy rain to the passenger side. When he sat in Milo was holding the millennium clock.

'What is it, Daddy?'

'I'm not really sure. I don't even know if it works.'

Milo pressed his eyes against the black rectangle as if trying to see beyond.

'Is it a scary thing?'

'No, it's a silly thing. Just a kind of clock. I have to get batteries for it. Anyway, never mind that, you're getting your first driving lesson. Ready? Take hold of the wheel.'

Milo handed over the clock, and put his little hands on the wheel. Joe guided him along.

'Now, this car is so powerful you have to be really careful. You know it's probably the most powerful car in the world. But listen. You hear how quiet the engine is? Mmmmmmm . . . can you make that sound? . . . Mmmmmmm . . .'

Milo made the sound along with his daddy.

'OK, you're going straight along the road. Now there's a little bend, so turn the wheel left . . . left, yeah, that's it, nice and slow . . . well done, what a driver! Now in a minute we're going to go right . . .'

Joe managed to run the clock down until about 5.40. He decided that was enough. If he took it nice and slowly round the lake, they would arrive back with just a few minutes to spare. Perfectly respectable. A great day out. Fifty kph all the way, he eyed the dashboard clock most of the journey home. Milo just stared out the window, in his own world. He seemed content though, yeah? Hard to tell with such a silent kid; still, maybe better this way than a whining brat. Joe turned into the drive of the cottage at four minutes to six. He saw Juliet come to the window. By the time he and Milo had unbuckled and stepped out of the car, she had opened the front door, and was calling.

'Quick, Milo. Out of the rain.'

Joe hugged him.

'See you soon.'

'Thanks, Daddy. It was brilliant.'

He ran to his mother. She ushered him inside. Joe didn't approach, but nodded to say everything had been great. Her smile and little wave goodbye were reasonably warm. Joe started the car and reversed quickly. Suddenly he saw Juliet gesturing for him to stop. He did. She gestured him to hold on and disappeared inside. She returned a couple of seconds later opening an umbrella. She ran down to the car.

'Did you get batteries for the weird clock?'

'No, I forgot.'

'Could I see it again?'

He passed it to her. Juliet looked at the battery chamber. 'Yeah. Hold on.'

She was already trotting back to the cottage when Joe felt a strong need to call her back. If her intention was to put batteries in the clock something urged him to stop her. He called out, his voice tighter than he would have expected.

'It's fine, don't worry. Juliet!'

She paid no attention and disappeared inside. Joe opened his door, then closed it again. For God's sake, following would be bonkersville, he thought. What was the problem with putting batteries in the clock? He didn't even know if the thing would work. The next moment a little smiling procession emerged from the cottage. Milo was in front holding the clock proudly. Juliet walked behind, carrying the umbrella over Milo's head. Joe saw the bright red light of the digital readout. Juliet said, 'The batteries for the transistor. I thought they looked like the right size. It seems to work all right – sort of.'

They were now near enough for Joe to see the numbers clearly. 5472715 registered in his brain as it quickly changed.

5472714 . . . 13 . . . 12 . . .

Juliet shrugged.

'Well, it works. It started up straight away as soon as the batteries were put in. Any idea what you're supposed to do with it?'

Joe didn't know. He didn't know why those particular numbers had appeared. He wasn't even sure exactly what the clock was now counting down to. His brain was suddenly too agitated to compute immediately how many weeks or months almost five and a half million seconds translated into. Instinct told him, not very many.

23

It was much later than Joe Power thought when he finally left Lillie's. Six minutes to four, how completely fucked was that? The last time he'd looked at his watch it was way before two, he couldn't remember exactly now, but way earlier, as he weaved Marianna on to the dance floor, certain that he was 'on'. She had approached him, yeah? She had let her eyes linger when he first noticed her on the far side of the circular bar. A few minutes later she had just happened to be standing next to him. It was so obvious. He hadn't even been particularly drunk at that stage, so there was no way he had misread the signals.

Joe's anger couldn't find focus. His headache was stoking it. He noticed, as he turned up Wicklow Street, that his fists were clenched. He felt his dick still semi-hard against his jeans. Even though he had been a long time off the scene, he still had a nose for the game and, as far as he was concerned, she had been into him for sure for sure. When they kissed for fuck's sake, when their lips touched, he felt her tongue snake out and tickle his teeth. Her fingers dug into his arse. It was all as Joe had remembered from years before. Better actually. Simpler. Faster. More direct. Best of all, Marianna couldn't have been more than mid-twenties. It felt like he had never been away. Once they got to exchanging mobile numbers, it seemed reasonable to presume it was just a question of deciding the old his place her place conundrum. Joe was easy either way.

'So, will we head?'

'You want to leave?'

'Well, you know. It's later than you think.'

She had looked at him for a few seconds before replying. 'Yeah, you're right.'

Which seemed to settle it. And then, with the exit door in sight. 'Do you mind walking me to the taxi-rank?'

That sounded odd in Joe's ears. Although the way she said it didn't sound like a brush-off. Was he misunderstanding something? Marianna had let her arms hang about his neck and had drawn him in closer. Her whisper was clear despite the noise all round.

'Look, Joe. I'd really like to see you again. Like really. Over the weekend even. Tomorrow if you like. I'll make time. But I'm like, going to go home now.'

What was he supposed to say to that?

In the doorway of Tower Records Joe saw a bundle with a young man's sleeping head sticking out. He was wrapped up well enough. All organized. What was someone his age doing living like that? Why didn't he get his act together? Joe had heard about a new fad in Dublin, night-club guys pissing on homeless guys just for fun. Only now could he appreciate what satisfaction there might be in lobbing it out and aiming a hot angry piss at this fucker, or gobbing something rancid on to his head. How long had he spent with that bitch? Two, two and a half hours? What a waste of time. How many double vodkas and Coke? Nearly four o'clock and here he was alone; no better off than fuckface snoozing there. Joe swayed on towards Georges Street. Part of his brain was insisting that the smart move would be to wave down a taxi immediately, get home and into bed a.s.a.p. Write off the night and start again tomorrow. Another part kept him hanging on, stumbling on through the night.

Gays were swarming outside the George as Joe crossed

the road. It occurred to him that if he was to go in there, chances were he could have his cock sucked no problem, even at this hour. As if to confirm this, he was pretty sure he got a sly look back from a guy passing with his pal. Joe stopped and let his eyes close, listening, swaying a little. Same old thump as in Lillie's, same buzz of chat-up bullshit, only everyone being guys they just got there faster, and no messing. Same drink, same drugs probably. So why not? What if he didn't even look down at whoever it was? He could just close his eyes like this and remember Marianna; not the crap at the end obviously, but the moment when, easing closer to her as she had perched on the bar stool, nudging his hard-on against the inside of her thigh, he had felt her press back. Any decent pair of lips would do if he could summon up that image again. He'd often thought that a big plus for gays was that obviously they were better at cocksucking than most women. Surely, having one themselves, they knew exactly what a cock required. Joe opened his eyes. Men were everywhere, clusters, couples, hopeful glancing loners. The problem was though, even the prettiest, campiest disco-bunny was still basically, disappointingly, guy-shaped. Closing his eyes wouldn't help, not if he had seen him in the first place. Maybe . . . maybe if truly he did not know whether it was a man or a woman, it might work; disembodied strong full lips, a brazen little flicking tongue, and teasing teeth.

It suddenly occurred to Joe that he had been standing there for a long time. Someone he knew might have passed in a car and spotted him. That would shed new light on the marriage break-up right enough. Joe Power on the pull outside the George on a Friday night. Juicy news. Funny actually. Some of the gays from the ad agencies might be in there right now, dancing the night away; Trevor perhaps, with that ancient boyfriend of his. If they came out and saw him . . . Joe realized he didn't like that so much. Go home, Power, for fuck's sake, go home! His brain screamed. He pushed on and turned left on Dame Street. There was a bit of a gale force blowing down from Christchurch. Everyone seemed to be huddling into a chosen mate, touching and cuddling. The huge queue at the Drinklink opposite the Olympia seemed entirely composed of snogging couples of one preference or another. Everyone else was having a party and everyone else had someone. Had he made a wrong call? Maybe he should have walked Marianna to a taxi-rank. Maybe she'd have changed her mind at the last minute. Joe suddenly thought, oh fuck, no! What if it was a little test? Some bullshit game to make herself feel like she wasn't a slut? They'd get to the taxi-rank and once she was sure he was a decent guy, content to kiss and say goodnight, she'd change her mind all of a sudden and go back to his place. Fuck, no! No way! Why hadn't he just made a date? He'd have set himself up for the rest of the weekend at least. No, no, he had been right. That wasn't what he wanted. No time for dates and all that rigmarole. He had been totally right. He had done the right thing. No messing. He had left her in no doubt how he felt.

'Are you serious?'

'Yes, but listen, don't think that –'

'After . . . after what . . . how long? So . . . like . . . what? You were just wasting my time? Prickin' around?'

'Sorry?'

'What time is it now?'

'What?'

'It's too late, that's what time it is? So what am I supposed to do now? How am I going to get myself a fuck at this stage, you cunt?'

He felt himself fighting the wind as he passed City Hall. He'd have been home long ago if he'd grabbed a taxi as soon as he left Lillie's. If he hadn't been in such a rage. Now he was stuck in between. He didn't want to walk any more, but he was so close to home that he would just get grief from a taxi driver for the low fare. He had to decide now before taking another step. He looked up and down Dame Street. He made a deal with himself. If a cab appeared now he would go for it and risk the grief. If nothing came in the next . . . he chose thirty seconds . . . in thirty seconds then he would walk on. He started to count down, thirty, twenty-nine, twenty-eight, muttering without moving his lips. At fifteen a cab with a light on appeared, coming from Christ-church. He waved, still counting down. As the taxi drew closer, he realized that the driver had either decided to ignore him, or somehow, hadn't seen him. Joe samba'd out on to the road, waving more forcefully, ten . . . nine . . . eight, interrupting his countdown to shout. Hey! Hey!! The driver looked briefly, gave him two fingers and continued on towards College Green.

By the time Joe stumbled across the LUAS line at Smith-field, his brain had more or less shut down, apart from the steady thump of pain. It was beyond allowing him any sense of how long it had taken him to walk home, or what time it would be when he arrived. His legs kept going just long enough to walk him into the lift, and out at the top floor to his front door, through the little hall, into the living room, before falling on to the sofa. As soon as he settled himself he saw, shining from the corner, out of the darkness, the bright red numbers; one digit winking as it changed second by second.

3446927 . . . 26 . . . 25 . . .

Down, down, down. How long was left, Joe wondered,

in days and hours? There was no way he could even begin to work that out right now. He could just about recall that he had recently calculated when exactly, to the hour and second, the clock would reach zero, but he was in no condition to remember what the answer was. It was infinitely easier to close his eyes; just blot those little numbers out. Over the last few weeks the clock had become, inevitably, almost ritually, the first thing he looked at every time he returned to his apartment. It was always on his mind as he reached his front door. Sometimes he would even find himself thinking about it as he crossed Market Square to his apartment building. It was annoying but there seemed to be nothing Joe could do about it. Once it drifted into his conscious mind he could hardly pretend it wasn't there, and trying to distract himself just felt fake. So he went with it. Sometimes he tried to turn it into a little game. He would try to guess what the precise number would be when he arrived in the apartment. He was frighteningly close once or twice. Tonight, thanks to vatloads of drink, the farce with Marianna, and the misery of the walk home, Joe had succeeded in not thinking about the clock at all, until now, flopped on the sofa, he saw it.

His head ached, he was sore to the bone. He felt old. He tried to picture Marianna. Somehow he managed to summon her up. She had come back with him after all and here she was straddling his lap, looking unblinking at him in the way that had made him so horny earlier in Lillie's. She tugged at his belt. Joe unbuttoned her top, but as he slid it back, he saw, past her bare shoulder, the clock winking away, and Marianna was gone. Joe groaned and twisted on the sofa. His dick was already out, so he pulled on it, trying to summon up some other image. The last time with Juliet? When was it, before that final end? Forget that. Before the long silences. Before the rows before the long silences. When was it? Where? In Brighton Vale, or Longford? Then he saw her.

She's walking towards him sipping orange juice, in the kitchen at Brighton Vale. Of course. Always that morning. But that wasn't the last time, was it? No, but it was the last best time; out-of-the-blue sex. What had come over her? He is still in his dressing-gown, lounging against the worktop, pouring coffee, listening to some radio discussion about the Port Tunnel. Juliet fingers the collar of his gown, leans in to lick his nipple. Joe thinking she is just messing, laughs, but it feels nice all the same. Now his other nipple, lingering this time, her lips closing, sucking gently, and he knows she's not teasing. He reaches down and presses a buttock in each hand. She relaxes against him, unzipping her jeans. Slipping his hands into the back pockets he pushes down gently, she shyly parts his dressing-gown, and slides her finger and thumb along his dick. The ache begins. There can be no stopping now. It would be too cruel a joke. Juliet locks her arms around his neck, and he takes her entire weight as she hitches her legs up and curls them round his hips. He has to reach forward and turn off the radio. There is no way he can continue with someone talking in the background about tunnel leaks and cost overruns. Juliet laughs. The only sounds now are the clock on the fridge and, distantly, the sea. He swings Juliet round against the worktop and pushes, pushes.

The image strong, almost hearing her breath in his ear, Joe lay back, stretching his toes, clinging to the memory. He was so very nearly hard now. He turned his head in search of Juliet's lips, imagining her tongue edging out between her teeth to meet his mouth. Then her eyes became red digits, flaring and winking.

3446592 ... 91 ... 90 ...

And the moment died. Joe stopped pulling. His soft little penis shrivelled and tipped left. He would not get Juliet back now.

'When exactly did you become so shallow?'

That was what she had said to him that night. Whatever the fuck that was supposed to mean. Some bullshit talk hiding something else. Not another guy, he knew that, it was never that; just something else. Of course it had made him angry. Of course it had. Of course. Joe belched. Acid shot into his mouth. He turned quickly on his stomach and spat the sourness on to the carpet. He wished he could just sleep now, forget; go out like a light, just like that, immediately. No chance. He would have to do something about the clock. He could just dump it, throw it away, forget all about it. Except that he had already lodged zero time in his brain. It came to him now. November 2nd, 18.15 and 39 seconds. Throwing the clock away would do nothing to help him forget that, even if it was just nonsense. Which it was.

Leaving the cottage that evening, Joe hadn't been able to wait. He had to satisfy his curiosity. No sooner had he driven away from Juliet and Milo than he looked for somewhere to pull in. He wanted to examine the clock, now that it was working. Spotting a lane as he passed, he stopped and reversed back, so quickly that the back wheel almost went into a ditch. He picked up the clock and turned it round and round. There was nothing to press, no way of adjusting it. When he shook it nothing happened. The bright red seconds just kept ticking down. He found a biro and scribbled down the last two digits at a glance, 82. Having nailed those, he could add in the other numbers at more leisure, 5472482.

Five million, four hundred and seventy-two thousand, four hundred and eighty-two seconds.

Eighty-six thousand, four hundred seconds in a day. A quick head calculation told him sixty-three days, eight hours and about eight minutes. Jesus! The clock would reach zero in slightly more than two months. Early November. What then? What did it mean? If he placed any significance in the old man's story, then it could mean that Juliet had only slightly more than two months to live. Joe didn't believe that, surely? No, he didn't. It was a joke, of course. Juliet was not going to die so soon. That was nonsense. All the way back to Dublin it was hard not to keep glancing down at the seconds ticking away. The first thing Joe did when he got home a couple of hours later was to sit at the dining table with a pen and some paper. He placed the millennium clock in front of him. Then he dialled the talking clock.

'At the signal it will be twenty thirty-eight and twenty seconds.'

He wrote down 20 38 20 as the clock spoke and then focused on quickly writing the last two digits from the count-down clock as the beep went. 37. Then he added the other numbers. 5464537. He calculated exactly how many days, hours, minutes and seconds the number represented. By adding the result to the time from the talking clock, Joe was able to work out accurately that the clock would reach zero at 18.15 and 39 seconds on the 2nd of November 2005. He felt quite elated at his efforts. Of course it was just a game. He had been curious. Now he knew. Except it was impossible to leave it at that. All that night he couldn't help watching the seconds tick away, wondering if zero time had any significance at all. OK, what if the old man's story had some kind of truth in it? Joe tried to take it step by step. Juliet would die suddenly, at thirty-five years of age. OK, and if this happened? What then? How would he feel? His ex-wife, married for six years, lived with for nearly three before that, a proper going out couple for two years before that; most of their adult lives intertwined and suddenly she is gone just like that. It was impossible to imagine what kind of loss or breach it would be. Jesus! He'd be left with Milo. He would become his sole responsibility once Juliet was dead. What did he feel about that? It was getting all too serious, much too complicated. It was way beyond a game. Joe, to stop these thoughts, had put the clock on the floor behind him and switched on Sky News. Non-stop New Orleans. There were people on the roofs of flooded houses, reaching up, waving desperately at the TV camera as it floated by above them, hovered a moment, then moved on elsewhere in search of more devastation.

Was that really three weeks ago already? Curled on the sofa now, barely aware of drool gathering at the corner of his mouth, Joe couldn't imagine himself ever standing up again. The movement would be too painful. He shivered and belched more acid. The pain from the back of his head had moved down his neck and spread across his hunched shoulders. Somehow his groping hand found the remote control. He flicked on to distract himself from the clock. There were still hurricanes on Sky News; different ones. The latest, called Hurricane Rita, was ripping through Texas. There seemed to be a never-ending supply this autumn. What was going on? Joe thought. Something was not right. Everything seemed so fucked. He knew he would have to do something about that clock. He would have to nail it one way or the other. That was the thing. He couldn't go on this way, just waiting for it to reach zero, and then . . . then . . . Joe was finding it really hard now to keep his thoughts going. The clock . . . the clock. Yes. If only he could do something. Check it out. He would have to . . . He felt so sick. He fell unconscious. Some time during the rest of the night Joe must have walked or crawled to his bedroom, somehow he must have pulled his clothes off bit by bit as he went. Maybe it was lucky that he hadn't quite reached the bed when he pissed himself. It meant the bed was dry and comfy and delicious when he curled up, leaving the problem of the dark spreading stain on the bedroom carpet for another time.

22

Rory, Shane, and someone he had met a couple of times before called Raymond, were the only guys Joe Power could tempt back to the apartment after the pub. Shane never refused the offer of free drink, so he was well up for it. Rory agreed to come because, after the marriage break-up, he had told Joe he was going to be his go-to guy, a typical Rory Americanism, apparently promising support and concern twenty-four seven. Tonight, however, the go-to guy couldn't carry out his dude mission until he'd phoned his wife, Lisa, for permission to be home later than expected. A couple of months before, Joe had discovered something scary but impressive about Lisa. While never openly taking sides between Juliet and himself, she had contrived never to speak directly to him since, a tactic so finely achieved that he had been in her company several times and never copped it. The realization had come one sunny afternoon when he'd bumped into them walking on Dún Laoghaire pier with their three children.

There are big hi's and smiles as Joe tries to remember the kids' names. Lorcan? Yes, the eldest, and Siobhán the girl is easy, but the little guy? Blank. It's another Gaelic name, he's sure, one of the weirder ones. Flustered, Joe rushes to speak, and the words he hears escape from his mouth sound not pleasantly joshing as intended, but insinuating and faintly boorish.

'Hey, Lisa, I haven't missed the big birthday, have I? The old three five?'

Lisa doesn't look at him. She turns to Rory, her tone amused, mock-scolding.

'Rory, what are you like? Have you put an ad in the papers about this birthday? You know I don't want any fuss.'

Then, instead of turning back to look at Joe, she suddenly steps past Rory to grab her youngest.

'Tréalach!'

That's it. Stupid fucking name. Apparently Tréalach urgently needs something wiped from his chin. Joe now realizes that at the moment they met, Lisa may have been smiling, but she wasn't looking directly at him. She may have made greeting noises, but she never actually said, 'Hello, Joe.' Now, as Rory blabbers to fill the silence, Lisa remains with her back to them, focused, like any good mother, on child management, and when Rory is rather quickly reduced to 'We must hook up soon, Joe,' she manages to be still distracted by that scamp Tréalach, and so is out of reach for the farewell pecks-on-the-cheek routine. Backing away, waving, Joe listens carefully, sifting through the soundtrack of goodbyes. Rory and the children come through loud and clear, but not Lisa. She has Tréalach in her arms and is looking at him, lifting his hand to wave, making encouraging sounds.

'Day-day! Say day-day. Goo-ood boy. Who's the best boy. Day-day!'

Once Joe spotted what she was at, he was even more impressed with her performance on subsequent encounters. Once or twice he had amused himself by trying to find a form of question that would force her to address him directly. Lisa was way ahead of that game.

Joe: 'Are you ready for another drink there, Lisa?'

Lisa: 'You know guys, I'd better not have any more, or I'll regret it in the morning. Won't I, Rory?'

Joe: 'What class is Siobhán in now, Lisa?'

Lisa: 'Siobhán, come here and tell the man what class you're in, and who your teacher is.'

Tell the man. She was even finding ways to avoid saying his name. It was simple and elegant. And implacable. He loathed Lisa but had to admire her balls.

Looking out through the bar window at go-to guy on his mobile hardly getting a word in, just listening and nodding, Joe suddenly felt the thrill of his personal freedom. He didn't have to take crap from anyone any more. He felt contempt for some of his other mates who had sloped off at closing time, home to their wives and girlfriends. Steve and Mark and Cian. Especially Cian, who had said, 'Yeah, yeah, brilliant,' when Joe invited him back, and then slyly disappeared. It was lucky that this Raymond guy was the kind of sad fuck who latched on to people he barely knew, because at least he made it a foursome. Less than four would have been pathetic, hardly worth playing the game. Why were more of them not intrigued by Joe's promise of a mystical object with a mysterious story?

Throughout the night, by drifting away from the group on the pretence of checking out girls, or seeing someone he knew, or going to the toilet, Joe had managed to abandon half-finished drinks, without the others noticing. He had insisted on buying the last couple of rounds and got triples for everyone, while his whiskey and ginger was just ginger. He was as good as sober. There would be no repeat of last night. He intended to see and remember everything clearly.

'Jesus, Joe, you should get yourself a cleaning lady.'

Back at Smithfield, go-to guy trailed after Joe to the kitchen, alert for evidence of the pathos of single life so he could offer advice.

'Lisa found this fantastic Lithuanian girl. Takes such a load off you know. And especially for you, I mean, like, now.'

Go-to guy offered his most understanding face. Joe imag-ined head-butting it. As an empathetic hand approached Joe's shoulder he shoved a bottle of wine into it and spun him round.

'Take that in. Glasses are on the table.'

Shane, in the living room, had found Talking Heads and wanted everyone in the building to know about it. 'Psycho Killer' drilled through the flimsy walls.

'And tell Shane turn it down.'

Joe gathered whiskey, vodka, brandy and Bacardi. He poured himself a ginger ale. Adrenalin demanded a real drink but he controlled the urge. In the living room the guys were drinking and swaying and staring at the clock in the centre of the table. Before going out that evening, Joe had placed it there, and beside it, a deck of cards and several packs of batteries.

3395739 · · · 38 · · · 37 · · ·

Shane roared along with David Byrne. *Don't touch me I'm a real live wire.* Go-to guy listened to Raymond shite on.

'It's pretty wild, yeah. It's like some kind of a podule. Kind of futuristic but retro at the same time –'

'Sit down, guys. This, as you've probably guessed, is the mystery object I told you about.'

'Mind if I –'

Raymond reached towards the clock. Joe picked it up.

'No touch. Don't spoil the suspense. Sit down, sit down.'

Joe went to the CD player and changed Talking Heads for the *Blade Runner* soundtrack. Better for atmosphere. They all sat down and he placed the clock in front of him so that the others could see the VDU.

'OK, my privileged friends, prepare for a story beyond your understanding. Pour yourselves a good stiff drink while

I tell you the Affair of the Car Boot Sale, the Gay Barrister and the Clock of Doom.'

They ooohed drunkenly, but they were in. Drinks were poured. Joe sipped his ginger ale and began. How to tell this story had occupied his mind since, still feeling putrid, he had crawled out of bed late this afternoon, and started phoning around. He knew how to lasso the limited attention span of his drunken friends. The setting and events had to have about them a large element of the bizarre, so the millennium party became in the telling a mythic midlands orgy. The characters had to be larger than life, so his wrinkled old car boot sale man spoke with exaggerated Longford belligerence, and the cursed barrister's voice dripped with fruity innuendo. Above all, the attention and curiosity of his audience had to be focused on the McGuffin of the narrative: the clock. Now as he reached the dark climax at the turn of the millennium, with poor old Maurice expiring on the road outside his house, the clock still clutched in his hand, Joe simultaneously unwrapped the batteries and doled them out two by two. Then, enjoying the attentive silence, he picked up the pack of cards and began shuffling, as he concluded.

'One fact seems indisputable. The barrister died at the same moment the clock reached zero. So was it just the coincidence to end all coincidences? Or did this . . .'

His hand touched the hard white plastic.

'. . . actually foretell his time of death? Who among you is willing to risk finding out? Are you in? Or out?'

He resumed shuffling. Shane bellowed.

'What the fuck are you on about?'

'Do you want to find out how long you have left to live? Do you believe the clock will tell you?'

49

'Of course not. It's complete shite. Good story though. Did it really happen?'

'Gospel. So, do you want to play?'

'Yeah, sure. What's the game?'

'Simple. Turn of a card. The high man gets to choose. He can either set the clock going himself, or choose someone else who has to do it.'

'And who made up these rules?'

'Me. It's my clock, my apartment, my booze.'

Raymond spoke.

'How come it's working already?'

Joe had the lie prepared.

'You don't think this is the first time I've played this game, do you?'

'So is that your number?'

'That'd be telling. Come on, let's do it.'

No one had noticed that as he talked and shuffled, Joe had held some cards intact, between thumb and index finger. He had arranged these cards earlier, a four, a nine, a Queen and, for himself, the fourth and highest card, the King of clubs. No point in leaving things to chance. Now, as he placed the deck on the table, they dropped safely on top. Joe looked to his left. Thankfully, go-to guy's sensitive gaze had dissolved back to Rory with a drunken grin.

'Off the top, Rory.'

'Me first yeah? Fair enough. OK. All right.'

His hand hovered. As Shane started heckling, he turned the card.

It was the King of clubs.

'Yes!'

'Nice one.'

'No beating that.'

'There might be an ace.'

'Yeah right.'

Joe could not speak. How had he fucked that up? Raymond was next, not that it mattered now. Rory would be the high man unless a real miracle occurred. How had the King ended up on top?

'A nine. No good.'

The pack was pushed towards Shane. The *Blade Runner* soundtrack was starting to grate on Joe's nerves; as was Shane's volume level.

'OK, we know an ace is a bit of a long shot, so can I say now, if you end up high man Rory and you're too chick-chick-chicken to have a go yourself, as I suspect you might be, then pick me. I relish the opportunity, do you hear me? I relish it. Can I cut the cards?'

'No. Off the top like the rest of us.'

Shane lifted his card, looked, and threw it down, disgusted. The four of diamonds.

'Fuck. OK Rory, remember what I said. Joe, you're only wasting your time.'

In this moment Joe understood how total his frustration was that events were no longer in his control, and how painful it felt to have to play it for laughs; close his eyes, hum mysteriously and tap the top of the deck several times. He opened his eyes and turned a card, aching for a miracle.

'Oooh! Queen of spades, the dark lady. Close, but no cigar pal.'

'Not to be, Joe.'

'OK. You're the man, Rory.'

Shane pushed the clock towards him.

'Come on, don't be a chicken, go for it.'

It was childish, risible, this dread Joe felt at the thought he might be chosen. It was just a game. He spoke to drown out his inner agitation.

'OK, OK, shut up, let the man think, give him some space. Quiet! Rory. It's up to you. You can elect to remove these batteries and set the Clock of Doom in motion yourself. You might find out something very interesting, maybe frightening, maybe life changing –'

'Use it or lose it, Rory.'

'Shane, for fuck's sake let him think. Or. You can nominate one of us to do the deed. Take your time.'

Blade Runner was really doing Joe's head in now. He stood up and went to switch it off. Out of sight, out of the line of fire. At last silence. Even Shane had shut up. Joe stared at the few lingering carefully groomed hairs on the back of Rory's head, as if to send a message to his addled brain. Choose Raymond.

'Aaah! What the fuck.'

Rory picked up the clock and opened the battery chamber. Joe slowly came back to the table, genuinely amazed. Anything could happen now.

3394524 . . . 23 . . . 22 . . .

The VDU went black as Rory wrenched the old batteries out and tossed them towards the centre of the table. He picked up his batteries, clicked one in, eyeballed Joe, then clicked in the second. He stared at the clock, squinting.

'Well, what is it?'

'I can't work it out. My brain is fucked. How long is that?'

He turned the clock round.

158780826 . . . 25 . . . 24 . . .

While the others were having difficulty even saying the number out loud, sober Joe silently worked out the ball park. A year was thirty-one million seconds, so one hundred and fifty-eight million meant five years and some change. If it meant anything. The others scrambled drunkenly for the calculators on their mobile phones. So, Joe thought, what had he discovered? Nothing. A totally different number had come up. So what? Why? Maybe his oldest friend would not live to see forty-five, or maybe it was as simple as the difference between Rory's new batteries, and Juliet's used ones. Raymond was first in with the result of his calculations.

'Five point nought three four years.'

'What's point nought three four of a year?'

'Not a lot.'

'You going down in five, my friend. Not much time left for you.'

Rory, laughing, reached for whiskey.

'I'd better make that will, so.'

The others laughed too; Shane loudly, Raymond nervously. Joe managed a laughing sound. This was not how he had imagined it. This did not feel like fun. Rory finished off his drink, and wiped a hand across his sweaty dome. The thick curls of his teenage years long gone, the tangle of straw that Joe's mother had once fondled satirically.

'Rory Duggan, you'll break hearts with that beautiful wild head of hair.'

If she was alive, what would his teasing mother say now to cautious balding go-to guy, scared-shitless-of-his-wife guy, as he meandered placidly into dreary middle age? Never mind about him, Joe thought, what would she say to me about what I have become? Rory picked up the cards and began to shuffle.

'Right, that's my future taken care of. Let's see who's next.'

Joe wanted to say, stop, everyone go home now. Rory put the deck down.

'Raymond.'

Raymond stared at the cards.

'Off the top.'

Raymond looked at the others. Joe was grateful for the honest fear he saw in his eyes. Raymond whinnied. He shook his head.

'Nah, nah, nah.'

'Come on, play the game.'

To Joe's relief Raymond stood up.

'Nah. Listen, I'm wrecked, guys, I'm going to head –'

'Ah, for fuck's sake.' Shane reached over and grabbed the clock. 'You fucking baby. Forget the cards. I'll do it.'

He showed everyone the VDU.

'Your number, Rory my man, a hundred and fifty-eight million blah right? OK, here goes. Who's betting it'll be in around the same?'

He yanked out the batteries. Joe wanted to grab the clock from him but he didn't dare. He would look such a fool.

'And the Clock of Doom tells me –'

Click. Click. The red glow from the VDU made Shane's wide eyes look bloodshot. The silence seemed to last a very long time before he turned the clock round and put it down for the others to see.

1640824041 . . . 40 . . . 39 . . .

'Jesus. This is too weird.'

It was Raymond, still standing at the table. Joe looked at Rory, at his tired squinting eyes. He could almost hear his brain straining to crank up, to add up. One thousand, six hundred and forty million, eight hundred and twenty-four thousand and . . . thirty-four . . . thirty-three . . . A door opened and slammed. Raymond was gone. Thirty-two seconds.

'What's going on, Joe?'

Shane's voice was quiet at last. Unsure. There was no way

54

Joe could work out in his head exactly what this number meant in years and months and weeks and hours. He didn't want to. All he was sure of was that his old school-pal was going to enjoy a very long life.

21

It was Christmas in October at Joe Power's Sounds Alive! studio. A buzz of street crowds, carolling, and discreetly in the distance, sleigh bells, filled the space. Two actresses, Gretta and Sue, laughed merrily and called 'Happy Christmas, Gráinne, Happy Christmas, Helen,' to each other.

'Thanks girls. Perfecto.'

Through the studio glass, the actresses acknowledged Joe's thumbs-up. He turned to Eunice, Trevor's ageing number two from the ad agency. Alarmingly white teeth gleamed from the walnut that was her face.

'Happy?'

'I love it.'

'Yeah, decent take. One problem though.'

Eunice sighed.

'What?'

'Three seconds over, I'm afraid.'

Eunice moaned.

'No, it has to be thirty exactly. Can you do that thing where you speed it up and no one notices?'

'Ten per cent faster? Technically yes, but my guess is the performance won't feel right.'

'Let's hear it.'

Joe opened the studio mike and spoke to Gretta and Sue.

'Take a break, girls. That was fantastic, but we might need another one. Nothing to do with you. Techie stuff.'

The girls nodded and went off to the kitchen. Joe adjusted the playback speed by ten per cent and replayed the simple tale of Helen and Gráinne, two young mothers and old friends, who bump into each other on Henry Street and greet each other with squealing surprise. 'Helen!' 'Gráinne!' They immediately praise the charm of the festive streetlights, share joy at the traditional Christmas tree on O'Connell Street, and, most of all, gush about the miraculous displays in the shop windows. Such is their pleasure at this serendipitous seasonal encounter, they decide instantly to pause for a relaxing coffee and a natter about the year gone by. Joe would drop in the tag line for the ad later, using a male actor with a velvet anglo baritone. 'Dublin City Centre, a Christmas tradition.'

'Well, it's exactly thirty seconds now.'

Silence. Then a little dog whine of disappointment from Eunice.

'It's lost it, though, hasn't it? That lovely relaxed cheerful . . . festive quality. Now it sounds just a bit rushed.'

'Which kinda defeats the whole purpose.'

'What do you suggest, Joe?'

'I've no magic formula, Eunice. The actors have to play it three seconds faster.'

'But then they'll be under pressure to speak faster. They'll lose the performance.'

'Probably. You could drop some words. About six would do it.'

'Six words. What six words?'

'Any six words. An "and" here, a "but" there.'

'But the script is agreed. Trevor will go mad if I change it now.'

Ooooh, Trevor will go mad! Poor old cigarette-stained Eunice, Joe thought, scared of Trevor's beagle yap.

'Well, I can't alter Time. Do you want to leave it at thirty-three seconds?'

Eunice hated it when the world didn't turn her way.

'But it's a thirty-second script. We were sure it was.'

Joe knew he did not really need to state the obvious, so he didn't. He also knew he had a session with Online Overseas Properties in ten minutes, but now was not the time to mention that. Never hassle the client.

'I'd better call Trevor.'

Which was what Joe had expected her to say. In the end it was always Trevor who decided.

'I'll grab a coffee. Give me a shout when there's a plan.'

'You're sure six words will do it?'

'Just tell him we're three seconds over.'

Joe was a little pissed off. If Trevor had been here they would be finished this long ago. Why had he stopped handling the studio end lately? He used to be totally hands-on and, in fairness, was great fun to work with. In the kitchen two more actors, Robert and Dave, had arrived for the Online Overseas Property session. They were sitting round the little table with Gretta and Sue.

'Stand by, girls. We have to lose three seconds. Eunice is making a crisis call.'

The girls grinned and nodded. They had a good attitude. Joe poured himself a coffee, listening to the chat. Robert was speaking.

'. . . He knows someone in the cast. He comes backstage afterward to say hi. You don't know him, but you recognize his name when you hear it, because, and this is the important bit, you happen to be friendly with his latest girlfriend.'

'This really happened, didn't it?'

'No, it's purely hypothetical. Anyway, everyone goes to the bar, but eventually the only ones left are you and this guy –'

'And he tries it on? It so happened to you.'

'No – what happens is, this other girl comes over and starts chatting him up. And he seems interested, OK? So now . . . do you a) Say something to let him know you're friendly with his girlfriend? b) Say nothing and just wait to see what happens?'

'Well, "b", obviously. For the crack.'

'OK, but if you say nothing, and he does get off with this girl, what then? Do you tell his girlfriend or keep schtum?'

Joe had heard the actors play this parlour game lots of times, when they were left hanging around. The dilemmas always seemed to be about sex in some form or other. Gretta caught his eye just as she was saying that she would definitely keep schtum. What happened on tour, stayed on tour. He smiled at her. Gretta said, 'What about you Joe? What would you do?'

'Me. Well, first off, if I thought I had a chance with the girl myself, I'd definitely let him know that I knew his girlfriend, to make him back off. But if I thought there was nothing doing, I'd say nothing, and just go and be a sad drunk on my own.'

The actors laughed. Naturally. He was the boss of Sounds Alive! and put a lot of work their way. Joe suddenly heard himself say, 'I have one for you. May I?'

He was a bit shocked at the sound of his own words. Now he would have to follow through. The actors were all looking at him, curious. Joe had never joined in this game before. As there was no way he was going to tell them the real story of the old man, the clock and Juliet, he would have to improvise some convincing parallel. His voice sounded false in his ears. If it had been a radio ad he would have stopped the take and gone again.

'OK, so . . . you go to a, ahh . . . a psychic . . . You're not normally into these kind of things, but you start to get impressed when the psychic tells you certain things. She, ahh . . . she knows how many brothers and sisters you have. Ahh . . . she's able to give their correct ages, say. Then she gives other, you know, little personal details about them that there's no way she could have known. So, by now you're impressed, OK? Then she drops a bombshell.'

Noticing the actors' attentive faces made Joe more confident. He could hear a certain relaxed authority in the flow of his words now. Believability. He knew where this thing was going.

'She tells you she has sad news, your sister is going to die soon. She gives you an exact date and time. Now . . . do you believe her, and whether you believe her or not, do you tell your sister what she said?'

Silence. This wasn't about sex. Joe wondered if he had just done something really stupid, if he had exposed himself in some way he would regret. Robert spoke first.

'Well, yeah, for a laugh.'

Sue jumped in immediately. 'No way, never.'

Now voices clamoured over each other.

'Like is his sister ill already? Has she got something?'

'No, this is completely out of the blue.'

'Are you told how she's going to die?'

'No. Just that it will happen on such a day, at such a time.'

'Yeah, I'd tell her, so she could do something about it?'

'But what could she do about it?'

'Make sure she stays at home out of harm's way. Locks herself in safely.'

'OK. And the house goes on fire?'

'I'd tell her so she can at least prepare herself.'

'Like how? Confess her sins and so on?'

'Well . . . whatever. Sort out her will.'

'Fair enough, I suppose.'

'No, but then you ruin whatever is left of her life. How long does she have, Joe?'

Joe thought carefully before answering this question. He thought the true time would be too shocking.

'Say . . . six weeks.'

'Right. So if you tell her, then for the last six weeks of her life, all the poor woman would be able to think about is her death. What's the point?'

'Choice is the point. Wouldn't you like to know if it was you?'

'No way.'

'But it would mean you could, you know, do things, tie up all the loose ends.'

'Forget the loose ends. You could just have a blow-out holiday. Screw all round.'

'How shallow are you?'

Joe tried to dampen the anger in his tone as he interrupted.

'Maybe it's not shallow. What if you tell her and then it doesn't happen? What if it turns out the psychic is wrong?'

'Ah now, that's a real head-fuck. So hold on, is it for real or not?'

'That's the point. You can't know for sure until it happens. Or doesn't.'

Gretta's voice came clean through; simple, sensible.

'Then definitely, you're better off saying nothing. Think of it this way. Not knowing when we are going to die is the norm. That's the way it is for all of us. There is no choice.'

'Ah . . . what about people on death row who are told their date of execution?'

'They're still not like, absolutely one hundred per cent sure.'

'Yeah, there's always going to be some little bit of hope.'

'Exactly my point. We prefer not to know.'

*

The discussion continued, even more intense and enthusiastic. Joe, listening, noticed how pleased he was that the actors were finding this dilemma more fascinating than the usual cheating-on-your-partner stuff. It flattered their egos to feel they were dealing with something profound, metaphysical, something about which opinion didn't inevitably divide along a male-female axis. Of course nothing they said was very illuminating. Almost everything proposed had been considered by him over the last few weeks. Had he expected to hear a magic solution? Why had he opened his mouth at all? Joe wasn't sure. For relief, he suspected; just to hear the problem that had been burning his brain talked about aloud; to hear voices other than his own spin this thing round and round. Joe was very conscious that time was running out fast. It was October 26th. He had less than a week to decide. Why not tell Juliet the whole story? Let her make up her own mind about it. If only he could just play the dispassionate narrator; let her listen and decide the truth. It would never be that simple, of course. How would he explain to Juliet why he'd waited seven weeks before saying anything? The closer to zero time, the less it seemed like a game.

The moment Milo and Juliet came out of the cottage with the clock was when he should have said something. He could have told the whole story, made a big joke about it. If she worried afterwards, that would be her own business. Joe had let another good chance go by three weeks ago, on Milo's fifth birthday. The second official access visit had been scheduled for several days before, but Juliet had readily agreed to him coming on the birthday itself. As the 1st of October was a Saturday, Milo would have no school, so Joe could collect him that morning around ten, and return with him at three, when a surprise party would be waiting at the cottage; all his new Longford school-friends and their parents. Joe was welcome to stay on for the party if he wished. It was an excellent plan, and organizing details for Milo's big day had led to a number of surprisingly relaxed phone conversations between Juliet and himself. Probably because, after his night with the boys, the number on the clock was over 1,600 million, looking at the countdown was having far less effect on Joe, even when it happened to come into his eyeline during one of these phone calls. The constant drip-drip of seconds made little or no impression on such a huge total. So it wasn't seeing the clock that made Joe Power uneasy during his chats with his ex-wife. It was the precise date and time that lit up in his brain every time he heard her voice on the other end of the line.

Wednesday November 2nd. 18.15 and 39 seconds.

They might chat at ease, but by the time each phone call ended, Joe would have worked out the hours, minutes and seconds between the present date and time, and zero time. He couldn't stop himself. Neither could he find the exact way to say anything about it to Juliet, because the truth was he still hadn't made up his mind whether he should tell her or not. He was of course suspicious of his own motives in this. Was it selfishness that made him hesitate, or was there a genuine dilemma? What was so bad about leaving it all to chance? During one phone conversation, he promised himself that if Juliet mentioned the clock in any way, he would take that as a cue to tell her the whole story. She never did.

Milo did.

'Daddy, you know the funny clock?'

It was on his birthday. Joe had collected him at the cottage, and was reversing quickly on to the road.

'Yeah?'

'Did you bring it?'

The car cut out. Joe focused on starting it again.

63

'No. It's in Dublin.'

'Mummy said it was a magic clock.'

'Maybe it is.'

Then Joe heard himself change subject as he changed gear.

'Hey, your birthday! Imagine. Five! Now the last time we were hanging out, I made a promise, so guess where I'm going to bring you today?'

He made a lip-smacking sound. Milo looked puzzled. Joe hit third gear.

'Your favourite?'

'McDonald's?'

'Yes. You want to go there straight away?'

Milo did. The clock was forgotten.

'Will I go faster?'

Milo said yes please. Joe hit fourth and the Maserati took off. For twenty minutes, until he spotted the big yellow arches, Joe controlled the conversation with a babble of questions about Milo's new school, his new friends, his alphabet, and living in the countryside. In McDonald's, tense and mentally exhausted already, he sipped watery coffee and watched his son feed. He tried to pretend that somehow he had managed to turn back time. It was still last month. He and Milo had made it to McDonald's at the first attempt after all. It was Happytime. As yet, there were no batteries in the countdown clock. The future held no particular fears. Truly, Joe wished it were so.

'Well? Joe? . . . Joe, is that enough?'

Eunice was tapping his upper arm.

'Sorry, sorry, Eunice, I was off somewhere.'

'We've cut four words completely, and we replaced "festivities" and "relaxation" with "cheer" and "break", which as Trevor says, will be much quicker to say.'

'That should do it.'

'Great. So will we . . . ?'

Joe nodded and turned to the actors. How much time had gone by? They were still discussing death, prophecy, knowing and not knowing.

'OK, ladies, we've made a few little cuts. Let's see how it works. Shouldn't be too long, guys.'

On the way back to the studio, Gretta moved alongside Joe. Her tone of voice seemed to assume a certain intimacy between them.

'I liked that dilemma. What made you think of it?'

Blow her out of the water, Joe thought. In the nicest way, of course.

'I didn't have to think of it. It happened.'

Gretta searched his face for signs of a secret smile. Joe said nothing more, guessing his answer would be interpreted as enigmatic wit. Sure enough, Gretta smiled.

'Yeah, right.'

It was her cheeky tone. The one she used for those ads where the boyfriend/partner was a moron and the girls, amusingly, always had the upper hand. Joe told himself that Juliet would probably react in exactly the same casual way, if he told her his story. In the cottage, after he had brought Milo home in time for his surprise birthday party, he had felt like such a stranger surrounded by the Longford mammies and their five-year-olds. He had watched Juliet move through the little party, dishing out cake and soft drinks, nattering with the other mammies as easy as a native. Once, catching his eye, she did the quick raised-eyebrows gesture that used to be their secret communication across crowded rooms in the old days. This moment only served as a reminder of how changed every other circumstance was. How plump and healthy Juliet seemed in this new life. If he tried to tell her the clock story, she would probably reply just like Gretta.

'Yeah, right.'

Or worse. She might suspect him, fear he was trying to unsettle things. No point in creating hassle when the whole thing was nonsense anyway. At the first sign that the party was winding down, he had taken the opportunity to get out of there; back to Dublin. Juliet had gone to the front door to see off a mother and child. He had followed.

'Listen, I'd better head.'

'Oh. Sure. I hope you had a nice time.'

'Yeah, I mean Milo's face when he saw . . . it was great. Worth the price of admission alone.'

'I know, he was overcome. All his school pals. It's been a great way in to the area you know. Everyone's so nice.'

Joe didn't know what to say next. He had no interest in any of this. Juliet had moved on, into some other world. She had taken Milo with her. Maybe she was as good as dead already.

'Yeah, well, see you in November.'

'Sure. The first weekend?'

'Yeah, maybe . . . actually I was thinking, during the week would suit me better.'

'But Milo'll be at school.'

'What time does he finish?'

'Two o'clock.'

'How about after that?'

'If you like, but I mean, November? The clocks will have gone back. It'll be getting dark very early.'

The clocks will have gone back? Jesus! Joe hadn't thought of that.

'What will you do with him?'

'Hmm? It'll be OK. We'll be fine. How about Wednesday the 2nd?'

Zero time was not 18.15. His calculations were out by an hour. Which way?

'If that's what you want, sure. Wednesday the 2nd.'

Joe couldn't help but contrast his confusion with his ex-wife's calm. Her shrug, her easy smile. Juliet seemed not to have a care in the world. It was as if the break-up had done her good.

'So we'll see you when . . . around three o'clock?'

Which way did the clock go, an hour earlier or later? Joe went blank and just stared dumb at Juliet. She gestured dismissively.

'Well, look, whenever. You can let me know.'

Of course he was hardly a mile down the road when it clicked that zero time would be an hour earlier: 17.15 and 39 seconds.

A hand squeezed his shoulder. Eunice was beaming down at him, Gretta and Sue were staring at him through the studio glass. Expectant. He hadn't a clue how the take had gone.

'That was great. Even better than before. Did you think so, Joe?'

'Absolutely, Eunice.'

'And how are we for time?'

Joe glanced down at the desk, then looked back at Eunice with professional pleasure.

'Exactly thirty seconds. Perfecto.'

20

Ten minutes was about as much time as Joe Power ever gave to buying an item of clothing. M & S occasionally suited him because its colour coding facilitated a quick in and out. He knew he was yellow for shirts and tops, turquoise for trousers and shorts. A fitting was hardly necessary, but usually he did a perfunctory one. This time there was a tightness as Joe pulled the trousers round his waist. He was able to button up, but his flesh pressed hard against the waistband, and there was resistance on the zip. He knew it would be uncomfortable sitting down. Maybe this was a different style of trousers; a smaller fit? Joe had been a thirty-four-inch waist for about five years now. Occasionally he had thought about getting it back down to the thirty-two of younger days, but he'd never bothered and Juliet hadn't complained. He was tall enough to carry it well. Thirty-four was fine. Staring at the mirror now, what he couldn't figure out was why his old trousers still fitted. Did they stretch with you? Maybe the labelling was a mistake? He put the old pair back on. OK, they did feel a little bit tighter, but nothing like the pair he had just tried. It would hardly be surprising if he had put some weight on in the last while; the shit he had been eating to go with the shit slushing round in his head. The skinny girl who guarded the dressing-room area took back the trousers with a smile.

'You don't want them?'

'I'll try something else.'

Joe selected four pairs of trousers this time, and took

them back to the dressing-room area, conscious of time passing and the tiniest sense of desperation. He truly had never minded being a thirty-four, certainly not enough to make any serious effort to reduce it, but he knew he didn't want to be a thirty-six. He pulled the curtain in the little booth and looked from trouser to trouser. Which was the best bet? On one label, he read encouraging words: 'comfort fit'. Once again he knew as he pulled them round his waist that they were still going to be too tight. He buttoned up. The waistband moved with his flesh a little better. It didn't resist him quite as much, but when he hunkered down the pressure was still very real. 'Comfort fit' wasn't going to do it. It was surely a waste of time now, but still, Joe tried on the other three pairs. He didn't even bother to button up the last. As soon as he felt the pressure on the waistband he let them drop and kicked them off on top of the others; a sad little pile in the corner of the changing booth. He sat down and stared at the mirror. Suddenly he looked fatter. His belly-button was disappearing in a line of flesh. Lank hair framed a puffy face. Miserable now, Joe thought of the first time his age and waist size had met, on his thirty-second birthday. It had been the same more or less since college, which was impressive. A few months later, buying his first size thirty-four had been mildly traumatic, but he got over it. He had known thirty-two could not last forever. On his thirty-fourth birthday he was still a thirty-four, which was good, and so it had continued. It felt right. This might be forever. So, what was he to do? The choices were stark. Buy nothing now, make do with the trousers he had, until he lost some weight, or give in for the moment; buy one pair of thirty-six and a belt. He could work his weight down notch by notch, back to thirty-four. It was a plan. Joe hauled himself up as straight as he could, pulling in his waist. That was all it took really. Better posture. Maybe a pony-tail. He wasn't far off the mark at all. It certainly wasn't irreversible. This time, when he handed back the four pairs of trousers, the skinny girl took them without comment. The expression on her face revealed nothing, either. What would she be thinking when he came back with the larger size? Poor fat bastard? Age catching up? Who ate all the pies? The colour code for thirty-six was a scary red. Joe chose a linen mix, black. He decided not to return to the changing-room.

The cold sun shone straight up a surprisingly quiet Grafton Street as he came out. It had been a bad start to the day. No longer wearing a watch, Joe checked his receipt for the time. 10.43. Nearly an hour to buy a pair of trousers. In less than seven hours Juliet might be dead. Joe decided he had better make time for a visit to the gym. He had concluded that there was no point in saying anything to her, unless he had something she might accept as evidence, which of course he didn't. Telling her about his game with the guys would hardly convince, even if he could convey how edgy the mood had been as Rory and Shane had left, or admit that none of them had been in touch since. It had occurred to him that there might be something on the net, other similar experiences. Ravings on blogs would not be evidence either, but at least it would mean that the idea was 'out there', that it wasn't just him losing it. Late one night he had googled 'countdown clock'. There were over six hundred and fifty thousand results, yet there was nothing directly related to his dilemma. There did seem to be a thriving market for countdown clocks. It was presented entirely as a fun thing, a way of preparing for special events. For $255 he could buy the CK 5000, which apparently was 'a great way to generate interest or excitement about an upcoming project or that special event'. Hallowe'en, New

Year, wedding days. Counting down a pregnancy seemed to be a particular favourite.

> *Looking forward to your Baby's Due Date? Now you can count down the time to this significant event! Celebrate the Baby's Due Date of your Wife, Daughter or Celebrity with style . . .*

Inevitably there was a website devoted to counting down to Christmas, but Joe found it a little more surprising that St Patrick's Day featured as a countdown favourite:

> *Are you excited about St Patrick's Day – the day when everyone is Irish? You don't need to be from the Land of Green to get excited about March 17, and our Countdown Clock will build your anticipation. Play our Irish jig! Re-enforce the importance of this event. Your anticipation will build as you count down the days, hours and minutes.*

Was that what Joe Power was feeling? Anticipation? Was he enjoying this? Nowhere in the six hundred and fifty thousand results could he find a hint of dread, depression or paranoia. Counting down time seemed to be just a big laugh. Even counting the days to retirement was presented as counting down to freedom. It wasn't as if Joe couldn't see the funny side. Who had thought of an online clock counting the seconds and minutes to Harry Potter's legal age? He laughed out loud at a website smartly titled www.backwardsbush.com, which simply featured a clock counting down to the end of the Bush presidency. It promised to make people feel better, because 'counting backwards makes time pass faster'. Joe's smile faded as he digested the truth of that. He'd had enough. He turned off his computer. Inevitably he looked over at the clock in the corner. It read:

1638374957 ... 56 ... 55 ...

With a number so large, each second lost seemed a mere one-cent coin slipping through the hole in a billionaire's pocket. But the billionaire was not Joe, the countdown in his head was very different and zero time was approaching much faster.

A few days later he had used some free time to visit the National Library. It didn't take long to find what he was looking for. On page seven of the *Irish Times* for Monday 3rd of January 2000 there was a short news piece with the headline:

TRAGIC DEATH OF DUBLIN BARRISTER

The article confirmed the bare details of the story the old man had told him.

Prominent Dublin barrister Maurice Nolan was killed in a road accident shortly after midnight on New Year's Day. The accident took place outside Mr Nolan's holiday home in Lanesborough, Co. Longford. He was crossing the road to the river frontage and boat pier which forms part of his property, when he was knocked down by a passing car. Shocked friends who were attending a New Year's Eve party in Mr Nolan's home say he died instantly.

Mr Nolan had been one of the country's leading criminal barristers for over thirty years, but it was his successful involvement in a number of recent high-profile celebrity libel suits that had brought him into the public eye. Mr Nolan was unmarried, and is survived by one sister. Funeral arrangements have yet to be announced.

Joe had also found an unsigned obituary in the *Irish Times* for the following Saturday, 8th of January 2000.

Maurice Nolan was rarely described as a sentimental man. To the many thousands of people who encountered him professionally during a remarkable career at the bar, he was incisive, relentlessly logical, ferociously intellectual, yet with an extraordinary ability to express complex arguments in simple terms. His court appearances served as inspirational master-classes for young barristers. A crowded public gallery was the norm whenever Maurice Nolan was in action.

Yet sentiment, not cerebration, was the core of the Maurice Nolan that many of his closest friends knew. He loved his country, not just the abstract idea of this independent Republic of which he was so proud, but the very hills and hedges, rivers and bog holes of it. He even gloried in our wretched weather, and loved retreating to his beloved Lanesborough at all times of the year, bullying friends to don their winter coats and wellies, and trek with him for hours in the rain, before rewarding them with a log fire, a generous warming tipple, and his sumptuous cooking. Love of friends and loyalty to friends was the touchstone of his existence. From the companions of early childhood, to his schoolmates at Rockwell, to his wide and brilliant college circle, we all fell under the spell of his shining star.

Friends attest to seeing Maurice with tears in his eyes while gazing at a favourite Jack B. Yeats. His constant visits to the National Gallery were matched only by his enthusiastic support for emerging Irish artists and sculptors. No colleague or acquaintance was safe from his sedulous salesmanship on behalf of the latest discovered talent. As a result, many have cause to be grateful to him for bullying them into purchasing Irish works of art that have, with the passage of time, grown in stature and value. His belief that the best of his nation should be celebrated and supported was a guiding principle of his very being. If Paris, Maurice's favourite other city, fed his intellect and his soul, then Dublin and Ireland constantly fed his heart. And he gorged on its delights . . .

Joe found it nauseating, and was still only halfway through. It seemed obvious there was nothing in it of interest to his quest, so he had skimmed through the rest, and was rewarded right at the surprising, if rather coy, conclusion.

Most of all Maurice was at peace in Díseart, his home in Rathgar, the happy home he shared with Roger, his friend and support for twenty-three years. It was truly his precious hideaway, and will seem sadly empty now . . .

Friend Roger? Roger who, though? Joe had wondered. And what did Díseart mean? Guys like Maurice, that whole generation, loved the bit of Gaeilge. Was Roger the friend who told the old man the story of the clock? How would he find him? He could hardly wander around the whole of Rathgar asking if anyone knew a house called Díseart. A bit of a dead end then. There was nothing he could show Juliet that would be remotely convincing.

Joe arrived at the gym, only to realize that he had no gear with him. He sat enraged, head down, fingers clenched around the steering-wheel. Was this a sign not to go in at all, another bad omen for the day ahead; more wasted time? He told himself not to drive away right now, he might only cause an accident. After a sustained effort to calm himself, his mind cleared enough to remember that there was some kind of sports shop in the gym. The thing now was to buy himself some new gear and get on with it. For the second time that morning Joe found himself shopping for clothes. This time he just bought quickly: large and cheap. He took a chance that everything would fit. He didn't really care how he looked. As it happened he didn't look all that bad, even in this hastily assembled gear. The situation was far from terminal. He was taking control of it before it got out of hand. Even looking at his reflection as he changed, Joe didn't feel that his body was much different. The gut was a bit thicker to be sure. That was hardly surprising. After all that he had been through with Juliet in the last six months, it was bound to have some effect. Thinking about it, Joe was happier that the consequences were physical rather than mental. That was much easier to put right. The other would be a right fuck-up.

He sized up the impressive choice of machinery in the gym, and decided to keep it simple: ten minutes running, ten on the bike, ten on the rowing machine. Burn off some calories. He set the running machine at a testing pace. It felt good. His heart got a bit of a jolt and was the better for it. He liked the sense that his leg muscles were getting a wake-up call. He began to open up his body more, lift his chest, swing his arms, make each stride longer. If he could see himself in a mirror now, Joe fancied he would look like a real runner. The more he ran, the more he was sure that in just a few hours' time, life would be back to normal. He would discover that the countdown clock was nothing more than a randomly dysfunctional piece of seventies kitsch. Juliet would not die. Once the deadline passed, and she was still right as rain, he might even be able to tell her all about it, give her a laugh. It might ease the overall scenario. Why couldn't she give up this ridiculous Longford thing? It had been a painful enough sacrifice to hand over Brighton Vale in the settlement, which, after all, had been his before he even met Juliet. That was bad enough, but at least as long as Juliet and Milo still lived there, he could visit easily, feel a connection with his old life. Juliet had robbed him of that when she decided to rent out his home to finance her little rural experiment. There was sweat now, and he felt his face hot and red. The thump-thump of his heart was exhilarating. He was past the halfway point and still felt fine. Three times a week. It was simple. A half hour three times a week and he would feel much better. 4.23 . . . 4.22 . . . 4.21 . . . Yes, in a few hours this whole crisis would be over, and he would realize that what had happened was that something had burrowed inside him, some personal doubt or fear had allowed foolish imaginings to invade his private place. He was glad now that he had called a halt to his research that day in the National Library. Imagine if he had gone on, trying to track down this guy, Maurice's old boyfriend? And if he had succeeded? What then? What would he have said to him? It would have been embarrassing; a bit ghoulish even.

Joe stepped off the running machine, breathing hard but raring to go. He rested for only thirty seconds before mounting the bike. There were a variety of computerized options. The most daunting looked to be a programme that replicated a slow steady incline. He chose it, and because he felt so good after the running, he opted for fifteen minutes rather than ten. The programme seemed easy at first. The feeling of cycling uphill was slight, the pressure on his leg muscles insignificant. About two minutes in, Joe began to sense the sting in the tail of this particular task. There was no respite. There were no little downhill sections where you could relax for a few seconds. Instead there was a reasonable, but relentless pressure. This time there was no sweat, his heartbeat remained more or less normal, but his calves began to ache. Joe craved a little rest. He regretted choosing fifteen minutes. He tried to focus his mind elsewhere. He foresaw himself at the cottage, later that day.

Standing at the open front door, he notices the clock in the kitchen; almost 5.15. Milo, hugging him. Joe taking his hand, turning to go. Then. He sniffs the air. He smells something. What could it be? He turns back to ask Juliet. She is reaching for a light switch, because it is dusk. Suddenly he understands exactly what the smell is, and what terrible accident is about to happen. He shouts at Juliet as he runs, flinging himself at her. He manages to slap her hand away as it touches the light switch. They both tumble over. She turns angrily to him, but then, suddenly, she too sniffs the air. It is the smell of gas. Juliet now realizes that his aggression was for her own good. She runs to the kitchen. A gas ring on the cooker has not been turned off properly. She embraces Joe with relief. Milo runs to them and they enfold him in a loving heartfelt family hug.

Wouldn't that be even better? Imagine if the countdown thing was actually true, but by being there at the right moment, Joe managed to alter the course of events, to be the hero who makes a difference? Even the satisfaction of such thoughts could not distract him from the now excruciating pain, as he pedalled upwards ever more slowly. His head hung, his hair drooped, tickling his cheeks and eyes. There was still more than five minutes to go. His leg muscles simply would not hold out that long. The constant pressure would be too much. Joe reminded himself that he had originally intended only to do ten minutes. Fifteen had been a wrong call. He knew that the thing now was to accept his mistake, and go back to the original sensible plan. In twenty seconds, ten minutes would be up. Pushing beyond the pain he was now enduring, Joe made a final drive, an Olympian lunging for the finishing line. At ten minutes exactly he stopped, released the handlebars, and taking his legs off the pedals, let them just dangle. Pain collided with relief and pleasure. It was some time before he felt capable of even stepping off the bike.

Rowing was the toughest of the three exercises – legs, back, arms and stomach muscles would all be forced into action. Joe was now regretting not having started with the rowing machine when he was fresh and eager. Over two minutes had passed since he stopped cycling. He had to go through with it. It would be really bad if he could not get through half an hour of fairly average workout. There was no way he was going to abandon it now. He sat down and stared at the computerized programmes, aware that he was really just delaying the ordeal. There were lots of options. He could choose a low level of difficulty and coast through the ten minutes. It was tempting. Was this it then? Was this how the process of giving up began? Not by actually giving up, which at least would be decisive and would suggest some kind of conviction, even courage, but simply by pretending to do something, while avoiding the possibility of risk and pain and failure. Joe could not do that. He chose to race against the machine at the highest level of difficulty.

Almost immediately he felt the pain along his spine. Every time he reached forward his stomach pushed down at his groin, making him feel grossly fat. The back movement was a relief by comparison: his arms coped easily with the pressure on the cord, and the stretch on his lower back was actually a kind of relieving pain. The pressure on his stomach was the part that felt most mortifying. Every thrust forward announced him as a fat ugly fuck and every stretch back became a bid for freedom. Each time his belly pressed down into his groin, it reminded him of the sexual humiliation that awaited him if he ever attempted to show himself to a woman in his present state, his penis receding under folds of fat. It wasn't that bad of course. He knew it wasn't that bad, but it was heading in that direction. The seconds ticked by so slowly. Every stroke was an aching struggle now, the strain on his lower back becoming unbearable. He sweated freely. He begged for the time to go faster. Three minutes left meant seven minutes already gone; two thirds of the way there. This should have been comforting, but Joe knew that every second of the time that remained would be lacerating because he had nothing left to give. He couldn't believe he had allowed himself to become so unfit in so short a time. It was as if he had tipped over some invisible barrier, not realizing how hard it would be ever to get back.

The jacuzzi had never felt so delicious. Once he sank into it Joe could not imagine ever getting out again. There was the added pleasure that because it was still morning, he was the only person there. It was his own private haven. He noticed that the large clock on the wall was directly in front of him. It was a simple classic design with clean readable numbers, a red second hand, and two black hands for minutes and hours. Joe stared at it for a long long time. He squinted to try and see the minute hand move but couldn't. He followed the second hand round. It seemed to be climbing determinedly to the top at twelve, then coasting all the way down to six before climbing again, but there was no sense that these highs and lows were of any significance in a larger journey. How comforting the traditional design of a clock was; how effortless the movement. Although each hand went round and round at different speeds, that scarcely seemed to matter because really, there was nowhere they needed to be; no final destination. The hands seemed to be moving forward certainly, but only to arrive again to a place they had been before. There was no starting point nor end point. There was no zero time. There were no days or weeks stretching into years. There were just three reassuring circular journeys; seconds and minutes and hours. Like going to work and returning home, the hands moved round forever in an endless unchanging routine. The traditional clock told time as if there was no beginning or end. It held no warnings for the future, nor regrets for the past, as if it had been designed that way so that people would never have to face the truth.

When Joe stopped staring at the movement of the clock and noticed real time again, it was ten minutes to one. He didn't know how long he had been sitting there, because he didn't recall what time it had been when he first looked at the clock. He was calm now, but dazed and still aching. He should go, to get ready for the trip to Longford. There were now three other people sitting in the jacuzzi. Joe had not noticed any of them arrive. There were two women and one man. They looked in their sixties, their skin pale and sagging, their voices cracked and thin, retired probably, off-peak members, filling in time.

Filling in time.

19

The thirty-six-inch trousers fitted perfectly. This was disappointing. Joe had left the gym with muscle pains, but also feeling cleansed and trim. He still had not eaten today. The least he had hoped for was that the new trousers would be on the loose side and would need tightening up with the new belt. No, the fit was just right. Soon after two in the afternoon Joe was ready to leave for Longford. On his balcony overlooking the square, he stood with his back against the railing, staring in at the clock in the corner of the living room.

1637503944 . . . 43 . . . 42 . . .

He wished this was Juliet's number and not Shane's, her life stretching out for fifty-two years. Birthdays in reverse, all far enough away to be fun. He could joke with her about it. Congratulations, only another fifty-one years to go! No pressure on Joe. But would he feel as significant as he did now? It was time to go. He put the clock into his shoulder-bag and left the apartment. The plan was to get to the cottage by about 4.30. This would allow for some chat with Juliet and an assessment of the situation. He might get a feel for what lay ahead. If it seemed right he could find an excuse to hang around the cottage, to be with her until after 5.15 and 39 seconds. At one point a couple of weeks ago this had been his absolute intention, to stay close so that he could influence the course of events if possible. Then it had occurred to him that just because he knew what might be the exact time of Juliet's death, it did not follow that she would be the only one to die. Was it not possible that depending on the circumstances, he and Milo could die also? Of all the fearful thoughts that had gone through his mind in the last few weeks this was the most terrifying. It opened a canyon of uncertainty in his brain. As a result of this, Joe knew that his purpose would be to take Milo away long before 5.15. They would return later to find whatever they would find.

It was 4.33 when he turned in the entrance to the cottage. Late dusk, turning very cold. The silence as he stepped out of the car felt self-conscious, ominous. Joe had to tell himself to cop on, that it was always quiet around here. Milo was not at the window, watching for his arrival. Had Juliet forgotten to tell him he was coming today? Where were they? Her old banger was there. He looked in the window. The living room was gloomy and empty. Had they gone for a walk? Joe decided to knock once before using his key. He felt edgy, full of doubts. He heard movement inside.

Milo answered the door. He looked sad.

'Mommy is sick.'

Joe's stomach lurched. So this was it? Was whatever it was, already happening?

'Is she all right? Where is she?'

'She's in bed. Her head is sick.'

'Joe, is that you?'

Juliet's distant voice sounded tired.

'Yes, it's me. Are you OK?'

As he spoke, Joe went past Milo towards the bedroom. The door was ajar. He stuck his head in. There were no lights on but he could make out the bundle that was Juliet wrapped under the duvet, her face only visible from the nose up.

'I'm zonked. I managed to get up to collect Milo from school. I fell straight into bed as soon as we got back.'

Milo also put his head round the door, looking very serious. Joe ruffled his hair.

'What is it?'

'Oh, shivers, headache, the works. Some kind of flu I suppose.'

'Have you seen a doctor?'

'I'll wait until tomorrow, see if it's any better. I'm really glad you're taking Milo. He's been very good, but he doesn't know what's happening really, do you, love? You've never seen Mummy sick before, have you?'

Milo shook his head. Joe tried not to show his agitation.

'Is there anything I can do?'

'Boil the kettle, would you, and make a hot drink in the biggest mug you can find with half a squeezed lemon, a spoon of honey and two Disprin.'

'Have you nothing else? Shouldn't you get the doctor to prescribe something?'

'Like I say, I'll see how I feel tomorrow.'

'But tomorrow might be too late –'

He heard the words coming out of his mouth before he knew he was going to speak. He heard Juliet smirk through the gloom.

'Joe, it's a bit of a winter bug. Relax.'

He didn't know what to say.

'Joe. The honey and lemon?'

'Yeah, right, sorry. Come on, Milo.'

The lemon was on top of a mound of fruit, brightly visible even before Joe switched on the kitchen light. He plugged in the kettle, found a knife and cut the lemon in half. Milo stood on a chair to get the jar of honey. Joe got a mug and a spoon. During all this he glanced up twice at the kitchen clock. He squeezed the juice into the mug. He let Milo spoon in the honey. Where was the Disprin? He tried to remember where they used to keep medicine. There was still no sound of the water boiling. Joe stared at the kettle, listening for the first hiss. Come on, he thought, how long does it take? He looked up at the clock again. 4.47. He walked quickly to the bedroom.

'Sorry, Jules. Where's the Disprin?'

'In the bathroom. Over the sink.'

He should have remembered that. He got the Disprin, returned and dropped two into the mug. They reacted with the lemon juice, hissing slowly into saliva. The kettle was starting to make little noises. It was nowhere near boiling. It occurred to Joe that he hadn't checked the amount of water in the kettle before switching it on. He lifted it up. It was nearly full, far more than he needed. He would save time that way. He poured off most of the water and set it down again. Joe winked at Milo, trying to keep his own panic under control. Finding Juliet in bed like that had been a shock, particularly in the circumstances. He told himself that just because she was sick didn't mean she was going to die in less than half an hour. In fact it more likely meant the opposite. Juliet was tucked up in bed, sweating it out, well out of harm's way. One thing was certain, though. Events had definitely altered his plans. He couldn't just take off with Milo now and leave her sick in bed. What if he did and she died? How could he explain that he just walked out on his sick ex-wife, and left her alone to suffer and die? That would be the kind of thing the tabloids would want to stick their snouts into. The cops might even decide to investigate. No, definitely he was stuck here now, at least until after zero time. He checked the clock. 4.50. Milo was brushing against him, looking up anxiously, and Joe suddenly saw himself, staring up at his mother making apple sponge in the darkening kitchen on a winter's evening, while he, not much older than Milo, anxiously waited to lick the spoon. Bubbling sounds from the kettle brought Joe back. He smiled down at his son.

'Here we go. Mummy'll feel much better after this.'

He grabbed the kettle as it switched itself off and filled the mug. He carried it, stirring as he went. The steam rising had a healthy honey lemon scent. The bedroom was now completely dark. Juliet sat up, took the mug and breathed in the vapour.

'Mmmmm . . . oh, that's good.'

'Do you want some light?'

'No it's fine. Fffsh. Hot.'

'Sorry.'

'It's OK. It should be hot. Well, thanks, you can head off.'

'No, we'll stay around in case you need anything.'

'Don't be silly. I'm fine now. I'll probably sleep after this, so I'm better off without Milo thumping around the house.'

'I'll keep him quiet. I'll read to him or something.'

'Will you just go.'

'Honestly, I don't mind staying around.'

'I know you don't mind. I'm just saying it's silly that's all . . .'

It was the second time Juliet had said 'silly'. Joe found this really annoying.

'. . . Because I'll be asleep, and you and Milo will be tip-toeing around afraid to wake me.'

Joe was aware of Milo's presence and didn't want any tension to become obvious. He couldn't resist stealing a glance at the clock radio. 4.57. This could become an actual row if he wasn't careful. In the circumstances that would be truly ludicrous.

'Well, OK, tell you what. We'll stay until you fall asleep and then we'll head out. Just in case you need anything.'

'Fair enough.'

Juliet's tone told Joe that she too wanted to avoid foolish argument. She finished off her drink and handed him the mug.

''There you go, Nurse Josephine.'

Juliet curled up and pulled the duvet round her.

'Mmmm, that feels better already.'

'Good. We'll be close by, won't we, Milo, in case Mummy needs us?'

Milo nodded. Joe put his finger to his lips, took the boy's hand, and tiptoed in an exaggerated way out of the bedroom. Once he sat down with Milo and his Letterland workbook, Joe began to feel ill at ease again. He tried his best to sound interested as Milo told him about the letters he had learned so far, Clever Cat, and Annie Apple, and Dippy Duck. Joe's mind kept drifting to what might go wrong. What if Juliet suddenly took a turn for the worse? There was no way the honey and lemon drink could have harmed her, was there? That would be just . . . He couldn't even finish that thought. Milo showed him Ticking Tess. When he made her sound, tk, tk, tk, it was a time bomb in Joe's head. He knew absolutely that he couldn't let Milo be there to see his mummy die, not that that was about to happen. There was no clock in the living room. Joe couldn't check the time. Sitting on the sofa with Milo's head on his shoulder, and the Letterland book on his lap, he felt trapped. He had to get away from the cottage. But he couldn't just go. He couldn't just drive away for fun. Under pressure, inspiration came.

'Sorry, Milo, I won't be a sec.'

He got up and went quickly to the bedroom. He put his head in. The clock radio showed 5.06. Joe whispered.

'Are you asleep yet?'

'Nearly. If this headache would go away, I'd be fine.'

'Listen, where is the nearest doctor?'

'I haven't a clue. Joe, I'll be grand.'

Nobody could complain about him leaving Juliet to find her a doctor. It would be the perfect excuse.

'Look, I'll take Milo out. We'll ask up at the village about a doctor. At least get a name and a number for you. So you have it.'

Juliet sighed.

'Fine yeah, if you want to.'

'We won't be too long.'

'Take your time.'

Joe told Milo to get his coat and scarf. When Milo asked what about Mummy, Joe told him they were going to find a doctor who would come and make Mummy better. He seemed happy with that. As he put on his own jacket, Joe checked that the gas cooker was completely turned off. He pulled plugs out of sockets. The whine of the wind seemed much louder now. The stress he felt screamed for some extravagant release, while another part of him felt utterly foolish to be in the grip of a kind of banshee superstition. When Milo reappeared in his coat and scarf, Joe grabbed his hand immediately and marched him out. He paused in the doorway, and looked back to make sure that he had forgotten nothing that might in any way become the cause of tragedy. The living room seemed utterly tranquil and safe. Joe quietly shut the cottage door. It was now very dark and the wind was cutting. There was no sign of stars or moon. Cloud cover, Joe presumed, as he guided his little boy to the car and popped him into the bucket seat. He was in a hurry now. He wanted to be well away by zero time. He jumped in and started the car. The car clock lit up. 17.13. He revved hard, attaching his seat belt with one hand. He looked back as he reversed fast. 'Belt up, Milo,' was the last thing he said.

The Maserati shot back on to the black road. The little boy's left profile burned white in the headlights of an oncoming car. Joe suddenly remembered that just as he had turned on his engine, he had registered the sound of a distant car. There was no time for any other thought before he heard the first shattering moment of impact and lost consciousness.

**Extract from a humorous article entitled
'Letters from Home', by Joe Power, published in
a college magazine, February 1987**

In my experience mothers don't write letters. They may
talk endlessly over the phone, but they never write
letters. That, it seems, has always been poor old
long-suffering Dad's fate.

> Dear (*insert own name*)
> I hope all's well. We're all in grand form.
> Pulling the divil by the tail. Not much news our
> end, but sure no news is good news they say!
> Weather not so bad. It was raining earlier but it
> seems to have cleared up now. How's college?
> Working hard I'm sure!! Mam says hello. Drop us a
> line anyway with all your latest. I'm sure there's
> a lot more happening with you up there, than us
> down here. We got a letter from Auntie (*insert
> name*) the other day. They're all well in (*insert
> as appropriate, Liverpool, Birmingham, Glasgow,
> Boston, Sydney etc.*). Mam says bring your washing
> down the next time you're coming. We'll expect you
> when we see you as per usual!!
> Sincerely yours,
> Dad, Daddy, Father, Pater (*whichever applies*)

Hapless fathers might get a better response if they
took a simpler, more direct, aggressive, perhaps even
legalistic approach to their sons' lack of effort on
the letter-writing front.

Dear Son

We urge you in the strongest terms to contact your Mother directly by phone, letter or telegram within 48 hours. If not, reluctantly, we will have to commence legal proceedings, resulting in potential loss of income on your part.

Yours etc.

A Father esq.

18

'Is time running out for Tony Blair?'

Joe Power heard the voice as he struggled to wake. He thought he recognized it.

'. . . defeated in the House of Commons for the first time since becoming Prime Minister eight years ago . . .'

Joe realized that he did not know the actual person who was speaking, he just recognized the special tone of voice. It was a newscaster; English, male.

'Following the New Labour rebels' astonishing victory, we ask our panel, is it the beginning of the end? . . .'

Joe began to remember. He was still in hospital. Was he out of high dependency? He seemed to be breathing OK now. Joe struggled to open his eyes. He saw the ceiling. The fluorescent lights were not on but there was a bluish glow in an otherwise dark room. Was it night then? He was on the flat of his back. He remembered being carefully wheeled into this room, his left arm encased in plaster of Paris. Joe tried a tiny careful tilt of his head and turned his eyes enough to see the arm was as he remembered it. He guessed it was sensible not to attempt any other moves. As long as he lay still he could breathe without pain. The nurse had spoken softly. Had she said the worst was over? She helped him swallow two pills; then came sleep. He did not know for how long, but it had been deep. It had been day, now it seemed it was night. Of course it might not be the same night. Could he really have slept that long? Some other voice, a woman's, was speaking now, reviewing the morning headlines. Joe wondered why was the television on at all? Was he in a private or public ward? Maybe there was someone else sitting there watching? Joe moved his eyes about as much as he could. He could see no other beds left or right, just walls. At the far corner of his vision, he managed to see, mounted high, the television. He couldn't bring his eyes low enough to confirm if anyone was sitting below it. Joe was getting agitated now. He wanted to shout out. Would he be able to? It seemed like a long time since he had spoken. He had to try. He couldn't bear to lie still like this, being forced to listen to *Newsnight* or Sky News or whatever it was. He framed the first word. The sound came out all right. It seemed to Joe a bit weak and croaky; like he was old.

'Turn it off.'

He tried again. He pushed himself to make it stronger.

'Turn it off.'

Nobody responded. No one stood up into vision. The voices on the television continued. This was worse than a nightmare. Joe was a man in pain, a man who needed pills to help him sleep. He had been in intensive care. Who turned on the stupid fucking television in his room?

'Joseph?'

The voice came from his left. Joseph? Who ever called him that? He flicked his eyes over, as far as they would go. A little man in his seventies was standing in the doorway, a plastic cup in his hand.

'You're awake. They said you might wake.'

Connie Power came towards the bed. He stood over Joe and offered a smile.

'I just went out for a cuppa. Wouldn't you know you'd wake as soon as my back was turned.'

'Turn it off.'

'What? Oh, right. Sorry. Sorry.'

He scurried to the TV set. Sorry, boss, sorry. Joe already wished that the first thing he had said to his father had not been an impatient order. Why hadn't he said something nice or ordinary, at least for a start-off? Still, the silence as the TV went off was heavenly. Joe waited for his father to reappear. He braced himself for the watery eyes full of concern. He told himself not to get annoyed when his father said something clichéd and useless. What else could the poor sod say in the circumstances?

'Silence is golden.'

His father closed in on him as he spoke. Joe felt a hand touch his arm lightly. He gave him a warm look. At least he hoped that's what it was. He told himself not to snap at him. There were things he wanted urgently to know; one thing above all. But it was Connie Power he was dealing with; a man who was hopeless in difficult situations. Joe was sure that his father would already have told himself that there was no point in upsetting a sick man. If the worst had happened . . . well, Connie would certainly not want to be the one to pass on the bad news.

'So you're over the worst of it?'

It had begun. Joe smiled and nodded. He wasn't sure how best to play this, his brain not really being in gear yet. For the moment he would say little and let his father do his thing.

'You've had a tough old time of it. We were a bit worried there for a while, but here you are now. You'll be as right as rain soon.'

Again Joe smiled and nodded. He decided he should offer some words. Make it like conversation.

'I will.'

Two nothing words, but it was enough. Connie continued more expansively.

'Of course they all came to see you. Babs drove me up on the Wednesday as soon as we heard. She stayed overnight, but she had to go back again on the Thursday 'cause she could only take the one day off . . .'

To get to anything resembling facts, truth, Joe realized he would have to ooze his way through this mudbath of chit-chat.

'. . . came back for the weekend with Mary and Catriona. We were laughing with Mrs Brady at the B & B. Every cloud has a silver lining for someone, says I. We have our troubles but here you are full for the weekend in the off-season.'

It was no surprise to Joe that his sisters had all travelled up from Cork. That would have been for his father, not him. Joe felt no resentment about this. They were perfect daughters and that was all there was to it. He was far more concerned about what was not being said. His father was on a roll now. There was no stopping the flow.

'They all send their best anyway and told me to call if you wanted any of them to come up to see you. But sure at the rate you're going you'll be out in a few days. There wasn't even much point in me hanging around either, but you know, I thought I might as well just in case. I enjoyed myself. Mrs Brady's very nice. She does a great breakfast.'

Connie's monologue shifted to Cavan and what a fine town it was. He had been great pals with a couple of Cavan lads in the FCA years ago, but never visited them after, even though there was a standing invitation. He couldn't even remember their names now. The staff in the hospital were top-notch, and they took his mobile number so he wouldn't have to wait around the hospital all day. They told him not to worry, they'd call if there was any news. The old mobiles really came into their own in these situations. Imagine, when Babs bought it for him, he thought he'd never have any use for it. No mention of Juliet. Nor, more significantly, Milo. Not even their names in passing. It wasn't the first time Joe had thought how different things would be if his father, not his mother, had been the first to go. Instead of the gentle reedy flow, stubbornly avoiding mention of anything bad, she would be sitting beside him, her eyes fixed on him, speaking in her here's-the-way-it-is style, framed more as statements than questions.

'So, Juliet hasn't been to see you.'

Of course her tone would hint at more to tell, an invitation to probe further if he wanted. And Milo? How would she have dealt with that? If it was the worst news, what would his mother, were she sitting there now, have said?

'Well? Do you want to hear about poor little Milo or would you prefer to leave it?'

That approach would have suited Joe. He often told himself that he would have visited Ballyphehane far more often in the last three years if it had been to see a widowed mother. Did he really miss her? He missed arguing with her. He never argued with his father. How could you when he never got to the point?

'Is it OK now? It sounds fine, is it?'

Joe had no clue what his father was asking. He had lost the thread. He looked into the nervous smiling face, hoping for a clue.

'It was very shallow there for a while.'

Shallow? What the fuck did he mean by shallow? Ah . . . breathing. Of course, his lungs. Joe nodded and sucked in some air as a kind of demonstration. He felt a little catch in his chest.

'It's fine.'

His father smiled and nodded.

'Good. Good. I thought it sounded better all right.'

'How long have I been here?'

'Here? In the hospital?'

'Yes.'

'Ah . . . including today . . . ten days now.'

Ten days? How could it be? Joe had no memories. There were images, a face mask, cold air pushing into his mouth, forcing him to gulp it back. Nurses' faces looming and receding. Pain? Not so much. He could not move. Dreamless sleep. Ten days. Jesus. When Joe focused again, he saw that his father's face now had a certain look. That search for the next thing to say. Like that night in the kitchen in Ballyphehane not long after the funeral. Alone together.

Connie is wiping crumbs from the table on to his palm. Just before he turns away to bring them to the pedal bin, he hesitates and Joe sees a certain look on his face that makes him realize what's going on, what is happening. His father feels some need to talk to him. This is awful. Uncle Mick and Auntie Susan are gone to bed so they can't save him. They've taken his room, he's trapped here, already tucked up in the old sofa-bed. Why can't Connie just follow them to bed, instead of collecting glasses and washing up? Joe shrinks further under the blankets, yawning by way of a hint. Connie continues his snail's pace cleaning operation. He keeps finding another little job to do. Leftover food is carefully wrapped and put into the fridge.

'Mick and Susan are looking well, aren't they?'

Joe replies pointedly, 'Yeah, amazing, especially after travelling from Australia, ha? They must be wrecked I suppose. We could all do with some sleep.'

If his father gets the hint he shows no sign of it. He's wiping down the oilcloth on the table. Meticulously. The clock is now a ticking crescendo, Connie's damp sponge swishes against the oilcloth, and upstairs, the toilet flushes. Joe wants to scream at him. Dad, go to bed now! I'm tired, I want to sleep. Then he sees that look, frightened and uncertain, sure, but with some kind of determination to keep going. Connie, having got rid of the crumbs, starts rearranging the cutlery in the drawer. Rattle rattle rattle. Joe suddenly feels cold. The only thing he wants his father to say right now is goodnight. He wants darkness and the room to himself. He lies back, pulling the blankets round. Should he yawn or close his eyes? Chance a pretend snore? His father is . . . hovering, playing for time, looking for a chance to proceed with this notion of talking. The only consolation is that he'll be unable to get the thing up and running unless Joe himself cooperates with the project. It's a question of holding out long enough, and not helping Connie to proceed. Joe hardens himself for the next few cruel minutes, confining all speech to minimal response. It's the only way; for his father's sake as well as for his own. Connie can find no more domestic tasks to occupy him. The exchanges between them falter more or less to silence. The endgame begins. First of all, the announcement of the intention to say goodnight, 'I'd better say goodnight so,' then the first of a series of actual goodnights, interrupted by solicitous inquiries. Has Joe everything he needs? Is the sofa comfortable enough? They will try not to wake him too early in the morning, although Uncle Mick is a notoriously early riser. Once back in Ireland he loves to go picking wild mushrooms before seven. Connie offers to pin a note to the door warning him not to wake Joe. The second goodnight is offered as the hand reaches teasingly for the light switch, only to pause at the final moment. Some advice about the eccentric ways of the recently acquired electric power shower has to be passed on, as well as a reminder of where the clean towels are kept. Joe continues to hold his nerve, his single-word replies now muffled underneath the blankets; grand, sure, fine, no problem. The third goodnight; surely the last? No. There is still time for some observations about the following day, and the possibility of sun, which has been threatening all week but has never really materialized. Hopefully tomorrow will be fine. The forecast is for fine at any rate. Scattered showers. Sunny spells. Joe hears a fourth goodnight.

''Night so.'

Only seconds yawn between these words and the blessed darkness, but they are tense and agonizing. It is still just about possible that Connie will blurt out something excruciating, making a doomed attempt at a bonding session unavoidable. What if he invokes in some vulgar sentimental way the memory of Joe's mother? That would be truly horrific. Joe hears the sigh of failure in his father's voice as he breathes a last goodnight and presses the light switch.

'Traumatic pneumothorax. I can say it but I can't spell it, sez you. They said you were in intensive care, and could I get here straight away. Sure between one thing and another, it was another four hours before Babs and myself arrived, and the worst was over at that stage . . .'

Connie's bedside rhythm had recovered. Sometimes under pressure he discovered a kind of momentum that kept the words coming. Joe knew he would be able to keep this up for a long time without sliding towards any dangerous subject matter. He remembered feeling some sorrow for Connie that night in the kitchen, although it was buried deep under the relief that his father had failed. Joe was still in no doubt it had been a narrow escape.

'. . . Mr O'Callaghan said it was touch and go for a while. If there had been any more of a delay with the ambulance or anything. The air was escaping from your lungs. There was only minutes in it, he said. It could have gone either way. Anyway he got you into the theatre quick time. A thoractomy. Never heard of that either.'

It was up to Joe. If he really wanted to find out about Milo he would have to confront his father directly, because it was clear that Connie Power would never bring up the subject. Which seemed to make it certain that the news was bad. But how bad? Was his little boy in intensive care somewhere? Had he sustained permanent damage? Or was it the worst news of all? Joe needed to know. It was all he wanted to know. He wished his father would just spit it out, get it over with. Lying helpless on his back, not knowing how long had passed since that last awful memory, a fear had been growing inside Joe even as his body breathed more easily and he felt more alive. It was a fear that he had got the clock thing all wrong. Perhaps disastrously wrong. What if it was never Juliet? What if the batteries had been inserted by Milo? The countdown was for him. If the worst was the case, and he was dead and had died more or less on impact, then . . . ? If Milo had died at zero time, did that make Joe an angel of death, literally ferrying him to his end? Right now only Connie could tell him the first, most important thing he needed to know. His avoidance already made it seem inevitable, but it could be otherwise too. There could be some other bizarre twist. Maybe Milo was still alive but damaged. Maybe Juliet, hearing the sound of the accident from her bed, had come running out and the shock had killed her somehow, a heart attack or something? Maybe in her grief she had taken her own life so that, after all, it was her life the clock had ticked away. Joe knew that there was no point in expecting his father to find courage and tell him. He would have to ask, and in a way that allowed no avoidance. Suddenly Connie stood up.

'I suppose I'd better be off. You need your sleep. Mrs Brady will be delighted to hear you're coming along so well. Can I get you anything before I go?'

Tears shone in his eyes, but the voice maintained its cheery tone. Joe wondered what the fuck would Mrs Brady care. Who was she to him? It was becoming a little harder to breathe. This was it then. Ask him now or wait again for God knows how long. It would be a long night if he didn't find out. He wasn't going to be left in the dark.

'Dad, what about Milo?'

Not that it was any surprise, but Joe saw immediately that of all the questions he could have asked, this was the least welcome. His father's face drained. He looked cornered. It was obvious he had no idea what to say. Joe waited. He knew for sure now that the scenario was very bad. Every second of silence made it worse. The only question was how bad. Was it the worst news of all? His father was unable to hold his gaze any longer. He dropped his eyes and head. His little frame seemed even slighter. Joe held on to the silence. Any word from him now would make it easier for his father and he wasn't having that. He wanted an answer. It was his right. He saw a tiny shake of the head. It could have been an involuntary quiver but it wasn't. Joe knew what it meant. Then came a little sigh, a catch of breath.

'I'm sorry, son.'

Probably because he knew that his only son now had his answer, Connie was able, finally, slowly, to look at Joe again.

'They're fairly sure it was instant. Juliet heard the crash. She ran out as quick as she could and by the time she got to the car, it was too late for the little lad. She called the ambulance straight away. It was some Latvian fellah driving the other car. He's OK, I hear. They don't know what they're at, these fellahs. Sure they're not even on the right side of the road half the time.'

Joe could hear the lack of conviction in his father's voice. He knew whose fault the collision was. Connie sat down again, and reached a very tentative hand towards Joe's arm. Unable to move much, Joe felt the pressure from inside his body more acutely. His heart was beating faster. His neck and shoulders now tense and hard. He needed to pee. Ideally he would have walked about and kicked something. That was impossible. Joe felt used, cursed in some way. Why him? Why had this been put on him? What had he done that was so bad? Everyone would blame him. Even his father probably blamed him deep down. They didn't know, did they, that it was written somewhere? Nobody but he understood the inevitability of it all. Poor little Milo. It was bad enough that his number was up after hardly any life at all, but why was Joe made to be the agent of his only son's death? That was sick. The pressure inside was affecting his breathing now. Joe felt his father let go of his arm. It was not fair. He was being fucked with; tortured, then kept alive enough to feel the pain even more. He had killed his own son. Joe was aware of the spasms jolting his body only because they reminded him how trapped he was. He could not sit up, let alone get out of bed. There was relief as well as a sting in his kidneys when he let go, but his breathing was becoming shorter and shorter. The face of a nurse appeared, his father's face behind her, soft, blubbering now. Useless old fucker, this is all your fault, Joe wanted to snarl. Somehow speech was now impossible. As he saw the nurse lift a face mask towards him, he couldn't even catch his breath enough to confess to the nurse that he had pissed himself. The mask pressed against his cheeks. The nurse held it there. The shock of its cool flow was disturbing at first, then pleasant. His body responded. Soon, apart from the uncomfortable wet cooling fast around his crotch and thighs, a certain calm returned. The nurse's face was smiling. He could just about hear soothing murmurs from her mouth. His father's face had disappeared, but Joe felt a hand touch his arm again, then slide down to his hand and grip it. His father had not held his hand since he was little, so very little. Joe never let him. Nothing he could do about it now. He wished he was dead.

17

'Time heals,' Babs whispered in Joe Power's ear as she rubbed his shoulder in gentle imitation of a hug. He knew she would have loved to give him a good sentimental clinch, but was probably nervous of collapsing his chest.

'Will you be able to get dressed on your own?'

The controlling tone of her voice was what Joe found depressing. Babs was here to take charge. The morning had started so well, with confirmation that he could go home. He hadn't thought about how his father would get back to Cork. It had never occurred to him that his sister would turn up to collect him. Babs must have left at around six this morning to be here now. She had even found time to buy Joe fresh clothes.

'We thought it would be better if you didn't have to put your old clothes on . . . you know.'

Her tone was designed to indicate that she understood how sad such a thing would be for him. Then a brighter note.

'We did the best we could in Dunnes. They'll do until we get you home.'

It most certainly had never occurred to Joe that he would be chauffeured back to Dublin by his sister and father. In so far as he had thought about it at all, he had assumed that, driving himself being out of the question, he would take a taxi.

'Do you need a hand getting dressed?'

No way.

'I'll be fine. Get yourselves a cup of tea. I won't be long.'

Joe backed them into the corridor and closed the door. He sat on the bed. Ah, fuck fuck fuck fuck fuck! What now? He intended to go back to the cottage before going to Dublin. There was no way he wanted Babs to drive him there or anywhere. Why hadn't his father just fucked off home earlier in the week like Joe had asked him to? Why couldn't they all let him alone? Dressing the top half of his body was no great problem, despite the plaster on the arm. Babs had been smart enough to keep it simple. She had bought a T-shirt, a short-sleeved shirt, and a baggy jumper. Joe quickly realized that trousers were going to be pretty awkward, and socks impossible. He went to the ward door and opened it a crack. Neither his sister nor his father were visible outside. He waited for a nurse to come into view. The first to pass, a tiny Filipina, seemed puzzled by his whisper until he explained why he needed her. She smiled at what she probably assumed was another example of the inhibition of Irish men. Joe lay back on the bed and allowed himself to be helped into his trousers, socks and shoes.

'Who will do this for you when you go home?'

Her voice was teasing, but Joe realized it was a fair point, something else he hadn't really thought about. He had been so focused for the last week on persuading everyone that he was getting well enough to be discharged. His ribs were healing fast, his breathing was fine, and now he could limp along with the help of just one crutch. He had pestered Mr O'Callaghan for several days to release him. He had brazenly pointed out that the shortage of acute hospital beds had become a national crisis. A & E was packed with misfortunes on trolleys and chairs waiting for a bed. Surely it was only proper to release his to some more deserving case? He had finally got his way. Now it seemed the problems were only beginning. He had nobody to come home to in Dublin. Or anywhere. Nobody he wanted. When he stood up to button his trousers he felt unwelcome pressure on his stomach. Christ, no. Surely he had not put on more weight? He managed just about to button up without revealing to the little nurse what a tight squeeze it was. How could he have put on weight after what he had been through? He would have to put up with it for now. He was grateful that the baggy jumper hid the bulge of flesh pressing over his waist-band. Joe thanked the nurse and limped out to find his father and sister. They were by the windows, looking out on to the garden area below. Babs was airing her views on the advantages of the smaller provincial hospital over the huge metropolitan centres.

'I don't care what state-of-the-art equipment they have in these super-hospitals, for most patients there's no substitute for a pleasant atmosphere, fresh air, and you know, that sense of community.'

There was no way Joe could suffer several more hours of this. What if they decided to stay with him for the night? It was quite likely. They might feel it would be wrong to leave him on his own. Oh Christ. Oh sweet Jesus no! Smiles and gentle hugs masked the soaring panic. For as long as it took to get down to reception and out to the parking area, Joe allowed himself to feel slightly better. The journey felt like a great escape, away from this wretched imprisonment. He had always hated the idea of it, and the last week had confirmed all his prejudices. Hospital was a smelly nether world, full of mopes. Some were just unlucky like himself, others had ended up here after too many years of bad life choices. Every time he ventured from his room he saw the creatures and heard their moans, the whirr of their wheelchairs, the hollow tinkle of urine on bedpans. Some lay silent under covers, just dissolving it seemed to him. Leaving it now, Joe knew he couldn't bear even the air of the place.

'You have to hand it to them. They did a great job on you all the same. I can't believe you're out so fast.'

Joe wasn't going to pass any comment now that might encourage debate or argument. He was not going to engage at all if he could help it. His father chimed in.

'The staff were fantastic. Really lovely.'

They passed visitors on their way to the wards. Joe had discovered over the last week that he hated them most of all. It was the way they all came bouncing in, so obviously feeling good about themselves, with their patronizing gifts of magazines, Lucozade, grapes. A couple of days before, Joe had seen a teenager giving an iPod to some poor shriv-elled old bastard; his father or uncle probably. Whoever he was tried to hide his bewilderment as the smug skinny shit demonstrated how it worked, and explained that he had downloaded all Johnny Cash's early stuff especially for him.

'Do you need anything, before we head out?'

Babs's creepily solicitous hand on his had stalled them near the franchise shop in the reception area. There was a queue as usual. A little goldmine, was how a patient from Cavan had described it to Joe one day.

'No. I'm fine.'

He was so close to freedom now. Once through the door and past several dreary coughing women standing under the awning, clutching the tops of their dressing-gowns with one hand to stave off the cold, while lighting up with the other, Joe felt the chill of November with the pleasure of a boy in an ad for mints. Zing! His heart lightened. Already he felt better able to deal with the prison guards on either side of him. He was now quite certain that he didn't want his father and sister coming to the cottage with him. In fact, he didn't even want them to know that he intended going there. They were already approaching Babs's car, so, on the basis that it was better to deal with it sooner rather than later, he said as casually as he could, even before she unlocked the door, 'Well, have a good trip home. If you could drop me to a cab office in the town that'd be perfect.'

He knew this wouldn't do it of course. It was just the first salvo. He waited for the 'Nonsense, of course we're going to drive you back to Dublin' reply. Babs and his father glanced at each other. It was no surprise who was left to do the talking.

'What are you saying, Joe? We're bringing you home . . .'

Joe opened his mouth to express mock surprise at the plan, and begin his ready-made protest that Dublin was way out of their way, and far too much trouble, and they had such a long journey ahead of them to get to Cork by nightfall. Besides, a taxi would whiz him home in no time. He failed to say any of this, however, because Babs had continued speaking.

'. . . We're taking you to Rochestown Road. I've the spare room set up for you and all.'

Joe could not speak. Babs came round the car to him.

'Sure for God's sake Joe, going back to Dublin now? On your own? You didn't think we'd do that to you, did you? Oh, Joe love.'

She pawed him. Still carefully, gently.

'After what you've been through.'

Now the November air chilled Joe to the bone. How was he to get out of this? He had expected them to insist strongly on taking him back to Dublin, but he had also calculated that the prospect of relieving them of the burden of all that extra driving, and in particular tempting Babs with the possibility of getting back to her kid so much faster, would eventually wear them down. As long as he was able to reassure their consciences sufficiently, he would eventually get his way.

That plan was dead in the water now. Absolutely fucked.

Babs and his father had clearly talked the whole thing through. They might even have assumed that Joe would be delighted with the thoughtfulness of the arrangement. Babs and Dick had such a beautiful home on Rochestown Road. He could imagine them discussing it over the phone. Or rather, his father listening while Babs talked. Babs would have made a big deal about Juliet, how angry she must be with Joe. One had to have sympathy for her, of course. How else could a mother feel in such circumstances? Imagine if Dick . . . she couldn't even bear to think about how she might react. Babs would have impressed on his father the idea that, however bad the situation would be if it happened in the context of a secure married environment, it was so much more unimaginably terrible when one was in poor Joe's situation. However thoughtless or foolish he had been, and let's face it, the accident had been his fault really, the family couldn't leave him completely isolated, exposed like that.

As Joe spoke, he saw Babs open the passenger door, with a little smile and an older sister shake of the head.

'No, honestly, I'd be better off back in Dublin.'

'Will you get in. It's fine. Dick and I are looking forward to having you.'

His father had already opened the back door on the other side, but hadn't sat in yet, perhaps in case Joe needed assistance. He was baring his teeth also. It dawned on Joe that further discussion was utterly useless. Both father and sister had an air about them. Plans had been laid. Perhaps any moment now more family members were going to appear from behind cars and shout, 'Surprise!' Verbal resistance was futile. Joe took the only option he felt was available to him. He turned and limped away as fast as he could. It didn't take long for Babs to catch up with him. His father wasn't far behind.

'Joe, stop. What's the matter?'

Joe kept limping along. The path to the entrance was long and meandering. He couldn't even see the front gates yet.

'Joe!'

Babs' claw curled round his shoulder now, almost daring to restrain him. Next thing Joe felt his father grasp his good arm more decisively. So they were going to use force.

'I'm going home to Dublin.'

'But Joe, that's madness. You'll be all on your own. You'll be much better off with us. It's no trouble, I promise you. Dick is delighted you're coming down.'

'Joe, Joe, are you annoyed we didn't tell you? Is that it? Sure we only decided it last night when I heard you might be getting out. We thought it would be a nice surprise for you.'

They were almost at the gates. Joe noticed covert glances from some arriving visitors as he wrestled free from restraint and raised his crutch high.

'Take your hands off me!'

He could tell that they knew he meant it. There was fear in their eyes now. They knew he would strike if either one of them attempted to take hold of him again. He backed away towards the gates. Passers-by were staring openly, but he didn't care. It was Babs and his father who needed to worry about that. It was more likely that he would be seen as some sort of victim in this drama. After all, he was the one with the bad leg and an arm in plaster. With an eye to propaganda and embarrassment value, he raised his voice.

'All I'm asking is that you stop harassing me.'

He limped on as quickly as he dared. The pressure on his stomach from the trousers waistband made fast motion very uncomfortable, but there was nothing to be done. When he next looked back he saw his father and sister returning to the car. Would that be the last he would see of them? He reached the gates and turned on to Railway Road. Now he slowed down, attempting full breaths. It was difficult. He opened the button at the top of his trousers to relieve the pressure. The zip held. How far was he from the town centre? Maybe a cab would appear and he wouldn't have to walk all the way. Babs' car passed him with infuriating ease and pulled in just ahead. His father got out and faced him nervously. Babs stayed at the wheel.

'Joe, please Joe. Listen for a sec.'

Joe stopped. He didn't really want to muscle his way past the little man. He sensed there might be a compromise suggestion on the way. Surely they would be glad to get rid of him at this stage?

'Joe, honestly, the way things were, we thought you'd be delighted to come back with us. We only want the best thing for you. You've had an awful couple of weeks of it. Look ... Mr O'Callaghan told me he'd let you out only if there was someone to take care of you, do you understand?'

Joe understood the threat. It was come with them or go back inside.

'He said you needed plenty of time for peace and rest ... and he said maybe ...'

Connie Power struggled with his next words. He tiptoed.

'Now I mean obviously only if you wanted ... but he suggested maybe there'd be no harm ... if you got someone to ... talk to ... you know ... kind of counselling.'

Joe thought about how long the walk might be to the town centre, and how inevitable it was that Babs and his father would pursue him in the car. There was going to be no easy way out, was there? A much better plan came to him, a tactic from his adolescence that he should have thought of before. Never waste time arguing the toss with parents. Just agree, then do what you like anyway. He walked towards his father. He bent down to look in the passenger door at Babs. He showed her his trouser top.

'These are too tight. Look. I can't even button up.'

'Oh, I'm sorry Joe. I had it in my head you were a thirty-four.'

This was such a relief. Babs had bought him a thirty-four, which meant he hadn't put on more weight. In fact he had probably lost some, because unlike in M & S two weeks ago, he had actually been able to close these trousers, albeit with discomfort. He smiled at Babs and looked humble.

'I have to get a bigger pair. I can't breathe properly if I sit down with these.'

'Of course, come on. Will Dunnes do?'

Joe nodded. His father helped him into the passenger seat. He gave him a little reassuring pat on his shoulder before closing the door. Babs pulled back out on to the road.

'We had to clear out Daíthí's toys, you wouldn't believe the amount of stuff that child has, but the room is looking lovely for you. And Daíthí is dying to see his Uncle Joe again.'

Joe tried to look pleased with that as he struggled to remember where the nearest cab office was. How close was it to Dunnes? He couldn't quite pin it down. He hoped that driving through the town might help him remember. Babs kept the chat going. Joe did his best to say the occasional nice thing. He was conscious of not overdoing it because he could tell that Babs was still wary, not fully convinced of his change of heart. She liked to think of herself as nobody's fool. They reached the roundabout and turned on to Farnham Street. Joe suddenly remembered that the cab office was first right and down that street somewhere. He searched for the name as they drove past. He caught it just in time: Abbey Street. If he was to get back there without either Babs or his father pursuing him, then he would have to escape from Dunnes stores undetected. He wasn't quite sure yet how to do that. Luck was with him on Connolly Street when Babs could not find parking near enough. She had to stop briefly at the entrance to let Joe and his father get out.

'I'll follow you in when I've found a parking spot.'

She added, with an attempt to sound amusingly arch, 'Mind him now, Dad.'

Menswear was at the far side. Joe was feeling a bit of a rush, his brain on high alert, surveying the shop, scanning for alternative exits. As he pretended to focus on the selection of trousers, he picked out the nearest exit. His eye traced the most direct path to it. He held up a size thirty-six to show his father.

'I'd better try it on just to be sure. I won't be a sec.'

He went to the changing area and pulled the curtain. Alone again, Joe took a calming breath. Now it was a matter of choosing the best moment. For comfort's sake he would have preferred to put on the larger trousers, but he might set off an alarm as he left the shop. Joe tossed the trousers on a chair, and peeped out. Connie was waiting right in his line of escape. A passing assistant stopped and asked him something. He shook his head and turned to nod towards the fitting-rooms. Joe pulled his eye away in time. When he peeked again his father had moved further away to a rail of jackets, having probably decided he would feel less conspicuous if he appeared to be browsing. Now was the perfect moment for escape. How long would it be before Connie turned round? Long enough for him to limp to the exit unseen? Joe forced himself to think of the seconds counting down to Babs's arrival, after which escape would become almost impossible. This drove him on. He stepped out from behind the curtains and walked quickly, directly. There was no point in checking for Babs as he came out on to the street. Either she would see him or not. The important thing was to get round the corner as fast as he could, then find Abbey Street. Head down and no hesitation was the way to go. Joe began to feel a sense of release. He was ahead of the game so far. Of course it wasn't over yet. Only a little head start, and it might not be long before either his father or sister would work out the cab office angle, after which it would be a question of how long it took them to find it. Joe didn't know if there was more than one in Cavan town.

Even though the woman in the cab office kept emphasizing that the client was a man with a crutch, it took twelve minutes thirty-eight seconds, according to the clock on the wall, before she tracked down someone willing to take him to Gowna and then Dublin. Because of the pressure against his stomach, Joe did not sit down. He stood staring at the clock, counting every second of the next five minutes and sixteen seconds until the woman nodded to him as a black Skoda pulled up outside. Joe's relief was tempered by fear that at the last moment, as he broke cover from the cab office, and crossed the pavement to the car, he would be spotted. It also occurred to him that he should request discretion from the woman about his destination. He decided this might backfire. She might wonder why, begin to panic, and phone the Gardaí. The whole thing could get out of hand. He was already worried that she had been looking at him strangely. Better to keep it simple. Babs never drove fast when she had Connie in the car, so even if they found the cab office and figured out he was headed for the cottage, they wouldn't catch him up. He would encourage the driver to go as fast as possible. He had no intention of delaying at the cottage anyway. Head down, he limped across the path and fell into the back seat. He tried to sit so as to put as little pressure on the trousers zip as possible.

'Begod now, you've been in the wars.'

It was an annoying little voice with too much treble in it. The face in the rear view mirror wasn't any more attractive. The pink balding head peeping up over the top of the headrest suggested a man of seventy at least.

'And not as much as a jacket on you. You'll freeze.'

Joe suspected it was going to be a long, slow, tedious drive.

'Gowna and Dublin. You know now it'll cost you?'

'That's fine.'

'Gowna is thirty, and Dublin from here is two twenty, so Gowna'd be much the same, so that makes two fifty. Tell you what, I'll do you two forty for the whole job.'

It only now occurred to Joe that he had no more than thirty euro in his wallet.

'Perfect.'

'Fair enough. Long as you know what you're letting your-self in for.'

Joe wondered if there was anything he could say that might persuade this old fuck to get going, and put the boot down.

'Sure. And if there's any way you could –'

Mid-sentence, they bolted from the kerb at what seemed a dizzying speed on such a narrow street and spun around on to Connolly Street. Joe glanced left and for a couple of seconds was fairly sure he saw his father and sister a hundred yards or so away at a street corner, before the bald driver ran an orange light, veering towards the Athlone road.

'Will you be stopping long in Gowna? It's just that we'd be far better off getting to Dublin before the dark.'

Joe assured him he would do his best to be as quick as he could. The cottage was beyond Gowna, near the lake. He just had to collect something. Working out the journey time himself, Joe figured twenty-five minutes to the cottage, or less at the rate they were going, a few minutes there, on the road again before half one. They could be in Dublin by half three, in which case he could go straight to the cemetery and not have to wait another day. That would be good.

'So, you had some class of an accident?'

Joe decided not to waste time composing a fake story. The man would see the Maserati at the cottage anyway.

'Yeah, got a bit of a bash. I was lucky, I suppose.'

The bald driver took the awkward left and right chicane at Casey's steakhouse without a pause. Joe was scared but glad.

'It wasn't one of them East Europeans, was it? Those feckers are around every corner with their old bangers on the wrong side of the road. They should –'

It would have been simpler to say yes, it was a Latvian. It would even have been true. Joe didn't know why he cut across the man's speech.

'No. It was my own fault.'

Though it had not been his intention, his words had the gratifying effect of silencing the bald driver for another few miles. They also set Joe off on a whole new line of thought. He considered the 'what ifs' that had dominated his mind ever since he had recovered sufficiently to allow clear thought.

What if . . . he had never bought the clock? Might Milo

be still alive, or had that been inevitable, one way or another?

What if . . . OK, say he bought the clock but then just ignored everything that happened afterwards; let events unfold? He would not have been at the cottage that day at all. What then? Or would Milo's death simply have taken a different form?

What if . . . it had occurred to him before it was too late that Milo rather than Juliet might have restarted the clock. This burdened him most of all; that he had been so blind to that now-obvious possibility. He still didn't know if it was so. This was the most important thing he had yet to find out. His problem was, the only person who could tell him was Juliet. How he might get to talk to her about this or anything he had no idea. The image of Milo carrying the clock from the cottage that day was now constant. Why, why had it not crossed his mind, even as a remote possibility? He could so easily have checked it, even that day in the cottage, with Juliet lying in bed. It could have been so casual and seemingly unimportant. At worst Juliet would have thought it was Joe making stupid small talk. Her reply might have changed everything. Beyond any shadow of doubt he would never have set off in the car with Milo at that moment if . . . If. What would have happened? Would everything now be all right? Would Milo have remained safe? Was it possible that such significant events could be made to turn out differently?

What if . . . it was simply all his fault?

They turned off the main Athlone road through an impressive pair of fifteen-foot-high danger signs that framed the little country road. Having arrived near Gowna so fast, Joe felt a little guilty that the driver's continuing silence might be a sign of hurt feelings. He decided to make amends with a casual friendly remark.

'You must know these roads like the back of your hand?'

The single syllable squeak sounded like agreement, but certainly didn't invite any further chat. Joe disliked the chilly atmosphere, but had no desire to talk crap for the next few hours either. What he wanted was a friendly silence, broken only by occasional inquiries from the bald driver about his needs and comfort.

'If I could drive as well as you, I mightn't be in the state I'm in.'

If this combination of flattery and self-abasement didn't help, then Joe would just leave it be.

'Fifty-two years, and never troubled an insurance company even the once.'

The thaw had set in. They were on speaking terms again. The question now would be how to keep it in check, as the little voice piped on.

'No offence meant now to yourself and your troubles, but if people just had proper control over what they were doing there'd be no accidents at all. And it's getting worse you know, not better. The thing about people these days is that they have no control. That's why it's all getting out of hand. No respect for others.'

Joe told himself he only had to suffer this for another couple of minutes. Soon the bald driver would need precise directions for the cottage. The journey had taken just twenty minutes. He was way ahead of the game. The 'for sale' sign was the first thing Joe noticed as they approached. His father had mentioned something about it in his roundabout way. It didn't upset Joe to see it. It was just another odd detail in a strange day. They pulled up at the entrance. When the bald driver saw him struggle to get out of the car, he stepped out and helped.

'Thanks. I won't be long.'

Looking up the drive Joe couldn't see the Maserati. He felt panic again. Had it been towed away? He limped towards the cottage, angling to see round the corner. There it was. His instant relief had to compete with another darker feeling as he looked at the wreck of his beautiful car. The whole passenger side was a squashed beer can, the door window and front windscreen both shattered. Joe saw dark spatters inside that could only be blood. The poor kid never stood a chance. Not the remotest. Joe came round to the driver side. He presumed that the keys would not be still in the car. They were not. Who had them? The Gardaí probably. What now? How would he get the boot open?

'Janey, that was some wallop.'

Shock seemed to send the pitch of the bald driver's voice even higher. Of course the old fucker's curiosity had got the better of him. He had to come and have a little look-see.

'Well, you don't need me to tell you how lucky you were the whack was all on the passenger side. Blessed entirely you were.'

There was no reply Joe could make to that. For some reason he was allowed a precious few seconds' silence. Just as the little whine began again Joe turned and interrupted.

'I'm so stupid. I came down especially to get something out of the boot. I've gone and forgot the keys. Would you believe it?'

He tapped the boot in frustration. He looked at the bald driver as if a last forlorn hope had occurred to him.

'You haven't anything I could open this with, do you?'

'I'll have a look.'

He came back with a selection of implements, obviously enlivened by the task. This was not a run-of-the-mill fare.

'Do you want me to try? There's not much you can do with only the one good hand.'

Joe felt he should agree. He watched impatiently as his driver tried to prise away the lock using some kind of a wrench. Soon the metal was bent, and gaps were opened, but the lock itself held. Joe picked up a small axe from the little armoury.

'Let me try this. I won't need two hands.'

He raised the axe high and attacked the lock ferociously. He hacked and hacked and hacked. He did not want to stop. Even the stab he felt across his shoulder with every blow renewed him. The trickles of sweat were a blinding relief. They might have been tears. When he finally cut through the lock and the boot lifted, he was sorry it was over, even though a spasm up his arm muscle made him drop the axe, and his body sagged against the car. He realized the silence from the bald driver was a nervous one. He wiped his brow and tried to smile.

'You know the way sometimes, you won't let it get the better of you.'

Joe looked into the boot. His shoulder-bag was there. He zipped it open, reached in, and lifted back the towel to uncover the millennium clock. He turned it face up. It was still working.

1635952746 . . . 45 . . . 44 . . .

It seemed like all the time in the world.

Joe zipped up the bag, picked up his crutch and went back to the cab. When he got himself settled he looked at the car clock. It was just after 1.20. The bald driver sat in and started up without a word. This time Joe could sense the silence was edgy, perhaps even slightly fearful. He closed his eyes, genuinely needing to rest them, but also so he could pretend to be asleep. He heard how fast they were going from the engine revs and the occasional whip of branches against the window. His driver was obviously anxious to get this journey over with as quickly as possible. That suited Joe perfectly. His mind drifted. Where were Babs and his father now? He hoped they had been sensible and decided to go back to Cork. Surely Babs would have got the hump at what she would have called 'Joe's antics'. Of course his father could be quietly obstinate. They might still be in Cavan sitting in Babs' car, she saying, 'Let's go home,' he saying, 'Do you think, maybe we should have one more look around,' trying to force him to leave as pointless as it had been for Joe to try prising information out of him about Milo's funeral. What way did the man's head work? Was Joe supposed to be angry that the funeral happened without him? Jesus, what was Juliet to do? Of course she had to go ahead with it. Who knew when he would get out of hospital, and what his state of mind would be? Joe had wanted to grab his father and shake him. It had taken days to get any actual details out of him about the funeral. Finally Connie muttered something about not having talked directly to Juliet because she was crying so much he didn't think he should intrude, and anyway her parents had come over to him and had a bit of a chat. Very friendly in Connie's opinion. They had had a good suggestion.

'They thought it might be for the best, you know for now, if any communication between you and Juliet went through them.'

So. Was that how it was to be then. It had taken a great deal of interrogation from Joe for his father to let that much out. What was the man afraid of? That Joe would be so devastated he might self-harm, or fall into a coma and never recover? Juliet's position was completely understandable. How else was she going to feel after what had happened? It was the most normal reaction possible in such a situation.

That's what made his father so infuriating. First instinct always dive for cover, say nothing, keep in by the wall. Why could he not just tell his grown-up married and separated son what was what? Then everyone on both sides, if you had to talk about sides, knew where they stood. The way his father doled out information, Joe still couldn't even be sure that he had named the correct cemetery. Mount Jerome he had said. There had been a big crowd and loads of flowers. It sounded heartbreaking.

The bald driver spoke. His tone was stiff as he inquired if Joe wanted to use the new toll road.

'It's entirely up to yourself. I couldn't say how much time you'll save, if it's worth the money at all.'

'Yeah, well, let's give it a go.'

'If you like now. It's your money.'

Joe understood the hint and searched his pocket. He found a fiver. The trousers zip pinched at his flesh as he leaned forward to hand it over. On the new motorway they would surely make even better time. He would soon be back in his apartment, showered, shaved and fed; safe. He could work things out then. The toll road was almost empty. Joe warmed to the curious perfect silence of this brand-new motorway. The low-lying November sun crept around the back of the car, casting its long shadow in front of them, as they travelled to where? The sensation was one of pleasant danger. The bald driver took the opportunity to push his speed beyond 120 kph. They would definitely reach Dublin before 3.30. There would be time to go to Mount Jerome before the sun went down. Even though that plan was pretty well settled in Joe's mind, once they arrived at the roundabout near Heuston station he felt so close to his Smithfield apartment that he was tempted to go home straight away. It was the thought of waking the following day, or the day after, with this task hanging over him, that convinced him otherwise.

'Hang a right here, please.'

He guided the bald driver towards Mount Jerome without mentioning the precise destination. He would stop at a bank machine as close to the cemetery as possible. They reached Harold's Cross bridge quickly. He spotted an AIB, and asked to stop. Everything was working out as planned, until Joe put the bank card in the slot, and shifted his hand to key in his personal code.

He could not remember it.

It should have been automatic. It was less a matter of knowing the number than, like a touch typist, knowing exactly where on the keypad to place his fingers. This was ridiculous. He had used that number for over ten years. He used it for all his cards. Was this some symptom, some side-effect from the drugs, the treatment? It was probably temporary, but what to do now? The bald bollocks had got out of the car when Joe got out. Glancing back, Joe could see him standing there staring, his shrivelled head the only part of him visible over the black roof. The transaction should take less than thirty seconds. Joe knew that. The bald driver would too. How much time had passed already? More than that definitely. Joe stared down at the numbers. What the fuck was it? It was clear now that it wasn't going to come to him just like that. His only choice was to think it through. Why had he chosen the number in the first place? His brain rattled through the possibilities. Age? Of course not, age changes. Birth date? Maybe. Day and month; 1002. Was that it? No, that wasn't ringing any bells. Day and year; 1068? Month and year; 0268? Christ, was it Juliet's date of birth? Not sure. It couldn't be anything to do with Milo, he was using the code long before he was born, before he was married now that he thought of it. Had the secret number any significance at all? Was it, say, related to his PPS number? Joe wanted to faint. If he could faint then at least it would be out of his hands. Someone else would have to take responsibility. There would be an ambulance. It would be an emergency. All thought of money would be put on the back burner. He would end up in hospital again . . . No way. His fingers had pressed 68. The year he was born. The fag end of the sixties as he always thought of it, when it was all turning sour, just his luck. Something about this number seemed right. 68 . . . what? What? He knew he had it. It was so close, something to do with 1968. Something. Images flashed, the blood pumping at his temples. His mother smiling with babe in arms. In front of their house. Not from life but a faded colour photograph. A little boy walking home from school on his own, reading as he went. In the door without taking his eyes off his book . . . the door. He had it. He remembered. He knew the shape of it on the keypad again. His fingers pressed 22. So simple. The number on his front door at home in Cork. He always loved chanting it as a child. The rhythm of it.

Twenty-two, Sycamore Road, Ballyphehane. Where he grew up.

The machine offered him choices. He pressed 'Other amounts' and requested four hundred euro. Joe turned and gestured helplessly at Baldy.

'Bloody machines. It's OK now.'

He turned back to collect his card and cash. He limped to the car holding out five fifties.

'That's fine.'

Now that it was all over and he had been paid above the odds, the bald driver seemed to relax. He dropped his eyes a little and tipped his shiny forehead in an oddly subservient way. He seemed suddenly to be a nice old codger. If you passed him on the street you would think he was harmless, a bit simple even. Joe acknowledged his thanks with a wave that he realized was patronizing. He turned and limped away before this old bald man with glasses, who for a brief stretch of time had been his driver, sat back into his car. 6822. He wouldn't forget that combination again in a hurry. It wasn't even four different numbers, only three. How could he have forgotten? Fucking hospitals. Someone should have warned him.

16

Mount Jerome was silent and seemed empty. The sun was now so low it appeared only in the gaps between a line of yew trees. As far as Joe could tell there was no other living person around. This was good. This way he could search without interference. No need to explain to anyone that he didn't know where his own son was buried. Once he found the newest section, he would look for the little wooden crosses they used until the time came to erect a headstone. Then he would search for the newest-looking mounds, and the freshest bunches of flowers. It was only . . . when? Eight – nine days ago.

The search took longer than he expected. The number of recently dead was surprising. Even after isolating the new graves he had to check more than a dozen before he found the cross with the name Milo Power on it. And the dates. More than seeing his boy's name, Joe shivered at the dates. October 2000–November 2005. It was the littlest, tiniest amount of time in the scheme of things. Joe laid down his crutch and joined his hands together in a formal way. He stared at the little cross, pressing his mind for appropriate images and memories; Juliet motioning him to come quietly and peep through the crack in the guest bedroom door, to see his mother sitting up in bed swaying baby Milo gently as she la-la'd the *Merry Widow* waltz; Joe, hoisting three-year-old Milo high, shouting, 'You're the winner!' after he had chased Babs' scraggly terrier around her garden grabbing at his tail. It was the only time he could remember Milo showing a bit of boyish aggressive spirit. Juliet of course had disapproved . . .

Enough.

This remembering was not taking Joe anywhere he wanted to go. There was something he wanted to feel that he could not. He knew the word that described it perfectly with its deep lonely German timbre: forlorn. Why could he not say, *I am forlorn*? Why, standing here in such tragic circumstance, was his forehead cool, his eyes dry, his hands unshaking, his heartbeat normal? Joe just could not get there. Forlorn remained out of reach. Still, he had bothered to come. He had stood until it was almost night. He could hear bats. Some final gesture and he could go. Speaking aloud was not on, even though there was no one around to hear. A silent prayer didn't feel right either. He could kiss his son's name? Maybe. It was the best he could think of in the near darkness. It wasn't exactly inspired but it might feel right. He limped around to the head of the grave and leaned forward towards the little cross. He held it steady with his hand, and bent further and lower to bring his lips to it. As he kissed the place where his little boy's name was, he felt the zip pop. His trousers opened and slid down, stopping just below his knees.

15

Having never been to the Yacht bar before, Joe wasn't sure how long it would take to get there from his place. It was 7.30 now, would half an hour be enough? The taxi driver seemed confident.

'Ah yeah, sure it's only Clontarf. Unless the traffic is mad altogether.'

It was the first time Joe had left his apartment since he had arrived back from Mount Jerome, under cover of darkness, his jumper tugged far down to cover his burst flies. He had pulled in his waist and squeezed the top button shut to hold his trousers up. Now, a week later, he still had a little red weal just below the navel where the button had bitten into his flesh. He was emerging tonight to meet Gretta. From the tone of her answering-machine message and their subsequent short phone conversation, Joe was confident that there was a distinct possibility of getting fucked for the first time in months. An arm in a cast might be problematic but surely not insurmountable. It might even make for a few tension-relieving laughs at a critical moment.

Was there another reason he might have decided to meet Gretta? Aware of how long he had been lodging inside his own head with the ticking clock, Joe was no longer sure he was capable of letting another person near his secret places. Nonetheless he had been wondering if the possibility existed that he might want to 'talk'. This might mean nothing more than normal social interaction; chit-chat, flirting. He had not spoken to anyone in a week, apart from delivery people, and an estate agent to ask him to put the Sounds Alive! studio on the market. He had avoided talking to his father and to Babs, instead sending e-mails apologizing for his behaviour. He begged very convincingly for some quiet time, promising to visit his GP regularly. Apart from these contacts Joe had simply let time go by in his apartment. Being there began to have the aura of a very comfortable waiting-room between past and future. This was necessary. Until Juliet would agree to talk to him he could not move on. Juliet was not responding. Three messages to her mobile, several e-mails and an inevitably pained conversation with his ex-mother-in-law had got him nowhere. 'It will take time,' was the best Laura could offer. She even managed to sound very faintly sympathetic, as though it was her considered view that Joe was not a total monster. Just as she was saying goodbye she remembered something.

'Oh Joe – your car, you know, in Longford. I presume you're waiting for the insurance people to come and examine it?'

Joe had not thought about that at all.

'Ah . . . no.'

'Of course . . . well . . . I'm sure you can hardly bear to deal with these things, but it's just that there it is, parked outside the cottage and . . . well . . . you see, Juliet has people coming to view the place in the next few days and . . . you know . . .'

Joe knew exactly. No point in upsetting a prospective buyer with the jagged reality of a crushed car outside the front door. Here was a chance to seem reasonable and helpful. Soften up Juliet. He made an instant decision.

'I won't be bothering with insurance. No point. I'll get one of the local garages to come and take it away for scrap.'

'Oh that's really kind of you, but we couldn't ask you to go to all that trouble, Joe. We'll organize that ourselves.'

The phone call ended very positively. Joe thought it was a lucky stroke that his ex-mother-in-law had remembered to mention the car, as his reaction surely cast him in a favourable light. Bottom line right now, however, he still had no prospect of talking directly to Juliet, no way of confirming his theory that it was Milo who had restarted the clock, and so triggered the countdown to his death. What Joe needed was certainty. He had begun to believe that it was so. In fact with each passing hour he was becoming as sure as sure could be that it must be so. But . . . a word, a nod of confirmation from Juliet would end all speculation. Once that happened anything was possible. He could even reveal to her the whole extraordinary story. She might begin to accept that there should be no blame. They were all just victims of horrible fate. What might happen between them then? Being honest with himself, Joe knew he thought less about the future of his relationship with Juliet than about what he would do with the clock once he confirmed whether or not it really had this strange predictive power. Would he, for example, have the courage to take a pair of batteries and call up his own destiny? In genuine honesty, Joe could not answer this. It was true that since returning to the apartment he had not looked at the clock. It lay covered in his bag. Of course not looking at it didn't stop the seconds ticking away. It didn't keep it from his mind as he tried to sleep; less than four hours every night for a week now. Each day he felt a little more groggy and listless. He dozed sometimes in the afternoon dusk, lounging on the sofa. A couple of times he had turned on his laptop only to slump forward within minutes, eyes closing. He had stopped using it at all once he became sure that Juliet would not make contact that way. His only interaction with fresh air and the outside world was to step out on to his balcony and take full breaths. This helped him feel better. The cold November blast at his kidneys almost always made him want to piss. On several nights he suppressed the urge to slip his dick between the bars of the balcony railing and spray on the little Smithfield revellers below.

Around the time he began to limp about the apartment without a crutch, Joe wondered if perhaps some sort of social interaction would be good, and he immediately thought of Gretta's answering-machine message. It had been one of fifteen waiting for him the night he returned from the cemetery. Having popped open the trousers button to relieve the cutting pressure on his belly, kicked off his shoes, stepped out of the fallen trousers as he dragged the baggy jumper one-handed over his head, Joe took a breath that was really a heartfelt relieved sigh. His battered semi-naked body felt freedom again, security in his nest. He had choices for the first time in weeks. He could limp out on to the balcony and watch the Smithfield torches burn high in the sky as the nightlife buzzed about below, play Prince or Talking Heads full blast, dig shit food out of the freezer, or just pick up the phone and order in. He could strip and have an admittedly awkward shower, or a wank, or both. He could – looking around his home enjoying these thoughts, and noticing the flashing '15' on his answering machine – listen to his messages. Or not, was his next thought. He really was in no mood, but something nagged at him. What if there was a message from Juliet in there? Unlikely of course, but still . . . There might also be something recent from his father or Babs, confirming whether or not they had returned home to Cork. That would be worth knowing. It would kill off any residual unease that they would suddenly come buzzing at his door; Florence Nightingales with fangs. If there was something he absolutely didn't want to hear he could always fast forward through it. Was there really any likelihood that Juliet would have called? Virtually none. Still. He went to the machine and pressed the 'new messages' button. As it happened he never bothered to fast forward. Instead he stretched on the sofa letting the messages run, with their constant reminders of dates and times passed, and the possibilities of futures that would never happen now. There was a sound engineer from London he knew vaguely called Simon, who said he would be passing through Dublin next week, which was now last week, and would be available for a pint and a natter. Sonia, who he hadn't heard from in years, called with a coy request for a freebie. Would he mix a low-budget short that some new girlfriend of hers had shot? Like immediately, which was nine days ago, because they had to meet a deadline for some Polish short film festival. A giggly message from college pal Grace announced that she and her partner Brian had returned from their amazing six-month Far East adventure, and were inviting people over on Thursday to see the fab photos and eat Vietnamese food. Last Thursday. Far from being depressed by such cheery communiqués, Joe enjoyed the parallel reality they suggested. Later there was a change in tone with a second message from a sombre, apologetic, deeply embarrassed Grace, who had finally heard the news. Four of the old pals checked in and bit the bullet. Rory first of course, then Shane, Cian and Steve. What could the poor fuckers say, now that their old pal had killed his only child and nearly died himself. What a dilemma for them. Joe could hear in all their messages a pattern of inarticulacy, pauses, sighs and mumbles, as if they were all performing in some dodgy Irish version of *The OC*.

'Hey Joe, old buddy . . . listen, what can I say . . . (breath) So sorry, man . . . I don't know when you'll get this but you know, ah . . . just to say . . . like you know I'm I'm I'm here for you, yeah . . . (sigh) I mean any time, you know, really any time . . . Jesus man . . . like if you want to have a pint or whatever, talk you know . . . (a kind of breathy sigh)'

Joe understood where exactly his mates were in all this. Probably thinking, 'Thank Christ it didn't happen to me.' He knew he would not be taking up any of these invitations; for their sake as well as his.

In the midst of all this cringe-making male unease, Gretta's phone message sounded mercifully different. Her clean fluent voice was a relief as well as a surprise. He recognized it straight away of course. That was a large part of the shock. To him her voice was heard on radio, announcing supermarket special offers, or sniggering with her girlie pals about their silly husbands, or advising investors, in crisp tones, that terms and conditions applied. It was a voice from his studio life. It felt odd hearing it at home on his answering machine, speaking one-to-one.

'Hello, Joe. This is Gretta, you know, Gretta Downey? I know you're not in Dublin right now, I just wanted to leave a message to say that when you get back, and hopefully that'll be very soon, if you need anything, please, please don't hesitate to call. If there's anything I can do for you, yeah? I keep thinking, you know, about that conversation we had in the studio that day. And then . . . well . . . really strange how things happen. Anyway, my number is . . .'

What was all that about? Why? Joe had no idea. Finally, from earlier that day, there were two messages, one curt from Babs, announcing that she and Daddy were now going home and they might have to inform the HSE about the situation, then later whining from his father, confirming their arrival at Rochestown Road, pleading with him to get in touch, and emphasizing how worried they were. Joe replayed Gretta's message several times. He couldn't help but detect a sexual undercurrent in her tone, which became more marked each time he listened. As a good voice-over artist, she would have known exactly how to pitch it.

The taxi turned left from the North Circular on to Bally-bough Road. Joe still hadn't decided if it was the possibility of sex was driving him outdoors tonight, or the opportunity of sharing his story with Gretta? Without any doubt that motivation was lurking there. It had been part of his decision to return Gretta's phone message in the first place, and certainly propelled his spontaneous decision, during that call, to arrange a date. Joe remembered the key dialogue exchange word for word.

'I'm beginning to wonder will I ever go out again? I wouldn't need to. You can have a whole life delivered to your door these days if you want.'

'I know. And it can be so tempting not to have to make any effort at all. Still, what's out there can be kinda tempting as well.'

It was the fact that she said 'tempting' twice, propelled Joe.

'Yeah, maybe I should let myself be tempted. Would it be good for me?'

'Wouldn't do any harm. Seriously Joe, you should. I have some free time this week if you want to hook up. If it helps.'

Done and dusted. Gretta suggested the Yacht. Close to her apartment, she said. Not much room for doubt there.

The taxi was now at the Clontarf end of Fairview Park and Joe knew only one thing for sure. If he did start to reveal his story, then there would be no sex. In Joe's mind the two things were mutually exclusive. Either or; fucking or talking.

'Very sad, wasn't it? Dying at that age?'

The taxi-man's words shocked Joe out of his thoughts. What the fuck? The eyes staring at him from the rear-view mirror seemed to require an answer.

'Hm?'

'I tell you something, I don't mind admitting it, I was in tears myself now. How about you?'

Joe did not know what he was supposed to say. Was he dreaming this? He didn't know this man, did he? Why was he saying these things?

'The wife of course couldn't figure me at all. No empathy there, you know what I mean? "Sure he brought it on himself," she says, and OK, we know that, but I mean fuck it you know, which of us hasn't been there or thereabouts, ha?'

The eyes in the rear-view lit up as car headlights flashed by. Joe was scared.

'You probably don't remember him in his prime, do you? What are you, early forties?'

Early forties? Joe couldn't stop himself interrupting.

'Thirty-seven. I'm thirty-seven.'

The taxi-man took the correction in his stride.

'Ah well, there you go. You wouldn't remember the great days at all. I mean I saw him live in Lansdowne Road in 1968. Man U. v. Waterford in the European Cup. Can you imagine it? Man U. v. Waterford! It couldn't happen these days. Ah, here we are.'

Because the taxi pulled in at that moment and he could see the sign for the Yacht directly outside, and the taxi-man stopped the meter at €11.60, Joe knew he was not dreaming. So what was he hearing? Was his brain scrambling everything, making nonsense of whatever was being said to him? Was there some kind of collapse coming? A stroke? Should he have stayed at home? The taxi-man had turned for his fare. He was smiling at the memory.

'Man U. won 3–1 that night. Bestie had a fantastic goal disallowed.'

Joe handed over a ten and a five euro note. He had to respond in some way. He decided to sound interested and impressed.

'Wow! No, you're fine.'

He waved away the offer of change. Bestie? Was all this about George Best? He'd brought it on himself, the taxi-man's wife had said. Had something happened to George Best? If so, then clearly the taxi-driver assumed Joe knew all about it. The problem was he couldn't pretend he knew because he didn't know what it was he was supposed to know. Was George Best dead?

'Poor fucker, ha? But when your number's up. Sure what was ahead of him? You know what I mean?'

Someone was definitely dead. Joe nodded and made a noise of agreement.

'I tell you the God's-honest truth though. I'm feeling fine as far as I know, touch wood, but . . . I'm only three years younger like. Got me thinking about things, I can tell you. Anyway thanks. Have a nice one.'

Joe stood on the pavement as the taxi pulled away, still trying to piece it all together.

'Lost in thought?'

Gretta was only twenty yards away walking towards him, smiling. She had made quite an effort. With impressive results.

'Hi . . . yeah, sorry. How are you?'

Gretta looked at his arm.

'Fantastic. More important, how are you feeling?'

Her tone was subtly intimate, a little breathy. Like an ad she had done for tampons once.

'Mmm, well . . . what's to say . . . mending, I suppose.'

He was aware of assuming a little-boy-lost look, and got an understanding smile as reward.

'If it helps to talk about stuff, I'm a very good listener.'

Joe suddenly discovered the answer to his dilemma. He shook his head.

'Talking about it is probably the last thing I want to do. I wouldn't mind a laugh though.'

Now her understanding smile broadened to something cheekier and a little giggle stole into her voice.

'I can do laughs. Like the pony-tail by the way. Suits you.'

As they turned to go into the bar, a kiss on the cheek seemed right. Gretta leant in to him quite easily. He just about caught her scent. Complex, he figured the word was. Certainly not cloying or sweet. Expensive. Joe couldn't even remember what he had put on. He had just grabbed a bottle and sprayed. It was probably something Juliet bought for him. What age was she? He had never thought about this before. Gretta's voice age was thirties housewife; middle-class with a nice warm rural undertone. It was a voice in the comfortable reassuring category, with nice comic possibilities when required; ideal for lots of products. Looking at her now he would have said she was probably thirtyish. He followed her inside. The nagging in his head would not go away. The more he thought about it, the more he was sure that George Best must have died. It was the only thing that made sense.

'So . . . where will we sit?'

Gretta was smiling at him. He didn't know for how long. He had better sort this thing out, because it would not go away. He gestured to a quiet corner near a large circular window.

'Listen, can I ask what might be a really stupid question?

On the way here the taxi driver was talking, and I hadn't a clue what he was on about –'

'Wouldn't worry about that. I always just switch off –'

'No, but you know when you think there's something you're supposed to know and you don't? Like you're out of the loop? Anyway just to ask, you've heard of George Best obviously?'

'Doh . . . I think so, yeah.'

'Did he . . . ah, has he . . . been in the news again?'

Gretta looked genuinely shocked.

'Are you taking the piss?'

'No. I told you it would be a stupid question. Look, I haven't been paying attention to anything lately.'

'You haven't even turned on a radio in the last few days?'

'No.'

'Right, yeah. Wow. Still, that's amazing. I mean it was everywhere. It's a bit of an achievement not to have heard about it at all like. He died two days ago. You really didn't know?'

'No.'

'Fair dues. You must be the only person in Ireland – no, in the whole British Isles – who didn't know. What'll you have?'

Joe really needed a drink now. He had avoided it since leaving hospital. There had been no specific instructions, but it had seemed like the right thing to do.

'Jameson and a little bottle of ginger. Don't pour it in. No ice.'

Gretta grinned, presumably at the precision of the instruction, and went to the bar. Nice fit to her jeans. She moved well. Maybe she wasn't even thirty? His eye caught Sky News on a TV over the bar. He could just read the rolling text at the bottom of the screen; arrangements for George Best's funeral in Belfast. Turning away he saw a Sunday paper left behind on a nearby seat. The headline was large.

TEARS FOR THE BELFAST BOY

Suddenly it was everywhere. How could Joe not have known that George Best had died? He looked around at the people in the bar, mostly couples. He watched their lips moving. Were they all talking about poor old Bestie and how tragic it was, and how he was the best footballer that ever lived, except maybe Pele and Maradona but definitely as good at least, and him and Miss World naked in the hotel room with all the money on the bed and the porter who brought him champagne asking, 'George, where did it all go wrong?' Until a few minutes ago all this had passed Joe by. It was as if he had slipped away from the real world for a few days. Was that so bad? Did he really need to know about George Best's death, or any other? He had his own dead to occupy his mind.

Watching Gretta slide through the crowd, expertly guarding their drinks, Joe knew he had to sort his head out fast; make a decision. A fuck, even a slightly uncomfortable fuck, might be the perfect relief. To curl his free arm around Gretta's naked shoulders and press her skin against his seemed very attractive, and might be just what he needed, now that he had vetoed the night of therapy option. That had been absolutely the right move. The prospect of listening to himself talk about himself for hours was, in retrospect, grim. A third new option loomed, however, even as Joe clinked his glass of Jameson with just a trickle of ginger against Gretta's double vodka with not a lot of Coke. He could have a drink or two, chit-chat about nothing, and get back

138

to his apartment as quickly as seemed polite. Alone. Yes. That was tempting. Anything else was beginning to seem like too much work, physically or mentally.

Now that Gretta knew what was required of her, she seemed to have worked out an approach. Her face twinkled and her tone was very 'I'm going to be frank'. She held her hands up, palms towards Joe.

'Now, present company excluded, OK?'

His nod gave her permission to launch forth.

'But . . . but . . . what is it with Dublin men – sorry, men in Dublin – these days?'

She was happy to expand without waiting for a reply. It seemed there was no shortage of good bodies and pretty faces. Dress sense had definitely improved. Guys worked out and took care of their skin. This was all good. Gretta was totally for that, but she was sensing more and more that there seemed to be some kind of trade-off.

'I mean, when a guy joins a gym, is it like a rule that he hands in his personality as part payment?'

Guys were no fun any more. It seemed they were under the impression that laughing inanely all the time meant they were fun. Also, if they kept talking about how much fun everything was, then that in itself made it fun, apparently. And what was 'fun' anyway; or 'craic', or being 'mad'? Guys were determined to declare themselves 'mad' or had friends who were 'mad'. Gretta, naturally, had a theory.

'Irish men used to have this inbuilt inferiority complex. They never really thought they could compete in the looks department, you know, at the highest level. So they made real efforts to have personalities. But some time around the late nineties young Irish guys began to believe they were sexy. Maybe it was the whole Colin Farrell, Westlife thing. Anyway, so now they go out to clubs, and like, hardwired into their thinking, is, "I am sexy. I am fit. Girls are so hot for me." It's as if last thing before they leave the gym, they check themselves out in the mirror, and they just love what they see.'

'So you think they think they don't have to try so hard?'

'Not exactly, because they try really hard to show you how fit they are. No, they just don't think it's important to be interesting. Or worse, they don't even know what interesting is any more.'

'Is this just a more up-to-date way of saying, they're only after the one thing?'

'No. Although of course they are only after the one thing, and hey, I don't mind that. I just wish they'd realize how much better the one thing could be. Sometimes I want to jump on to a bar with a megaphone and shout, "Come on Dublin guys. I can see you work out. I love what you've done to your hair, your teeth are to die for. You smell so good. Now before I sleep with you, will you please show me something about you that's actually interesting."'

'So we're boring?'

Gretta did the palms out thing again as if warding off a blow.

'Ah-ah. I said present company excluded.'

'But they can't all be like that. What about foreign guys? Aren't they interesting? And exotic?'

'You know I used to think that. Two years ago I'd have been one of the "once you go black you never look back" brigade. And of course some of the Poles are gorgeous. Those cheekbones! But now I'm thinking, maybe . . . maybe we need another fifty years to let the whole melting pot thing sort itself out. You know, language, status, all that. Is he going to be deported in the morning? Has he a wife back in Cracow he hasn't told me about? It's a buzz in the short term, and by short term I mean a night or two, but you know, beyond that, it just gets kind of messy.'

After the amusing travails of single girlhood in Dublin came the hilarious up-and-down world of the freelance actor. Gretta gradually unveiled more and more of her chosen persona. Anecdotes hinted at a sensitive, but witty and tuned-in girl, who could stand back from the craziness of her chosen profession and see the crap for what it was, but still love it. She laughed at others' obsession with success. A lot. She told many stories which revealed other people's obsession with success, laughing helplessly at each one. The way she told them made Joe laugh too, encouraging her to tell more. There were so very many examples of her actor friends' obsessive ambition. All so hilarious. Joe was relieved at how the evening was panning out. Very soon after Gretta had sat down with their first drink, he concluded that the call of his invitingly silent apartment was irresistible. Gretta's lips were tempting certainly; he would like to feel her fresh clean skin. At one point she gave her mouth a rest and crossed her legs as she sat back sipping her nearly neat vodka. The line along her thigh to her arse was so tantalizing that Joe nearly gave in and reached his hand out to touch her somewhere, to begin something. He didn't. It was nearly half nine already. He would easily make it past ten. Earlier on he had worried that the time would drag and energy would falter. Escape would be harder if a pall of failure hung over the evening. An uneasy silence might pull him into the kind of conversation he did not want to have. Ten o'clock seemed very far away at ten past eight. Thanks to Gretta, the time flew. She was genuinely entertaining. There certainly was no danger of a silence. Even when Joe found nothing of interest in a particular anecdote, he could amuse himself by counting the number of times she used the word

'I'. He counted sixty-one in one uninterrupted three-minute sequence, with quite a few 'me's' sprinkled along the way. Once ten o'clock passed, Joe felt safe. Now all he needed was an opening that would lead to a wind-up, that would lead to a friendly goodnight, that would send him home free. He knew that that process would probably take half an hour or so, but that was OK.

Gretta had moved on to the ancient world of the Celt. Did Joe know that in the Celtic system November was the start of the year? Joe did not. *Samhain*, the time of darkness. Of course darkness had a very different resonance in the Celtic imagination. It did not have the same connotations of danger and fear. Because we in the modern world had created artificial light, we foolishly wanted to be in the light all the time. We were literally afraid of the dark. We could no longer appreciate the positive power of darkness the way the Celts could. To them it was a natural part of the year's cycle, from *Samhain*, the time of darkness, to *Bealtaine*, the time of light. The time of darkness was, to the Celt, nature's way of encouraging rest and contemplation, of consideration. It was a time when man's natural desire to fight and dominate nature had to be tempered, and the feminine virtues came to the fore. Gretta believed strongly that we should embrace the dark and all it had to offer; a space to rest and think and restore one's spiritual energy ready for the active time, the time of light. Joe had two unspoken responses to this. First he was amused. He imagined Gretta out in Galway somewhere, at some Festival of the Spirit of Women with a cod ancient Irish name like Meanma, or Broinn, tucking into a week of workshops, lectures and female vocalists. His second response was to be wary. Was she trying to lead him somewhere with all this talk of embracing the darkness? He was not going to be drawn down a path with no obvious exit point, stuck in her apartment at four in the morning, pissed and saying things he would later regret. It had even occurred to him that this could end up being all about Gretta. Not wanting to talk about himself, was he merely giving her the opening to talk about herself?

The fear Joe felt at that moment was cold and damp.

It was time to execute his exit plan. He grimaced and rubbed his leg. Enough for Gretta, even in mid-sentence, to notice, and drop her voice to her most soothing contralto.

'Is it sore?'

Joe was a brave little soldier.

'Not so much sore. Just stiff. It's probably not good to be in one position so long.'

He stood up. Grimaced again. He rubbed the back of his thigh.

'Ooh. That shot up.'

He limped away a few steps and limped back.

'Listen, I think I'd better call it a night.'

'Oh. Really?'

'Yeah, I'm just realizing how much it's taken out of me. Lucky there's no smoking, or I'm not sure my chest would have taken it. Breathing's still a bit of an effort sometimes, you know.'

He picked up his jacket. Gretta stood, at a loss for words for the first time tonight. Joe decided he would be as pointed as he dared.

'Physically, I'm just not up to speed yet. But listen, I had a lovely time.'

One-handed, the jacket was on. Gretta had little choice but to pick up her bag and coat.

'And I am getting better every day, believe me. Next time I'll be able to keep up, I swear.'

'Well, it was great. I really enjoyed it. Listen, I'm just at the corner of Castle Avenue. Why don't you come back to my place and call a cab from there?'

Luckily as they stepped out the door he noticed an unoccupied taxi going by.

'No, look, it'll be faster just to flag one down here. I don't want to walk any more than I have to.'

'Of course.'

If she stayed now to wait until Joe got a cab that would ruin things. Surely she must know that? Apparently not. Gretta had no intention of saying goodnight yet. They stood together looking up and down a now taxi-less road. How long would she linger? Why, for God's sake? To eke out another few pointless minutes? To hold his hand as he got into a taxi? To wave him goodbye? Joe decided to move her on. He wanted his being alone time to start now. He took Gretta's hand and squeezed. He drew her near.

'So can I ring you again when I'm a hundred per cent, maybe once I get these stitches taken out?'

'Please do.'

'Really?'

'Absolutely.'

It needed a kiss to finish things off. He had to give her that at least. As it happened it felt really nice. He let it go on, barely stopping himself from sliding his good hand down her back. His other arm pressed against her breast, but the sling and the plaster cast meant he felt nothing. Her fingers began to slither through his hair. Time to stop. He eased away and met her eyes, trying to look like he was in the grip of powerful desires and struggling to hold back, which in fact he sort of was. He smiled and made the sound of a philosophical sigh.

'Go on, off with you.'

'I don't mind waiting with you.'

'No, go on. It's freezing. Really. I'd better cross here so they'll know I'm going towards town.'

He stretched his good arm, still holding her hand as he backed away on to the road. Finally he let go, as if reluctantly. A little wave and Joe turned away across the road. Hopefully by the time he got there Gretta would be walking away and that would be the end of that. Of course she looked back and they waved to each other one last time. What a lovely night. Joe was pretty sure Gretta had no idea he wouldn't be calling her again. She would sleep happy tonight. He thought of the quiet security of his apartment and knew he had made the right choice. Clontarf Road was uncommonly empty even for a Sunday night. Gretta was disappearing round the curve of the pavement, and there was no one else in sight. Only two cars were approaching from Clontarf village. Neither was a taxi. The cold was not so fresh now as chill. The silence was beginning to feel sinister. The first sign that something was not right came when Joe saw the second of the two approaching cars pull into the bus lane and begin to overtake on the inside. The cars were now only a couple of hundred yards away from him. As they came level with each other, they both speeded up dangerously. Joe took a step back. He was becoming wary but in no way expected what happened next. Something poked out of the window of the car on the inside lane. It pointed at the other car. Before Joe had time to work out what it was, rapid gunfire told him. It sounded like ten shots or so in a couple of seconds. Could that be? The side windows of the outside car exploded. It spun across the road and rammed a wall on the corner. The other car braked and stopped right in front of him. He could not, dared not move. Someone jumped out from the back, but it was the strange gun in his hand that took Joe's attention. It was pointed in the direction of the crashed car. A noisy rapid burst erupted. Then to his intense shock the man turned and Joe realized that the gun was raised and aimed at him. He was about to die and there was nothing he could do about it. A blast of a dozen bullets was about to blow him away. Joe's only thought as he saw the finger tug on the trigger was, 'So I get no warning.'

Had there been any sound? Perhaps a click? He had heard no gunfire. The man was staring at his gun. So was Joe. Had it jammed? Were there no bullets left? A creak signalled that the door of the Yacht had tentatively opened. A voice from inside the car started jabbering. Still staring at the barrel pointing in his direction, Joe heard the man's voice. Surprisingly soft. Amused.

'Lucky fuck.'

Then the gun and the man disappeared into the car. It pulled away, revving, and turned up Seaview Avenue, skimming by the silent crashed car. Joe paid no attention as some brave ones began to edge out of the Yacht. He didn't even have any interest in the bloodied figure that suddenly pushed his door open and collapsed out of the crashed car. Joe's brain was too energized, too exhilarated by a sudden extraordinary realization. The bloodied man distracted the attention of the growing crowd. It allowed Joe to back on to the darkness and silence of the grassy area of the seafront, and limp away unnoticed. He tried to calm himself enough to form the epiphany into a clean sentence.

'Until it is my time to die, I cannot die.'

Nothing could kill him. He had totally missed that message after the crash in Longford. Tonight he had been given another chance to understand. Who were those gunmen, those ugly angel messengers? Was it some gangland feud? Joe didn't care. These were details, fascinating for the tabloids, nothing to do with his story. What mattered was the utter clarity of his understanding. He couldn't die until it was his time. Until that time came he was safe. Invulnerable. Free. He hadn't thought of his situation in this way until now. The millennium clock wasn't a death sentence, it was a liberation. Joe felt a surge of power within himself. Now he couldn't wait to find out what his time-span was, how long his freedom would last. The sound of Garda sirens was getting louder as he flagged a taxi at the bottom of the Howth road. The driver was listening to a late-night phone-in on FM 104. Of course someone was giving out about immigrants. Joe caught the usual rasping whine and zoned out. He just thought, fucking twat, wasting his time bitching on the radio. He focused his mind on the clock waiting for him in the bag in his apartment. Time ticking away. What would his fate be? How long had he left? How many years of guaranteed life? Why had he never thought of it like that before?

His hand shook as he pushed in the front door key. Not even bothering to close the door after him, he just limped quickly to the bedroom, opened his bag and pulled out the clock. Placing it on the kitchen table, Joe Power sat and basked in the significance of the moment. Should he tell Shane and maybe even Rory, share this extraordinary insight with them? Lucky Shane, imagine how he would behave once he realized that he could not die until all his one thousand six hundred million seconds ticked away. Joe wasn't going to find out his reaction. His mind was already elsewhere, trying to recall what he had done with the batteries. Jesus! He hadn't put them in the car, had he? The clock ticked down another thirty-six seconds before he remembered. Sure enough they were in a drawer in the kitchen. Joe put the batteries on the table next to the clock.

He calmed himself. Could he put aside his doubts and questions? Should he wait until he'd spoken to Juliet? Be more certain. 'What's the worst that could happen?' He echoed the tag line of an ad campaign that he admired. He picked up the clock, turned it upside down, and prised out the batteries. That was the easy part done. He gazed at the VDU, black and empty again, as it had been the day he bought it. He breathed deeply, feeling again the exhilaration of that moment, scarcely an hour before, when someone had failed to kill him. The voice had whispered, 'Lucky fuck.' He was wrong. Luck had nothing to do with it. Joe whispered aloud.

'Until my time comes to die, I cannot die.'

He turned the clock upside down again. He picked up a battery and inserted it. He picked up the second battery and didn't hesitate. Once it clicked into place, Joe turned the clock upright on the table as the VDU flashed into life.

14

Parisians drive too fast and have no patience. This thought spurred Joe Power on as he stepped from the kerb and, staring straight ahead, limped across Rue Soufflot. He savoured the full-blooded soundscape that followed: wheel-screech, horns and angry voices. One car stopped inches from him. He did not flinch. On the contrary, he felt a buzz. Not today, he thought. I'm not dying today. Without looking in their direction he raised his walking-stick and shook it at the drivers. They responded with even more hysterical horn-blowing. The frisson, he thought, was not quite as heart-pumping as his night-walk to the Liberty Hall end of the boardwalk in Dublin a few nights before, but it was fun nonetheless. Now he had to make sure that he did not lose his quarry, who had so suddenly disappeared round a corner. Sure enough, when Joe turned right at what he saw was Rue St Jacques, there was the man in the charcoal cashmere overcoat, still no more than a hundred yards away, although walking more briskly now that he was going downhill. Joe's heart was beating faster, mostly with pleasure at his little stunt. He had enough faith in the clock at this stage to feel confident that he wouldn't be killed, but there was no guarantee that he wouldn't be injured. Certainly, on the Liffey boardwalk the other night he had known there was every chance that any one of the druggies hanging around could turn nasty and do him some damage. He had tried to appear nonchalant as he passed the main group. He stopped at the Butt Bridge end and leaned over the rail to look down into the murk of the Liffey. He felt intensely vulnerable as he hovered, listening. There was quite a lot of talk conducted at aggressive volume levels, although he could tell that none of them were conscious of this. He wondered if anyone was trying to figure out what he was doing there. Someone might decide he was an undercover cop, for example, in which case presumably there would be trouble. It was pleasurably scary. Joe turned round so he could see them, leaning his back against the railing. How easy it would be for any of them to push him over. There were two women and four men. A leather-faced man took a swaying step towards him. Roared.

'How's it going, man?'

'I'm grand.'

'Cold, yeah?'

'Sure is.'

'Fuckin' freezing.'

Leather-face stared at him for a long silence, although he was probably entirely unaware of how long.

'You jumping in, yeah?'

The question could probably be heard by the audience in the Abbey Theatre round the corner, but had no tone of threat. Joe sensed that if anything bad was to happen, it wouldn't be premeditated. That was what was most exciting about the whole set-up. His only conviction was that he wouldn't die. The rest was up for grabs.

'No. Just looking.'

'Right, yeah.'

Leather-face seemed to forget he had started a conversation. He turned and lurched back to the bench. That was it. No one else paid Joe any notice. He waited for another long minute. The group continued roaring at each other. The sense of danger waned and the cold wind became annoying. He decided to walk closer to them on his way back. Invade their space, just to see. There were a few salutes, and how're you's. That was it. Then he was back at the gap in the boardwalk wall. He stepped through and crossed the street. Waiting for the LUAS on Abbey Street, Joe decided to stare at a wiry pale teenager in a tracksuit. The pale teen stared back, but he was the first one to look away, using the approaching LUAS as his excuse. Confident, Joe watched him get on first and sit down. Once he was sure his gaze had been noticed, he stepped on to the tram, eyeballing him as he passed. He sat a couple of rows behind. Joe figured that now the pale teen would be a bit nervous, wondering what the story was with the fat fuck in the pony-tail. When he saw him try to glance back surreptitiously, nervously, a fresh tingle ran up Joe's arms and across his shoulders.

The man in the charcoal cashmere overcoat was still walking straight down Rue St Jacques. He crossed two intersections. Soon he would reach the Seine. Where was he going? At Boulevard St Germain the lights were red. Joe caught up with him, but stood a couple of feet behind, hoping the man would not turn. When the lights changed, Joe gave him a little head start before following again. He was definitely still headed towards the river. Ah! The Marais maybe? A bit early in the day, Joe thought, unless the old queen enjoyed a little boy-gazing over brunch? At Petit Pont all became clear. Joe felt he should have guessed from the start, even by the way he was dressed. The man in the charcoal cashmere coat crossed the bridge and swung right to Notre-Dame. It was nearly twelve o'clock. He was going to some pre-Christmas service. Joe was happy enough to rest for a while, having been on the go since early morning. There were about a dozen priests on the altar along with a large choir of men and boys, which seemed like a big deal for a weekday, even if it was nine days before Christmas. Joe settled in four rows behind his man, slightly at an angle so he could see him between heads. Joe had never particularly liked Notre-Dame. This was the first time he had sat in the seats reserved for worshippers. It was mostly full of well-heeled Parisiennes, but in fairness there were lots of poorer-looking immigrant faces and fresh-faced eager young American types. A Christmas mélange, Joe presumed.

A blond boy in a blue soutane stepped forward from the body of the choir. He looked eleven or twelve. He began to sing a French 'Kyrie eleison'. Joe wondered what was it about the sound of a boy soprano that was so extraordinarily beautiful? This was the first time he had heard one 'live' since childhood, the awe of midnight Mass in Ballyphehane, his mother's hands on his shoulders, pressing him reassuringly against her as they queued for communion and tiny Eric Brennan belted out 'O Holy Night', although probably not with such quality and composed confidence as Joe was hearing now. Certainly this blond angel on the altar probably didn't pick his nose between tunes like smelly old Eric. He tried to see if the man in the charcoal overcoat might have a tear in his eye as he gazed and listened. Very gay, very *Death in Venice*. The moment seemed like further confirmation that his detective work had been spot-on. This surely was Roger Merriman. He would soon find out. For now Joe was happy to close his eyes, to listen better, to hear more cleanly the purity and cold certainty in the boy's voice; his pleasure in his own sound. How long had it been since Joe heard anything so beautiful from a human being? He could not remember. He lived with sounds. Actors blessed with rich, mellow, resonant, soothing, sexy voices came to him every day. Was there not beauty there? Had he stopped listening to them? Or was it because these voices he worked with were, in the end, always just selling something? One of the talents Joe had always been proudest of as a commercials director was that he was alert to the tiniest underlying lie in an actor's tone. 'Sorry, don't believe you man (or gorgeous). One more time please,' was his frequent response and the ad agencies loved him for it. The truth was he no longer believed any of it: the lazy laddish voice designed to encourage lazy laddish twenty-somethings to choose a certain bank; the languid cool voice that was supposed to link your success to a certain car; the soothing older voice that made mums and dads trust its promise of a pleasure-filled retirement. In Dublin these days, there was no end to the stream of meretricious voices on the airwaves. Over the last five years he could have worked the studio twenty-four hours a day without satisfying the demand. How much shit had he filled his ears with over and over? Had this century created any new sounds that could be described as beautiful? He remembered his distaste the first time he had used dial-up internet. What was that scrum of sound, the gurgles and whirrs and rattles that elbowed each other until connection was established? It was so ugly. When he thought about the sound of Dublin over the last few years, it was of roadworks and building works, constant traffic noise, alarms and sirens, the tuneless yammering of stags and hens in Temple Bar.

The boy's soaring joy made Joe feel more relaxed and pain-free than he had done in a long time. Even the image of the millennium clock in his mind's eye seemed more gentle just now; the seconds not punching sternly down, but dissolving gently from one number to the next. If Joe could spend more of his time in this state, he might find contentment. The boy held unwaveringly what Joe realized was his final note, then allowed it to die softly. The usual hollow breathing, quiet coughing and shuffling filled the silence. Joe opened his eyes again.

The man in the cashmere coat was not to be seen.

Anxiety returned with force. Joe looked around, already feeling a tightness in his chest. Surely he had not left? For how long had he shut his eyes and let his mind drift? He stood up and shuffled past four pairs of knees, looking behind all the time hoping to spot his man exiting. Just as he reached the end of the row he glanced back towards the altar and saw him from the corner of his eye. He was sitting exactly where he had been. What was going on? Then Joe realized. While his eyes were closed more people had sat in the seats in front of him, and blocked his view. Now Joe did not know what to do next; push his way back, or withdraw to the back of the church? He felt so exposed and foolish, standing at the end of a row, out on a limb. There was no way he was going to risk losing his man now, not after all the investigative work he had put into locating him, not after getting up at five this morning to catch the early flight to Paris, not after pressing the buzzer beside the name Merriman, and lurking behind a car, watching for his face to appear at a window. What price a little rudeness to an irrelevant stranger after all that? So Joe nudged a shocked old hatchet-faced demoiselle, who stared at him and then at the others along the row. One weakling moved along, leaving his seat vacant. The others, apart from the old bitch, felt they had to do the same. She stayed put. The seat next to her was now free so Joe stepped across her, hearing a stage-whispered *'insupportable'*, as he sat down. He ignored her, keeping his eyes fixed on the part of the man in the charcoal overcoat that he could see. Now time ticked by way too slowly and painfully. At the end he stayed sitting as the congregation started to leave, eyes fixed on the man in the charcoal cashmere coat. When he moved, Joe moved, slipping in directly behind him. No way was he going to lose sight of him again. Once outside, the man walked back across the river. Surely he wasn't going straight home? That wouldn't suit Joe at all. His only options in that situation would be to approach him in the street, or call at his apartment. Neither was ideal. What Joe had hoped for, and assumed, this being Paris, was that his man would go for coffee, sitting himself outside some art nouveau brasserie bar on the corner of a busy boulevard, making it easy to approach him. At that moment the man stepped into a *salon de thé*. Joe approached the window. La Fourmi Ailée. The place was lined with bookshelves, with an old wooden staircase leading to a mezzanine, intimate, winterish, somehow more London than Paris. The man was being seated. The waitress seemed to know him. This was the opportunity. Joe entered and found himself a seat, facing the man diagonally. Calmly he put his shoulder-bag beside him, opened it and took out the millennium clock.

67341637 ... 36 ... 35 ...

What was he about to find out? He placed the clock on the table, turning the bright red numbers towards the man he already thought of as Roger Merriman. The waitress came and blocked the view. Joe decided to order loudly enough for the man to notice his bad French, and Irish accent.

'*Café crème et un petit jus d'orange, s'il vous plaît.*'

The waitress moved away and revealed eyes already glancing discreetly in Joe's direction. Which meant he now saw the clock. Sometimes, even the most practised faces cannot hide the truth of a feeling or sensation. The moment the man saw the clock, Joe knew several things at once: that it was indeed Roger Merriman who was seated across from him; that the emotion he felt on seeing the clock seemed best described as the shock of recognition; when he raised his eyes to look at Joe he seemed unable to speak. The pause stayed unbroken. The success of this little stunt was so immediate and powerful that Joe didn't know what to say either. Roger Merriman looked at the clock again, perhaps checking to see how many seconds had elapsed in the silence. Joe wished he had planned a killer question.

'*La pendule. Elle est intéressant pour vous?*'

His French sounded childish, nervous. Not at all the effect intended. Roger Merriman barked back in an Irish accent and tone that Joe remembered from radio announcers when he was growing up.

'You're from Dublin?'

'Yes.'

'Well now. So am I.'

'I know.'

That was better. Roger Merriman's eyes briefly flashed fear again. The question for Joe now was how to push his advantage to get the information he needed. Roger Merriman reverted to the clock once again. He gestured.

'Do you mind?'

Joe brought the clock to his table. He stared at it closely, but did not touch it. He focused for several seconds on the Millennium © trademark on the plinth. When he spoke again he had imposed a casual tone on his voice.

'What did you mean when you said you knew I was Irish?'

'Your name is Roger Merriman?'

The edge crept back into his voice.

'Yes. That is who I am.'

He was probably a little freaked out, which Joe thought was fair enough. Your day starts OK, apart from a buzz on your intercom and no one there when you answer. You take a peek out of the window, but you can see no one. It's odd, but you decide to forget about it and step out into the fresh chilly morning. You have a pleasant walk, spend a beautiful, maybe even transcendent hour in your little local church, and afterwards adjourn for a quiet tea in your favourite hidey-hole. The little incident with the buzzer is long forgotten. Then, suddenly, an unwelcome surprise.

'Do you recognize this?'

Pointing at the clock, Joe felt that he was behaving and sounding too much like a private eye. Now that he had the right man, he should stop asking questions and just try to explain his end of the story.

'Well, I know what it is, if that's what you mean. It's what was called a millennium clock. And looking at the trademark it seems very much like it might even be a seventies original. Which is strange . . .'

Roger gestured towards the clock.

'. . . Why is it still working?'

Now it was Joe's turn to be surprised.

'What do you mean? It has batteries in it. It works.'

Roger shook his head. He waved a patronizing hand and his voice assumed a similar tone.

'No, no, no. The batteries have nothing to do with the time mechanism. The batteries only power the visual display. Think of a DVD recorder and a TV set. The recorder will record without the TV set. One only needs that to see what one has recorded.'

Roger now seemed interested in the puzzle. He pointed at and gestured towards the clock as he spoke, but Joe noticed he still did not touch it.

'You see, these clocks were intended as a typically seventies, even more typically French, joke on the idea of modern technology and planned obsolescence. Something perfectly useless with a pre-ordained end. Isn't it obvious? The clock mechanism is sealed inside. Look, it cannot be adjusted. There are no buttons or switches. This was quite deliberate; pre-set, predetermined. All of these clocks were set to run until precisely midnight 2000, at which moment it was intended they would reach zero and, like the old song about the grandfather clock, stop short, never to go again. Because everything is disposable you see, even Time itself. In 1975 it seemed to some people like a very good twenty-five-year-long joke. Unfortunately for the company that made them, it was not a good enough joke or perhaps it was too good. It was touted as the kitsch hit of the seventies, but it never took off. The company went bankrupt. Of course for those few who had bought a millennium clock, its failure as a commercial product made them love it even more.'

Roger stopped talking, his eyes fixed on the clock. He had almost talked himself back into composure, but just failed. Joe could sense him fighting something powerful inside himself. The waitress arrived with tea.

'You say this clock shouldn't be working at all?'

'Hmm? Obviously not. This is 2005. If this is an original millennium clock, it would have stopped working five years ago. That was the whole point.'

'But it is working.'

'So it is.'

His tone sharpened.

'Did you buzz my apartment this morning?'

'Yes.'

'And?'

'I'm sorry. I didn't know how to explain myself over the intercom. I thought it would be better to approach you . . . well, more like this.'

'So why buzz my apartment?'

'I was trying to find out what you looked like.'

'So? Ah. You presumed I'd look out of the window.'

'It's what people tend to do in that situation, isn't it?'

'And you were . . . ?'

'Watching behind a parked car.'

Joe didn't add that the face which appeared briefly at the window had seemed so sad and worn that when the buffed and groomed old gent in the charcoal cashmere overcoat had stepped from the building twenty minutes later, he could not be certain it was the same person. The long grey hair had been the only decent clue. Looking at him now three feet away, Joe could once again see past the tonics and moisturizers to the pale despair in the eyes. Not that he felt sorry for him. The old queen would probably live longer than Joe.

'So you've been following me since? To ask me . . . what?'

'Well, first of all, you should know, if you haven't guessed already, this clock belonged to Maurice Nolan.'

Almost as if he knew what Joe was about to say, Roger seemed to be standing up and moving away even as the words 'Maurice Nolan' were spoken. He called loudly, pulling out his wallet. He took a ten euro note and waved it at the surprised waitress. He threw it on the table next to the millennium clock and walked away. Joe shoved the clock in his bag, grabbed his walking-stick and followed. Roger Merriman was already several hundred yards up Rue Dante, now moving much faster than Joe could. He tried to put on more speed but his dodgy leg protested. Soon Roger reached St Germain and disappeared to his right. Joe kept going but he knew already that he had lost him in the crowd. So stupid. More time lost. Standing on the corner of Rue Dante and Boulevard St Germain, sweating in the freezing air, breathing with difficulty, Joe could feel his life wasting away.

13

This time, having pressed the buzzer for Roger Merriman's apartment, Joe Power waited. He was hoping that Roger had gone home immediately and locked himself away. If this was not so, he had no idea where else to look. He might as well go back to Dublin and forget about it. There was no answer. He buzzed again. He buzzed a third time.

'Yes?'

The single word was a challenge.

'It's me. From Dublin. My name is Joe Power, by the way.'

'Would you mind leaving me alone.'

'I'm really sorry. I didn't explain myself properly –'

'I'm hanging up now. Please don't buzz again.'

'I thought you could help me, that's all. I think the clock is counting my life away.'

Roger hadn't hung up. He wasn't saying anything but at least he was listening now.

'My little boy died. He was only five. The clock counted down to zero at the same moment. I'm sure it's not coincidence. You might be the only other person who'd understand what I'm feeling –'

A click. He had hung up. Joe buzzed out of frustration. He stepped back on to the pavement to look up again towards the full-length apartment windows. This time no face appeared. Now the choice was simple: give up or wait on the street for however long it took. Joe knew he had neither the patience nor the time for that. Roger might even call the police. This man and Juliet were the only people who could help him. Neither, it seemed, would even speak to him. The door of the apartment building opened. Roger was wearing his overcoat.

'Lunch,' he said, pointing in the direction he wanted to go. They walked round the back of the Panthéon, silent until Roger spoke again.

'When did you come to Paris?'

'I flew in this morning.'

'You missed the riots then.'

Joe decided not to ask what riots. It was probably something he should know. He nodded.

'France is, as O'Casey in another context put it, in a state of chassis. Has been for some time. A cultural and intellectual crisis mostly, but now suddenly people abroad think Paris is burning and are scared to come here. It isn't burning, is it?'

'No.'

'Did you fly into Charles de Gaulle, or suffer Ryanair?'

'Charles de Gaulle.'

'How was it passing through the terrifying *banlieues* on the way in?'

'I took the RER. The journey was fine.'

'All quiet at Aulnay-sous-Bois? Of course. How did you find me, by the way?'

Joe was pleased rather than thrown by this sudden switch of subject. He had no fear of describing candidly his forty-eight-hour stint as a private eye. It had occurred to him that ad-man Trevor's ancient boyfriend would have been around the gay scene in the seventies and eighties and, as it was a pretty small scene then, he might remember Maurice and Roger. It was the first time Joe had spoken to Trevor since – well, for months, and he could hear uneasiness from the other end of the line. Milo was mentioned, which only made it harder for Joe to shift the conversation round to the real reason for his call. When he finally managed it he could hear a certain sniffiness in Trevor's response. He gave him the ancient boyfriend's mobile number, but the vibe was clearly that he disapproved and didn't want to be involved. Joe was a bit mystified. Did Trevor think he should just be sitting at home lamenting his tragedy? What the fuck would he know about losing a son anyway? All these thoughts returned to Joe as he told Roger his story, but he spoke none of them aloud. Nor did he mention that although the ancient boy-friend had remembered Maurice very well – 'How could I not, the charming old fraud?' – and even recalled that 'there was someone long-term, not that that meant anything', he couldn't for the life of him remember his name or anything about him. 'Obviously not worth remembering.' Nor did he have any idea where they lived in Dublin. 'Never on that particular invite list.' What Joe did tell Roger, quickly and simply, was how one contact had led to another, so that, within twenty-four hours, he had the name of a solicitor, Brian Young, who was indeed still only in his twenties. He had been a regular attender at their parties in the very late nineties. Roger was puzzled.

'Brian Young, I don't remember him.'

Joe was not surprised, but didn't say so. He thought it diplomatic not to mention that Brian Young had explained exactly why he had ended up at some of these parties. Brian was friendly with Fionn, and Maurice had quite a thing for Fionn, who for his part genuinely enjoyed Maurice's wit, was flattered by the attentions of an important man, and found it hard to resist these lavish occasions. Brian Young was brought along as a shield, to help prevent Maurice's attentions becoming too intimate. It was a laugh and he got mightily pissed for free. It was a whole other world to Brian at the time. In what had become a recurring theme, he didn't remember anything about Maurice's partner either. Not on his radar.

Joe did tell Roger that Brian Young had been able to bring him to Díseart in Rathgar. That was when he discovered that the beautiful old house had been rented out and that the owner now lived in Paris.

'You mean they gave you my address?'

'A teenage daughter. I think she thought it was the fastest way to get rid of me.'

'I don't know whether to be annoyed that I can be tracked down so easily by a complete stranger, or flattered that Dublin remembers me kindly.'

From the way he was greeted, Roger was obviously a regular at L'Écurie. He shared a brief joke with a man smoking in a corner, a dog at his feet; all very homely. Roger seemed much more at ease again. He didn't even glance at the menu.

'Mussels or steak?'

'Ah . . . Mussels.'

He didn't need to raise his voice as he called their order across the tiny cave-like room.

'So. The clock?'

Joe gave it to him. This time Roger picked it up deliberately. He turned it round and round, feeling it. His thoughts seemed to drift. For a few seconds he was very far away. He focused again on the digits.

67337966 . . . 65 . . . 64 . . .

When he spoke it was obvious to Joe that he had worked something out.

'So am I understanding you correctly? You . . . suspect that this is how long you have left to live?'

'Obviously I don't know for sure.'

'You are aware how such a theory might sound?'

'I must be. I haven't said it to anyone else.'

'That's probably sensible. Slightly more than two years to go is my calculation, right?'

'That's very impressive.'

'I'm good with numbers.'

'Early February 2008. The day before my fortieth birthday, as it happens.'

Roger smirked. Joe did not show his annoyance.

'Ah. I see. And the chilling significance of this makes you even more inclined to believe it.'

'Maybe.'

'Tell me this. What was your best hope? That I'd confirm this theory of yours, or rubbish it?'

Joe thought about that. Roger smiled.

'Isn't that interesting? I can tell that you don't mind the idea of knowing, even if what you know is that you will die young.'

'It feels like the truth to me already, and to know something like that is empowering. But there's still this nagging doubt –'

'Might that be because, really, you know the idea makes no sense?'

In Joe's ears, Roger was beginning to sound like a cunt. He had to work hard to keep his voice even.

'Then what about Maurice? What about my son?'

'Yes, what about your son?'

This time Joe told him everything, unedited, from the moment in Ballinalee when the old man took his goods from the boot of the car, to the night he inserted the batteries in the clock. Roger didn't interrupt. Joe could feel from his eyes that something was resonating. As if his words were an unwelcome reminder of things Roger Merriman thought or wished he had forgotten. By the time the story was finished, lunch had been eaten, espressos had arrived, the smoker with the dog was gone. The afternoon sun had come round and a narrow-angled beam was striking the wall behind Roger, grazing part of his forehead. There was a long silence.

'I remember that old man. Odd what made me tell him about the clock. Something in my conscience.'

'Because you thought it was true.'

'No. I'm afraid not.'

That tone again. It was really annoying. It had taken a lot out of Joe to tell his story. He had been shocked at how some of it sounded when spoken out loud. Only the comfort of talking to a stranger in a foreign place offered him protection. Now that it was done, he was not willing to let this old arse-bandit dismiss it with a sneer. He rummaged in his bag, pulled out a pack of batteries, and placed it down next to the clock. There was no hiding the challenge in his voice.

'All right then. You put the batteries in.'

'What would that prove?'

'That you really don't believe it. That you don't care what happens.'

'Good point. No. I don't believe in my own certainty that much.'

'Well then?'

'I can't prove you wrong. Let's just say, I'm not inclined to believe. The story you've just told me, it reminds me of something Maurice used often say when he came home from the first day of a trial, after he had heard the prosecution outline its case. He'd say, "Yes, they did well, they have a very strong case." There would be a little pause, then a smile, "But they haven't closed," and he'd move on to some other topic of conversation. Whenever he used those words I knew he would demolish them. You haven't closed, my friend. And I can't help you get rid of your nagging little doubt.'

The more he listened the more Joe was sure that the hint of smirk on his face and in his voice was a conscious effort to hide something. Some fear or doubt.

'But what did you feel that night, when it happened? He did die just as the clock got to zero, didn't he?'

'Yes.'

'Well? OK, time has passed, you feel differently now, but what did you feel at the time?'

The smirk faded. Roger's eyes seemed a little more watery. Joe pushed harder, holding the clock up . . .

'I'm not asking you to give me some piece of incontrovertible proof. I just want to know if, even for a moment, you believed there was a connection? So I know I'm not going mad here, that there might be something, some force at work with this thing. You said yourself that logically the clock shouldn't even be working. But it is. Look at it. And my son is dead because of it.'

Roger seemed to make up his mind about something. His voice lost its bark.

'And you want me to say the same about Maurice's death? What do I really believe? I wish I could believe what you are suggesting. I wish I could blame everything on some mysterious force, beyond our power to control, sending us messages in a white plastic clock. Even if it is mystically sphere-shaped. The force I blame was all too human.'

He paused, but Joe knew that was not from uncertainty. He was thinking about how to tell his story.

'There was this young man, frail, fine-haired. Rather improbably called Fionn. From the first time we met him

I knew Maurice would not be able to resist. He had what I suppose one might call intelligent good looks, at first glance something intense and thoughtful about him. I would guess you were like that when you were twenty-one. I would hope you don't have his other, more sinister qualities.'

Joe couldn't tell whether that was a serious question or a jokey comment. He was too focused on what was coming next to dwell on it.

'Maurice was lost to him, and to make things worse, I could tell he was wasting his time. The cover was definitely not an accurate guide to the book. The boy was vicious. At the party that millennium eve, it was he who grabbed the clock and ran upstairs. He led the jeering, knowing quite well how much that would hurt Maurice. People thought it was just petulance because his precious clock turned out to be faulty. But for Maurice the only important matter was the boy's betrayal. As everyone linked arms at midnight, I pretended to ignore Maurice hunched in his corner, but I was watching of course. He sat staring at his clock. I knew that all he was thinking about was who had waved it in his face and begun that humiliating chant. And . . . and I couldn't control my own jealous anger at how sad this was making him. I had to let Maurice know that I knew what was really going on, show him that I could always see inside his head.'

He paused. His eyes dropped to the clock.

'I still remember as I came up to him, the clock was flashing 43 . . . 42 . . . 41. I said, "I wouldn't worry about it, Mo darling. He wouldn't have fucked you even if the thing was working properly." He stared at me. For the last time as it turned out. I knew I had cut deep. He just stood up and walked out and . . . well. So you see, if I hadn't spoken as I did . . .'

He reached across. Three gentle fingers grazed the back of Joe's hand.

'All of which is to say, his death had nothing to do with the clock at all.'

The smirking ironic tone had returned.

12

Out of the blue, in the dead time between Christmas Day and New Year's Eve, the phone rang in Joe's apartment. Moments later he heard his ex-mother-in-law speak on the answering machine.

'Joe, this is Laura here. Laura Dolan . . . I wonder if you could call me some time today – hello?'

'Yes, hello Laura, this is Joe.'

'Oh you are there. Good. I'm ringing on behalf of Juliet, as you might guess.'

'Sure yeah, is she OK?'

'She's not so bad, Joe. She came to us for Christmas Day. It was a bit quiet this year, as you might imagine. Anyway, I won't delay. She asked me to ask you if you still wanted to meet her –'

'Yes, yes absolutely.'

'OK, well then, is tomorrow too soon?'

'No. That's fine.'

'Good. What time?'

'Any time.'

'Well, do you want to say a time?'

'Ah . . . eleven o'clock?'

'I'm sure that will be OK. I'll call again if it's not. Do you mind meeting her in Brighton Vale?'

'No.'

'Good . . . grand. Oh, there's something I'd better tell you, I suppose. Just so you don't get a shock tomorrow when you see the sign outside. As you might imagine, the house feels very different now, you know, after all that's happened. So Juliet has put it up for sale.'

'That's fine.'

If that was all, it was totally fine as far as Joe was concerned. His heart was singing. Juliet wanted to meet him. It had happened so much faster than he could have believed. He would have to think out carefully how to approach this encounter. He didn't want it to get messy, like Paris.

'I hope you don't feel . . . well, as you might imagine, I wouldn't want you to take it personally . . .'

Joe knew what his ex-mother-in-law was trying to say. She thought that because Joe had owned the house for three years before he even met Juliet, it might still have some kind of emotional resonance for him. Maybe she thought he resented the separation agreement, and would feel that Juliet had no right to sell the house. Joe wanted to assure her that he felt none of those things. He was even a little amused at the coincidence of both of them looking for answers to their traumas in property transactions. He selling the studio, and maybe even the apartment, she selling the cottage and Brighton Vale. They were both going to be cash-rich and childless. What was Brighton Vale worth now? Over two million anyway. Jesus, a hundred and sixty thousand old pounds he had paid in 1993. Who'd have believed it?

'Is that OK then?'

Joe, lost in his thoughts, had missed whatever his ex-mother-in-law had said. Was it important? He checked that he had the arrangements right.

'Sure, sure. So I'll call to the house at eleven tomorrow morning.'

'She'll be there. And how are you, Joe?'

'Well, you can imagine. Still here anyway, you know.'

'You decided not to go down to Cork for Christmas?'

His father and sisters had so bombarded him with messages that he was afraid they were going to travel up and
kidnap him. The lie that he had made an arrangement to
spend Christmas Day with Rory and Lisa had proved just
enough to fob them off.

'No, ah sure I haven't done that in years.'

'We were up at the grave Stephen's Day.'

'Yeah, I went myself . . . there before Christmas.'

'Poor little fellow . . .'

Joe heard a sob. He would have to end the call. He had
no time for this.

'Listen, I want to say thanks so much for everything. And
for being so understanding. You wouldn't believe how much
it's meant to me. I'll never forget it, I swear. Bye . . .'

Joe put down the phone before she could respond. Every
part of his body was feeling a tingle or a rush or some kind
of rhythmic beat. It was fantastic. He turned to look at the
clock, now placed permanently on top of the TV.

66095647 . . . 46 . . . 45 . . .

One word from Juliet tomorrow would decide his future.
He was sure he would be proved right. Over the last few
weeks, he had created in his mind shaky home video images
of the crucial moment.

*Inside the cottage; the clock on the kitchen table; Juliet with
batteries in her hand; Milo clamouring, 'Let me, let me'; Juliet
picking up the clock and turning it over; Milo watching excited
as she slides back the cover of the battery chamber; Juliet handing
him the batteries and pointing; Milo after a little trial and error
managing to get the first one to click in, then the second so easy;
Juliet closing the battery chamber, and (slow-motion) turning the
clock round so Milo can see the digits light up. He is thrilled.*

The scene was as real as memory for Joe now. He no longer considered the original option: that it was Juliet who put the batteries in. Occasionally, especially since Paris, he had reminded himself that he had to keep that scenario in mind. More and more he could feel himself drawn to the certainty and power the counting down offered him. On Christmas Eve night he had stood on his balcony rail, and considered letting himself fall off. Fortified by his belief that he was not yet due to die, Joe was fascinated by the prospect of what it would feel like to give himself to an experience like that, willingly. What injuries would he sustain? He knew from his recent experience that the pain component was less significant than people presumed, especially if the para-medics arrived quickly enough. What damage would be done, permanent or otherwise, from a four-story fall? He couldn't do it. Looking down, he realized his greatest fear was not that his faith in the clock would prove misguided, and that he would die after all, but that he might sustain some kind of permanent brain damage, making the rest of his lifespan completely unbearable. That would be too cruel a joke.

All going well, he would depart Brighton Vale tomorrow ready to live in total, and reasonably wealthy, freedom. Joe recognized his need for Juliet to think well of him, even perhaps forgive him, though he didn't expect that. He wanted their encounter to be as calm and friendly as was possible under the circumstances. He was a little concerned, from what her mother had said, that Juliet might think that Joe would resent her selling the house. Why should he? Juliet had got it as part of the settlement. That was the end of the matter. Signed, sealed, end of story. The settlement had been a total success as far as Joe was concerned, merci-fully quick, clean and decisive, unlike the break-up itself.

Everyone ended up satisfied. So he had given up lots, so what? That was fine by him. In return he had got his life back. He had always thought Juliet understood that that was how he felt. The proposal had been hers in the first place, after all, and as Joe now remembered, he had briefly thought, 'She can go fuck herself,' when it was first put to him by the negotiator. Juliet was not to know that though, because by the time he gave his formal response he had thought it over and realized that it was a viable and simple solution. So he had said yes without any more haggling, even though it was tough to be asked to hand over what had been, after all, his first real home. Surely Juliet wasn't imagining that, as well as the effects of all the recent trauma, he was also harbouring some resentment about old stuff? He would have to reassure her about that. Sell Brighton Vale and the best of luck. He hoped she would get three million for it. She might too. They could both be multimillionaires. If the sale of the studio went through quickly, he could pay off the mortgage on Smithfield, and still have several million left over. In less than twenty-four hours he could be like one of those guys in so many recent TV ad campaigns, the ones who go where they want, do as they please, leap across buildings, swim oceans, literally peel away and toss aside any impediment to their freedom and pleasure. Your world your way. Genuinely easy. Make your own rules. Joe knew that was marketing bullshit – naturally there was no such thing as total individual freedom without a price. But there was one significant difference between him and all the other fools. He knew the price now, and was prepared to pay it.

Joe decided he had better give some thought to clothes. He didn't want Juliet to draw any mistaken conclusions from how he looked. Recently he tended to hang around in his boxers. If he went out at all he just threw on roomy tracksuit bottoms and a woolly jumper. It was still annoying him that he couldn't seem to get back to his old waist size. He couldn't figure it out. It wasn't like he was over-eating. He had managed to make one trip to M & S just before going to Paris. He had wasted no time. He had simply grabbed a pair of red-code trousers, and quickly tried them on. They fitted perfectly, so he bought six of them. He would wear one of those tomorrow with one of the many elegant shirts Juliet had bought for him over the years. He hadn't worn any in a while. Surely they still fitted? In the bedroom he tried them, one after another, tossing them on the bed in frustration. They were all fine at the shoulders, but none of them would button at the waist any more, except for two non-fitted ones. Spending so much time in front of the mirror also made him realize how much he needed to shave. And shower. Maybe cut his hair? He wondered if he had started to smell.

The water trickling down his body was a darker grey than he had expected. Even the suds couldn't disguise the extent of the dirt. Joe figured it must be from his hair, which hadn't been washed in a long while. He liked the medicinal smell of tea tree. He was fascinated by how truly cleansing this shower felt, like a real transformation. The shave was the trickiest bit. Growth had become so thick he had to use two razors. He went at it gently. He definitely did not want to cut himself on this occasion. Once he could feel the softness of his skin again he was pleased. Even his eyes looked brighter. Juliet had been intoxicated with his eyes in the dreamy early days. 'Sweet almonds' she had called them, and always when they made love – even when, years later, they were just going through the motions – she would gaze into them as if drawing necessary sustenance from them. A little Optrex bath would be nice. He searched, even though he was pretty certain there was none. His attention was distracted when he spotted a not quite empty bottle of I Coloniali, an aftershave that Juliet had once given him. He had forgotten he had it. He slapped some on and wrapped a towel round his waist, intending to lie on the bed for a think, but the look of the bedlinen put him off. Did he have any clean stuff? He went to the living room instead, and lay down on the sofa. He felt himself drying nicely as he thought about how his meeting with Juliet might go. Why did she suddenly want to meet him? What did she want from him? Maybe she just needed to vent her feelings, which was fair enough. If so then she would start by being rather coldly angry and, depending on his response, she would build herself up to some outburst, righteous and intense. Possibly tearful. Joe decided that whatever it was she might need to get off her chest, he would certainly not fight back. He would be contrite. After all, he was contrite. As contrite as could be. His regrets were deep and true. Surely, surely Juliet understood that? He would bow down under every accusation until her storm eventually blew itself out. Then he could begin, slowly, carefully, to move the conversation round to that day, the day in question. Hopefully she wouldn't notice what he was doing. Once he had eased from her the information about Milo and the clock, well . . .

It occurred to him that there might be something more to this invitation. The fact that his ex-mother-in-law had mentioned selling the house might have some greater significance than he had first thought. Maybe Juliet wanted more. Maybe she was trying to use Milo's death as some kind of leverage to change the separation agreement, get a piece of Sounds Alive! also. Had she heard he was selling it? What if she was planning to exploit Joe's guilty feelings? If so, he'd be walking right into her trap by being too contrite. So. How would he gauge her intentions when they met? He would have to proceed much more carefully, keeping his feelings under wraps, while not seeming callous. Let her show her hand first . . .

This was madness. Joe knew that Juliet was not that kind of person. She had no slyness in her. If she wanted something from him, he would know about it very quickly. She would let him know exactly why she had asked to see him. He was losing the run of himself. Why was his mind not as relaxed as his body now was? Tomorrow would be fine. This was how it was meant to be. It was Christmas, New Year time. Juliet just wanted to begin a process; to make things all right again. Was tomorrow New Year's Eve? Joe realized he did not know exactly what day or date it was between Christmas and New Year. He hadn't been keeping track. Time for him now was the seconds ticking away on the millennium clock. So how many days had passed since Christmas? It was genuinely hard to say. He needed to find out. How could he time his arrival at Brighton Vale correctly if he didn't even know what time it was in the world right now? He turned on the computer, impatient to find out now, glancing at the millennium clock ticking away as he waited for it to load up. Twenty-eight precious seconds passed before he accessed Date and Time. It was Thursday, 29th of December 2005. 20:15:47. Joe glanced at the millennium clock.

66020353 . . .

And back to the computer clock. He let his eyes flick back and forth.

20:15:48 . . . 66020352 . . . 20:15:49 . . . 66020351 . . . 20:15:50 . . . 66020350 . . .

Which was true time? Joe switched off the computer. It took him very few seconds to work out that from now, he would be meeting Juliet in more or less fifty-three thousand and, say, a hundred seconds. With any luck, once he put on nice clean bedlinen, he would sleep peacefully through most of that.

Seconds after Joe woke, he began to realize that he was still on the sofa, and it was probably the middle of the night. He felt resentful. If he got up and walked straight to bed he might get to sleep again immediately, but he remembered that he had not changed the sheets. Resentment became rage. Something started to make him feel this was all Juliet's fault. It was she was keeping him dangling like this for no good reason. How much time was left to fill before he could meet her? Joe's anger gathered force. He thought of ringing and demanding that she meet him immediately. Now. After all, it was his life she was wasting; had she not done enough of that already? He controlled himself and went searching for clean bedlinen. On the top shelf of the wardrobe, he found sheets and a duvet cover still in their packaging. He couldn't remember ever having bought them, but he was glad of it now. Having ripped off the old soiled bedclothes, Joe saw the stain on the mattress. It was frustrating but he had to turn it over. The other side looked good as new. The fitted sheet tucked in easily and stretched smooth and white. The duvet was much more of a struggle, and needed a lot of aggressive shaking before it settled itself to a perfect fit inside the cover. Closing all the buttons was tedious. After that, the pillowcases were easy. Joe, sweating a little, was proud of his newly dressed bed. It was calling him. It would feel crisp and warm around his newly washed body. He would wake up fresh, ready for his rendezvous. Naked, he slid in. Time passed. Soon Joe began to accept that he was not going to fall asleep, no matter how easeful his bed now felt. Whether it was because of the nap on the sofa, some energizing effect of his activities since, or simply that his mind was full of childlike anticipation, he didn't know. What was clear to him was that it was still dark and he could not sleep. He got up in a temper and walked to the living room. The clock was the first thing he looked at:

65989184...

He couldn't be bothered doing the sums to work out how much time had passed. He switched on the computer again. It seemed to take forever to load up ... 4:57:37. He switched off, now feeling unbearably frustrated. Naked in the dark with another six hours to go, he could think of no way to fill in the time.

I I

The clock read 65985222 when Joe put it in his shoulder-bag and left the apartment. He figured if he took it nice and easy he should get to Brighton Vale at about the right time. The phone call to Juliet's parents had perhaps been a miscalculation. Her father had sounded groggy when he answered and his tone became strained and tight as he interrupted Joe's flow.

'If it's really so important to meet earlier, I'm sure ten rather than eleven would be fine for Juliet.'

It was clearly a take it or forget about the whole thing option. Although unsatisfactory from Joe's point of view, he had sensed that his call might be causing some negativity, and so had accepted, even pretending to be really grateful for the miserly one-hour time change.

It was dark and freezing cold, but dry at least. Smithfield was empty, quite silent. Joe didn't see another person until he reached the quays. Two Chinese men were just ahead, walking silently in the same direction. Beyond the Four Courts he passed a small group of men waiting for something or someone. They were smoking and muttering in an East European language. By the time Joe reached Ormond quay he had passed more Chinese and some darker faces; all silent, all moving with sober intent. Where would the country be without them? Joe thought, up and at it every morning, Christmas or New Year or whatever, opening the city, giving it a bit of a sweep-up, before the Irish decided to get their arses out of bed. No more than ten or twelve years ago, the only bodies you'd have spotted on the quays at this hour would have been hard-cases lurching for early doors, or young pricks, like himself at the time if he was honest, in tuxedos at the arse end of a long night out, looking to cap it all with the ritual of an early morning drink. Now we have our very own serf-race, Joe thought. Time to abuse them instead of ourselves. Stopping at the traffic island on O'Connell Bridge and gazing up towards the giant Christmas tree, now completely overshadowed by the Spire, then turning back towards Trinity College, Joe felt an intense energy flow through him. While most of Ireland slept in bloated contentment, and little immigrant folk scurried about the city focused only on today and what tiny improvements to their lot the next twenty-four hours might bring, he had chosen to take this lone journey across Dublin to claim his extraordinary future. Very soon, all going well, Joe Power would be a free individual, needing no one any more. Anything he might desire, he would get for himself. He felt a profound consciousness of his superiority, standing in the dark before dawn at the dead centre of the city. He walked on. By the time he reached the Grand Canal basin Joe was intensely pleased that he had chosen this way to fill the time before his meeting with Juliet. The air felt clean. He took big breaths and blew out slowly. He liked how quiet the streets were, yet he was glad to have escaped what he now realized was the claustrophobia of his apartment, and be able to look at occasional passing faces, especially as he was unlikely to meet anyone he might know.

A wiry lad was leaning over the bridge, staring up, apparently lost and dazed. Joe had to resist looking to see what exactly was attracting his attention. It was either the penthouses overlooking the canal basin – penthouses the wiry lad would never see inside unless he broke into them – or beyond the luxury apartment block to some distant star.

When Joe was no more than a few yards away, the wiry lad's eyes, quite suddenly and distinctly, shifted focus directly to him. The action itself was intended to unnerve. The wiry lad was no longer out of it as he had seemed to be, but alert and clearly dangerous. The gaze shifted briefly to Joe's shoulder-bag and immediately back to his face again. As yet there was no sign of a weapon. Maybe he was waiting to see if he would need to produce one. What pleased Joe most about himself in this moment was that, despite the clever eye-shifting shock tactic, he neither showed nor felt any fear. His only actual concern was that he did not want to get involved in any potentially messy violence now. Nothing should desecrate this time. Staring back, he continued walking towards the wiry lad at the same pace, hoping the little fuck would be thrown by the lack of any hesitation and uncertainty. They drew level. Joe was not impressed with the clichéd challenge.

'What're you looking at?'

Already it was clear, from the position of the right hand, that whatever weapon the wiry lad had, it was in his back pocket, or rammed down the ass of his trousers. Joe would know all about it in a couple of seconds unless he did something. It could get messy and he might have to kill him. The wiry lad was easily slight enough to be spun around once Joe grabbed his right arm, which he did. He rammed him against the bridge and pressed his entire weight hard on him. There it was, a knife tucked into the back of his jeans. The wiry lad was wriggling, trying to reach it with his free hand. Joe pulled it out, held it high, and dropped it into the canal basin. All the wriggle and fight went out of the wiry lad at that moment. His bony frame sagged against the bridge. It occurred to Joe that if anyone came along at that moment it would look like some horrible rape was taking place, with Joe as the vicious perpetrator. The difficulty was, if he let go could he be sure that the wiry lad had really had enough and would do the sensible thing, back off and let Joe continue his walk safely? That was not a chance worth taking. Grabbing the back of his jeans, he hoisted the bony body quickly, up and over the side of the bridge, into the water. He knew it must be freezing down there, but it was only a few yards to the dock if the guy was a half decent swimmer. As Joe walked on, he thought the screaming and splashing were unnaturally loud. It sounded a bit fake really.

The incident gave Joe more pep in his step. He noticed with pleasure how well his damaged leg was holding up. It was on the RER back to Charles de Gaulle that it had first occurred to him how much it had improved, given the punishment it had withstood that day. Using the *ascenseur* outside Roger Merriman's apartment had not been an option and Joe, impatient and without even thinking about it, had more or less raced down the emergency stairs, without any obvious negative effect. Now he found that he had got through silent Ringsend to Sandymount Strand more quickly than expected. It had been in his head to watch the sun rise over the sea, but here he was on the empty beach, and it was still quite dark. What the hell, he could wait. He hoisted himself on to an unbroken bit of wall at the disused baths. He had done exactly this with Juliet many years ago. When? Definitely not long after they first met, maybe ... God, 1995? As early as that? He took the clock out of his bag and placed it beside him, where she had sat. How long would it be before the sun appeared? He guessed less than half an hour, say one thousand, six hundred seconds. Had they stopped here on the way back to Brighton Vale? Was it the first time he took her there? Joe couldn't place the occasion. It had to have been an occasion — she was wearing an evening dress. He remembered it clearly because of the slit up the side. How he had ached to slide his hand in. Why hadn't he? Was the relationship still at the shy stage? They had walked barefoot across the strand arm in arm, so close they almost tripped over each other. Then they sat on the wall, kissing again and again. It must have been summer, Joe thought, it was never as cold as this, his arse was freezing. Though he couldn't be sure of the occasion or the time of year, he could still hear clearly the gentle timbre of Juliet's voice. She never seemed to raise it, it had no tinny insistence. It was before the time when young middle-class girls annoyingly pitched every end of sentence *like a question?* Joe believed in Juliet's voice, like his mother believed in prayer. He had fallen in love with the sound of her, especially on that night, melting with the gentle plash of the waves. The sun began to appear. He checked the clock and did a quick calculation. One thousand, five hundred and forty-seven seconds. He wasn't far out at all. Joe had to admit that this sunrise looked more genuinely beautiful than his romanticized memory of that other morning. The dramatic collision of winter sun and winter sky was always more heartbreaking. Shards of deep, deep orange light speared ruthlessly through cracks in smoky clouds: ice and fire. Maybe the cold seeping into him was making him feel dreary, but now Joe was sorry he had sat on the wall to watch this. Walking would warm him up.

Twenty years, almost all his Dublin life, had been spent around the area he was now passing through. Somewhere up Woodbine Road was where his first digs had been when he came to college. Then the famous house share with Shane and Cian for two years in Emmet Square. That had been legendary, until they were thrown out after the Gardaí had called during one of their classic parties. It spoiled a great set-up. That had started Joe thinking about buying his own place, even though he was only twenty-three. He was really enraged to discover he could be evicted just like that. He hated that landlord for years after, and even made revenge plans. They had had such a laugh there. He had bought his first car during that time, and drove home one night off his head, with Shane and Cian and three girls piled in. Jesus! That had to be the same night he was woken by Shane next to him in bed fucking the girl he had just fucked before falling asleep. He had totally forgotten that. In Blackrock village he tried to figure out the exact spot where briefly he had a bedsit overhead a shop, a newsagent's. What was it now? That landlady was sweet. A widow. She left him to himself, not like that bollocks in Emmet Square who thought he had a right to march into the house whenever he felt like it, 'just doing a few repairs'. Even though he had driven up and down the Rock road ever since he bought Brighton Vale, Joe hadn't thought about any of these places in years. It must be something to do with the hour of the morning, or some instinct that he was passing this way for the last time. That thought surprised him. At Seapoint DART station entrance Joe crossed the pedestrian bridge over the lines, and stepped down into Brighton Vale. It was the most perfect spot in Dublin to live as far as he was concerned: a cul-de-sac hidden below the Monkstown road with one row of villas overlooking the rocks and the sea. Beyond, a clear view of Howth Head. From the first time he saw it, his choice had been clear: buy this or just get the fuck out of Ireland. Go to the US and become a millionaire before he was thirty like Rory. Immature though he was at that time, Joe understood what a haven this was. A hundred and sixty thousand pounds was like a joke-price now, but at only twenty-four? Back then? Passing the faded old painted name on the side of the wall, he shocked himself with a terrible and angry sting of loss. Thirteen years of his life single and married and familied; all gone. Was it only ten months ago it had all come tumbling down? Or rather, feeling the familiarity of the house and the sound of the sea once again, was it so long ago? Two faces in a parked car darkened his mood further. Juliet's mother and father were sitting in their old blue Opel on the sea side of the road close to the house. What was this, Special Branch surveillance? What did they think was going to happen? Joe stopped and stared, making sure they noticed that he noticed them. First there was a little nod and smile. Then his ex-father-in-law got out and stood leaning on his door. He saluted casually. Joe realized with a shock that he could no longer remember the man's first name.

'Morning Joe. Good timing, almost ten. Did you get a DART?'

Joe decided to play relaxed. He nodded.

'Is Juliet inside?'

'She is indeed.'

'See you later so.'

'That's fine. Everything all right with you?'

Was that a casual inquiry or some pointed remark? Joe couldn't tell, but sensed his ex-father-in-law was looking at him in a peculiar way.

'Not bad. Thanks for arranging the earlier time.'

'Well, you were sounding a bit . . . anxious.'

Again was there a tone in that? Some inference? Joe couldn't be certain of what he was hearing. Not that he cared much. He just wanted to get into the house to Juliet. Let the Special Branch patrol outside if that made them happy. They were irrelevant. Fucking 1992 crock. Was he going to drive it until it fell apart in the middle of the road? Special agent ex-mother-in-law rolled down her electric window.

'Hello, Joe. How are you feeling?'

What was her first name? Had he not spoken it aloud on the phone last night?

'I'm feeling very good. Bit of a limp still. That's it really. No pain. Is it all right to go in?'

Ex-father-in-law tried to glance at his watch without appearing to.

'Of course, sure.'

Joe Power opened the gate and walked in. He climbed the six steps to his front door, which was newly painted, but in the same Sutcliffe green Joe had chosen long ago. He lifted the knocker and tapped it twice, politely, an expected guest. The door opened. Juliet's smile was already in place.

'Come in, Joe.'

There was a new carpet on the stairs. Something different on the wall. A different painting? At first glance Joe didn't care for it. He knew he should be saying something but he was stuck. He wasn't prepared for how hard it would be. What a struggle not to remember. The sound of the sea receded as Juliet closed the door, and he heard a door slam in the past. He had to keep focused on now. Now. His hand roamed the surface of the shoulder-bag, feeling for the security of the clock. Juliet reappeared in his view, her tone suddenly more intense.

'I am so sorry this has taken so long. I hope you understand. I kinda know you do. How hard it's been. I suppose my real fault was, I never thought about how hard it was for you too. I can see it now. It's written all over you.'

This was nice to hear. It was very hopeful that she was apologizing straight out, although this other thing about something written on him suggested to Joe that Juliet was still under strain. She had definitely lost some weight. Her eyes looked wary, or maybe a bit fearful. Joe couldn't quite put his finger on it. There was something else in her tone too, despite the gratifying apology. Whatever it was, it grated on him ever so slightly.

'Coffee?'

'Please.'

He let her lead the way to the kitchen. There didn't seem to be too many other alterations.

'Have you had breakfast?'

'No, I left early to walk out.'

'From where?'

There was the tone again. She was trying to disguise it this time. Trying to sound like it was just a casual question. Joe now regretted mentioning that he had walked. Yes it was an unusually long walk, but why should he have to explain himself? He decided that the best thing was just to move things on.

'Don't worry, I'm not hungry. Coffee is fine. I'm glad to see you looking so well.'

Juliet seemed to be staring at him. Then she smiled again.

'You don't have to pretend with me. I look awful and so do you. We've both been through it. I thought it was just me, but I can see now, how it's been for you. Oh, Joe, what are we going to do?'

Her voice was crying before the tears came, two glutinous blobs ballooning in the corners of her eyes, then spreading and filling. It was obvious to Joe that she was in a desperate state. He should hug her. If he held her face down into his chest she would feel him strong and protective. Instead, even as he reached towards her, Juliet had taken his face in her hands. She was looking at him intensely even through her tears. She was holding and caressing his face as if he was a little boy, pushing his hair back from his forehead. What did she think she was at? Now her tone was truly grating.

'I imagine you know what I was feeling and thinking about you at first. I went through – I can't even say. I suppose I wanted to make you the – I wanted everything to be your fault. So I persuaded myself you didn't care enough, when the truth was it was destroying you even more.'

The kettle whistled. Unbelievably, Juliet smiled under the tears and patted his face as she stepped away to make the coffee. It clicked with Joe what it was in her voice. It was this pitying thing. From the way she was behaving, not only was she not angry with him, it was like she felt sorry for him, or was concerned for him. Even the way she looked at him; that fixed *understanding* smile, as if he was someone who needed help. What kind of bollocks was this? This was worse than her contempt.

When exactly did you become so shallow?

Juliet rinsed the cafetière, and spooned in coffee. Not enough of course. Joe tried to deal with it without inferring criticism.

'I won't want much. Just half fill it.'

'Sure.'

He watched as she poured, a little tense. Would she stop halfway as he had suggested or would she pour on unthinkingly? He couldn't keep silent.

'That looks great. That's perfect.'

He nearly reached out a hand to stay her, but she stopped in time. Juliet put the kettle down and wiped her eyes. Making the coffee seemed to have helped calm her a little. She looked at Joe and smiled again. All this smiling was unsettling. She touched his face again.

'We can help each other, maybe. For Milo's sake.'

Just in time she had mentioned Milo's name. So he could be spoken of, that was good. It meant that somehow, Joe could bring conversation round to the clock. He would put up with this other stuff for now, no matter how annoying it was. Let poor old Juliet ramble on. He would keep his eye on the prize. It did occur to him that, in her present frail psychological state, there was no way he could even think of opening up to her about the clock, and what it meant. That would be a complete waste of time in the present circumstances. That made his task clearer, simpler. He would find out whether it was Juliet or, as he suspected, Milo had put the batteries in the clock that day. Once he had that information he could leave, get the hell out. As he followed her into the front room, he couldn't help wondering why she had moved the sofa to the other wall. Its new position didn't make sense to him. The room felt all wrong. Couldn't she see that it didn't work? Basic. Juliet raised her coffee mug.

'Is it OK for you?'

Joe nodded, thinking, yes, thanks to me not letting you put too much water in. Juliet sat down on the sofa. The morning sun was strong on her face. It caught some of her old beauty.

'About the funeral. You know I didn't do it to – well, for any bad reasons. Absolutely not. We just didn't know how long you would be in hospital and . . . well anyway you know the whole thing. But if there's anything you want to ask me about it. Anything you like. I'll try to tell you. If it helps.'

There was that tone again. What was it supposed to be? Patient understanding? Soothing counsel? Joe felt his fist clench. How was he supposed to respond to this? He did his best.

'What kind of coffin was it?'

'Just a little box, Joe. Simple, unvarnished. No handles or stuff. With his name on top. Milo Power. It was so small. I was able to carry it myself from the hearse to the grave. They didn't want me to, but it helped, you know. It was like he was asleep in my arms . . .'

She bowed her head. Joe tried to think of another question. He knew he had to stick with the funeral for a while.

'Were you able to say goodbye before they closed the coffin?'

Juliet nodded. She said nothing more for a moment.

'I suppose if they had let me I'd have just stood there for hours. It was Dad who sort of pulled me away. I don't mean pulled like that, I mean, you know, he pressed my arm and got me to turn away, and once I did that . . . I knew that was it. They always say that the undertakers do a beautiful job but they didn't. I mean I'm sure they did amazing things fixing up the injuries and so on, but . . . there was no life there. It wasn't Milo really. It was something stone cold and . . . I was only looking because it was the next best thing, like a wax figure or something. I think you'd have hated it.'

At last Juliet had got something absolutely right. He took her hand.

'Did anyone . . . say anything? A few words?'

'Dad wanted to read that Seamus Heaney poem, but I wouldn't let him. The priest of course said something. I wasn't listening. There was an awful lot of crying. There were people there, I hadn't a clue who they were, all crying.'

Joe decided to risk shifting the ground a little.

'I keep remembering his birthday party.'

'Yeah?'

'He hadn't a clue what was coming, and on the way back to the cottage I was deliberately being kind of, you know, dull, not much fun. I could tell he was a bit disappointed to be brought home so early especially on his birthday. Then when he walked into the cottage and saw all the faces.'

'He didn't know what was happening I think. He'd never heard of such a thing as a surprise party.'

'Next thing he's bouncing around the place. King of the castle.'

'Oh, he loved the attention all right.'

'I think he was really happy down in the cottage.'

'Do you think so, Joe? Really?'

Joe steeled himself. He half believed it anyway, so why not say it?

'From what I saw, sure.'

'Thanks for saying that. That means a lot. He was turning into a real little country boy.'

Joe thought, now. Maybe now. Tread carefully.

'I noticed it already on that first visit at the end of August, I hadn't seen him in a few months, and already something was different.'

'You weren't happy about it.'

'No, I wouldn't say that. But he was different somehow. Remember when the two of you came out that day with the clock, and he was holding it, and you were holding the umbrella over his head?'

'Yeah?'

Juliet looked slightly puzzled. Joe was nervous now. He could tell she wasn't sure where this was going. He had to nail this immediately.

'I remember thinking, I bet Milo wanted to be in charge, pestering you to let him put the batteries in, and carry the clock out.'

'Really, were you thinking all that?'

'Well, you know. It seemed funny to me. That idea.'

'Yeah, he was definitely becoming his own little person.'

She had lapsed again. Tears were near again. Joe still didn't have his answer.

'So . . . was I right?'

'Hm?'

She was distracted, not on the same wavelength. He would have to take a chance; be bald.

'Was I right? Did you let Milo put the batteries into the clock that day?'

Juliet looked at him like he had asked her something in another language. He wanted to shake her. She didn't seem to understand what he was asking. Wherever her mind was right now, it wasn't anywhere near that moment when the countdown clock had been set in motion. For luck, Joe pressed his hand against the clock inside the shoulder-bag. Did she even remember?

'Batteries? . . . Oh yeah, he put them in . . . There was all this "Let me, let me!" And then when the numbers popped up he was delighted. I told him they were magic numbers and he had to make a wish.'

Joe felt light. His whole self eased. It was OK. Everything was clear now. It was as he had believed and – yes, truthfully – hoped. Milo's number had come up, poor kid. That was what happened. After that there was nothing to be done. Joe noticed that Juliet seemed to be easing his head down on to her lap. She was caressing his hair and making a soothing sound. His bag had slipped on to the floor. He could make out a little bulge in the leather that was the clock, ticking away. His number. It was very comforting. Maybe after all this was the right time to show Juliet the clock, start to tell the story. Until this moment such a plan hadn't seemed possible, not with those odd smiles, and the uncomfortable undertone in Juliet's voice, but now . . . now he had got his answer. More than anything right now he wanted to reach his hand into the bag and pull out the clock. He was impatient to see precisely how much time was left. Joe recognized the little tinkling arpeggio he heard. The music sting that announced the arrival of a text message on a mobile phone always reminded him of a department store staff call. One of Juliet's hands stopped caressing and left his shoulder. A little laugh followed soon after. Clearly Juliet had just checked and read a message. This annoyed Joe sufficiently for him to look up. With her free hand, Juliet was texting. She smiled down at Joe and turned her mobile towards him so he could read her message. *All OK*. Juliet tried to sound throwaway.

'Dad. For his peace of mind.'

Joe sat up, then stood up. He walked away a few steps then turned back, his annoyance multiplying into rage. He pointed at the mobile phone. He was only inches away from being able to knock it out of her hand.

'He texted you?'

'Yeah.'

'About me?'

'No. It's OK, Joe. He was just concerned.'

'Concerned about what?'

'Look, it's nothing. He was just checking that everything was going OK. And look, I'm telling him yes it is.'

Now Joe batted the mobile phone from her hand. Now the smile disappeared from her face.

'And why wouldn't it be OK?' He bit hard on each letter, O – K.

'I can't believe you did that, Joe.'

'Oh sorry, maybe it's Daddy on patrol outside I should ask.'

Joe walked from the room quickly. Juliet followed.

'After everything. I can't believe you did that. He was just concerned.'

'So I hear. I'll go ask him about what.'

'Oh, for God's sake, we're all concerned.'

Joe thought, stop saying that word.

'Like who?'

'All of us. Why wouldn't we be? Look at you.'

Joe turned at the door.

'Who?'

'Who, who? Everyone left who still cares anything for you. They all spoke to me, Joe. They said I was the only one who could get you to listen. Jesus.'

Joe saw it all now. His anger was cold now. He had been set up.

'Who?'

'Don't come one step nearer. Your father and your sisters. They're at their wits' end. Rory and Lisa, Shane, Cian. Trevor phoned just before Christmas –'

Trevor? Joe could not believe what he was hearing.

'. . . and I tell myself things are not as bad as they think. But then as soon as I open the door . . .'

Juliet gestured to him. Joe could tell it was not just to his face, which he had shaved before leaving the apartment, or his carefully chosen clothes, or his belly, which fair enough, was a bit embarrassing. It was to the whole of him, inside and out. Joe Power had been set up. Not that it mattered, because he was a step ahead of all of them. He had got what he came for, so fuck his father and sisters, Juliet and her special agents, everyone. They didn't know what the deal was. Not a clue. Joe opened the door and walked out. Juliet called after him, her voice ringing in his ears like begging, but his eyes were on a bigger prize now. Her father opened the door of his wreck and started to heave himself out, but Joe was already well up the road, moving fast, nearly at the little pedestrian exit that would take him over the DART bridge, out of Brighton Vale and on to the beginning of the rest of his life. The calling had stopped. He didn't look back, not caring whether or not they were in pursuit. Nonetheless he walked quickly up the steps. From the bridge he heard the sound of a DART approaching. He looked down the track. It was just coming into Seapoint station, headed for Dublin. If he ran he might catch it. He was confident he would catch it, because it was going to be that sort of day. The ticket desk was shut, so there was no delay. He hopped over the barriers and on to the train as the doors closed. It was easy to find a seat alone in a carriage with just five people in it, two of them slumped dozing. He put the shoulder-bag on his lap and opened it. He took out the clock. His heart was beating fast, but he was floating. Confident. Positive. He was an individual set free. Nothing and no one else mattered except himself and the time he had left. It was a pleasure to gaze at the clock.

65967399 . . . 98 . . . 97 . . .

An amazing opportunity had come his way. As always with opportunity there was risk. So, he wondered, what now?

Essay in the future tense, written by Joseph Power for Mr Waters in 4th class, 1978

WHEN I GROW UP

When I grow up I will be rich. I will not be like those boys who think there better than the rest of us just because they get more pocket money. My Mam says never be a big show of. I will have my own football team and I will be nice to everyone. I will give all the players 50 pounds a week each. All the best players will come and play on my team, like Kevin Keegan and Steve Heighway, and we will win the cup. I will give the rest of my money to my mam for a new kitchen

10

Joe Power was beginning to think he couldn't spend his money fast enough. On the night before his trip to Cuba, he checked his bank accounts online. The total from various accounts, including interest, was four million two hundred and thirty-five thousand euro and forty-seven cents. Having sold Sounds Alive! and the Smithfield apartment, he had cleared five million two hundred thousand euro. This meant that he had spent less than a million euro in . . . how long? He glanced over at the clock and did an automatic calculation.

46260463 . . .

More than nineteen million seven hundred thousand seconds had passed since he had become free. He would need to spend at an even faster rate to get rid of it all by zero time. It was Joe's absolute intention to spend every cent. There was no one from his past life he wanted to benefit from any legacy, and he had no intention of forming any such relationship over his remaining time. Why was it so hard? How come other people seemed to have no trouble spending multiples of millions? Of course their circumstances were different. Joe was aware that he was a special case. Unique. The super-rich acquired costly entourages. They had friends and family who soaked up large chunks of cash. They were encouraged to make expensive long-term investments: property, shares, art. They were embarrassed into donating to charity. None of this applied to Joe any more. He was a pure individual, free of all responsibility. It was frustrating therefore to find that pursuing personal pleasure was not as expensive as one might have imagined. There were of course many ways to spend the money much faster, but were they of any real interest? Had any of his recent holidays been worth it? Prague? The Kenyan safari? Sandy Lane? The private helicopter to Ashford Castle for a weekend with ... what was her name? He couldn't be bothered trying to remember. All these trips, and others, had failed to match expectations, and were therefore a waste of his valuable diminishing time. Joe was sick of spending thousands ... millions of seconds packing and preparing, queuing in airports, going through ever more complicated, lengthy, mind-sapping security procedures, sitting uncomfortably in packed planes for far too long. If he was truly honest, only one trip had hit the spot. To his surprise, he had loved Havana, and it had lingered most in his memory. This was the only reason he was prepared to spend so much time going there again. He was a little afraid of second-time-round anticlimax, but felt he had to take that chance. He was becoming so bored. Joe gazed at the clock. He checked what it felt like to sit still for ten seconds, then twenty, then thirty. He stood up and stretched. The conundrum that dominated his life remained the same. He did not want his span to seep away quickly, yet it was only when he was happy, engaged, buzzing with life that it did so. Otherwise time dragged. As it was doing now.

It had been night for a little while, so Joe knew that soon it would be time to go to sleep, so as to wake up fresh for his journey. He was not in the mood for sleep yet. Neither did he want to sit at his computer teasing out the problem of how to spend his money faster. He desired some pleasure now. There were over a thousand CDs and DVDs on the shelves to his left, but he wasn't in the mood for any of them. He rarely was. Many were still in their seals. The greatest pleasure he had got from this collection was in buying them, all on one afternoon. The memory of it still allowed him occasional amusement, especially the expression on the face of the kid in HMV when Joe had explained what he wanted.

'I want all of these – the essential collection.'

Joe had handed him printouts from various internet sources, lists of the greatest, the most famous, the best-selling, the most influential music of the ages. The kid stared at the pieces of paper. Joe could tell he wasn't sure if this was some elaborate practical joke, one of those infantile hidden-camera TV show set-ups. He took out his then recently acquired gold card.

'Will it take long?'

The kid took the gold card. He seemed to decide he needed help with this one.

'I'll have to check what's in stock and stuff.'

Joe watched him hurry to the far end of the shop and go through a door. A few moments later a woman, fortyish, appeared. She came to Joe smiling a big bright smile. If Joe was a lunatic or prankster she would smoke him out.

'Hi. Well . . . this is unusual.'

'I suppose so.'

'We're a big shop, but most people just buy three or four CDs at a time.'

'I thought it would be quicker this way.'

'Well, yes, certainly. It will be very bulky.'

'That's OK. How long will it take to organize?'

'I suppose if a couple of the guys went at it maybe . . . half an hour. Do you know how many CDs there are altogether?'

'Not certain. Over eight hundred, I'd say.'

'And of course we may not have them all in stock,

although looking at the list, I would say we certainly have a lot of them –'

'I really would like to do this as quickly as possible.'

Joe had enjoyed the effect he was creating, but he was also at that early point in his new life when he was anxious to make time work too hard.

'Yes, of course.'

She handed the list to the kid.

'Gordon, quick as you can, and get James to help you.'

It became a very pleasurable two thousand seconds or so watching Gordon and James on their treasure hunt around the shop. Joe could tell that they began to enjoy it too. It became more and more competitive. They created individual piles and rushed back with their hands full, checking to see which of them was ahead. From the various lists only forty-seven selections proved impossible to find. This didn't bother Joe. He had enjoyed himself and foresaw millions of seconds of satisfaction from this collection. The manager, having deducted twelve thousand three hundred and forty-six euro, sixty-four cents from Joe's gold card, was now in a mood to be smilingly helpful. She suggested that if he drove round to the loading area, her boys could bring the goods to him there. Would that suit him?

That had been some afternoon, and once again the memory of it tickled Joe; time well spent. Admittedly he had listened to only part of just forty CDs or so. Why was that? It was puzzling how, in situations like now, a hiatus, it rarely pleasured him to curl up on the sofa, surrounded by the highest-spec audio-visual equipment, and listen to the finest music the world had ever produced, from whatever period in whatever style suited his mood. Why could he not be bothered to watch some film which by popular and critical consent was one of the greatest ever made? What did Joe want? His craving wasn't for haute cuisine or fine wines either. What about the gym? It might not be too late to go and refine even further the body he had been successfully sculpting. This was tempting. It was a continual pleasure for him to button his thirty-two-inch-waist jeans with ease, especially when sweated and cleansed after a workout. He was not one of those who stood at a mirror in the locker room gelling his hair and checking neurotically for tiny physical imperfections, but occasionally, when ready to go, he did enjoy five seconds of gazing. By any standard he looked fit. Compared to how his body had been, he was transformed. Tight, muscled, tanned. If he went to the gym, afterwards he could go to a club, indulge the easy power his improved body and money gave him. A fuck would not be out of the question, not by a long shot. Joe gave this scenario serious thought. If it was basic sexual relief he wanted, why bother to leave the apartment? He could log on to one of his porn sites and, for a few euro, enjoy a wank? Many times lately he had chosen this option over any kind of encounter with others. Much less time wasted for much the same amount of physical pleasure had been his calculation. Joe understood that what was tempting right now about a night-club was not the probability of sex, but the pleasure of seduction; the more resistant, the more uncertain the better. Sex would be no more than the necessary conclusion; proof of victory. Joe also recognized that this was a game where the more time it took – up to a point – the more enticing it was. This night he didn't have that much time to give it. He had a plane to catch when daylight came.

In truth Joe knew what he desired. It was in his head to go for a night-walk. So. Why not? The whole thing could be over and done with in four thousand seconds. Less.

Joe, having finally allowed the idea to become a conscious thought, sat down again and closed his eyes. He had been for his last night-walk not much more than a million seconds ago. That was not such a long time. He had been certain he would not feel the need again before he left for Cuba. Was the truth rather that he hoped he would not feel such a need? If so, why should he hope that? This was hard to answer. Joe was edgy now. He tried to distract his brain by thinking ahead to his journey. Via Heathrow it would be around fifty thousand seconds before he landed in Havana. He hated the thought of so much travel time but comforted himself with the promise that once he got through that ordeal, the rest would be pure pleasure; at least if his previous time there was any guide. Joe forced his mind to focus on what he would do once he arrived.

He takes an old Cadillac taxi from the airport to the Hotel Inglaterra. He checks in and showers quickly. It's now near darkness. He strolls to Calle Refugio, to the casa *particular run by Luis, who is delighted to welcome free-spending José back. He gives him the best of his three rooms. Finding a* jinetera *to spend the night with will take no time, although Joe knows he'll be satisfied only with Moniquita or Valeira, the girls who saved his sanity on that first trip. They made the fat slug he was then feel desirable. He turns and there they are suddenly, their pleasure in his company seemingly as real as ever. They offer kisses and laughter and a sensuality that normal prostitution, at least in Joe's limited previous experience, never achieves. Sometimes he returns to his room at the Inglaterra to siesta alone in the midday heat. Now it is night again and, elegantly dressed, he is enjoying the old colonial atmosphere of the hotel restaurant. He might spend a quiet night in. Or stroll across Parque Central on to Calle Obispo to drink, meet* chicas *and bring someone back to his room in the* casa particular. *It seems miraculous how in a city with armed cops on every corner, Joe can feel such an anonymous free spirit. Though largely purchased, the feeling seems pleasingly authentic.*

On his first visit, Havana's genius for embracing parallel realities had relaxed Joe. It had jogged a surprising nostalgia in him for Ireland when he was a happy little boy in the seventies. As the days and nights had passed, he had also appreciated the contentment of never watching TV, nor listening to radio, nor following the news. Not knowing what time it was had felt good. The sun rose and fell, night came and went, the millennium clock had kept him precisely informed. Since returning to Dublin he had continued that way. Millions of seconds later, Joe did not have to affect lack of knowledge or curiosity about what was happening in the world. His body and mind were cleansed of these things. His time in Havana had lulled him towards this state. Such an experience had been worth every cent, every second. He craved a renewal. Focused on these thoughts, he went to the kitchen. He checked the fridge, but there was nothing he wanted to eat. He considered making coffee but didn't actually start to make it. He could sense that Cuba was running its course as a means of keeping his mind occupied. Cuba was the future. Right now . . . now . . . now he wanted a night-walk. Yet he continued to resist this desire. He went back to his computer in a more determined mood. He would sort out his money question. That was what he would do. Now surely, was the perfect moment, this short time before he went to bed, before his long journey. By analysing more closely how he had been spending his money so far, it might be possible to work out a better plan, to spend more money in a more pleasurable way. It had to be done. Joe, determined, opened a new file. He sat back and tried to focus his mind, organize his thoughts. How exactly had he been spending his money? He typed:

```
1. Mercedes x 2 €284,000
```

That was an obvious start; a big item of expenditure.

How worried he had been that he would feel nervous getting behind a steering-wheel for the first time since the accident, but the Mercedes had been such a pleasurable drive that, from the moment he heard the engine, he had felt at ease. It had the comforting low growl of one's own dangerous but highly trained guard-dog. The purchase had made him think about Milo. It had been a brutally short life, and he had been such a placid decent boy. Beyond that there was no more to say or think, without drifting off the point. What had happened to Milo was simply how it worked. Time up. The same for himself soon enough, after all.

Joe thought about that first Merc, now in a car-pound somewhere. Were the guys who towed it away, or their bosses, mystified that he had never come to them? Was the PO box number he had left as his contact address after selling the Smithfield apartment, and never checked, stuffed with reminders and semi-threats of legal proceedings? Even though it was enjoyable to think about how it must be doing their heads in, that some guy called Joe Power could leave a virtually new Merc unclaimed, it still left a bad taste in the mouth to remember that the stupid woman who'd brought him back to her apartment hadn't warned him that it was twenty-four-hour pay and display on the street outside, which was why the car had been clamped in the first place. He had been left standing in the freezing cold having just snuck out of her apartment, while she slept. The clamping guy, sounding smug and under thirty, had said that it would be an hour at least before someone came to release the car.

Joe had shouted at him and bounced the mobile phone off the pavement. He had stood on it, full weight, and then walked away thinking, Fuck them, I'll collect the car when I feel like it. But it felt better just to go and buy himself another Merc. And of course, it was how the first night-walk began. A complete accident, an odd conjunction of disappointing sex, a clamped car and no available taxis. Joe allowed this memory to run. It was winter then, a very cold night. Was it before the first trip to Cuba? Was that woman the first he had been with since the last awful meeting with Juliet? The more time passed the harder it became to remember events in any kind of chronological order.

Joe stared at his lengthening expenditure list, knowing he could not shake off the urge to go out. Maybe a night-walk tonight was inevitable? And why not? He posed the question again. After all, maybe nothing would happen and that would be OK, just fine; that was the deal, surely? So why make a drama out of it? Why not just get himself ready and go? Was he afraid? In another effort to distract himself he began to type again, as quickly as he could think of things.

```
Flights . . . €50,000
Hotels . . . €60,000
Restaurants . . . €20,000
```

These figures were too rounded, more or less off the top of his head, the result of hasty agitated calculation, but they represented some sense of where his money was going.

```
Girls.
```

Having typed the word, he stopped to think. He deleted it and retyped:

```
Sex.
```

He thought about that for a little while. On-line porn hadn't actually cost too much in the scheme of things, maybe five thousand euro, straight-up prostitution had been at least twenty thousand euro, and then of course there was all the money he had lavished on entertaining girls, including stuff like the private helicopter to Ashford Castle for that point-less weekend with – he forced himself to remember – Naomi, was it? How much for all that? Fifty thousand euro easily. He typed:

Sex . . . €75,000

Joe knew this was becoming pointless. He could go on and on, flinging out figures like this easily, or, instead, spend tens of thousands of seconds painstakingly adding up meticulously researched real accounts. What did it matter? Joe stood again. He would go out for a night-walk. That was what he wanted now, so that was what he would do.

A phone rang. The ring tone was Gilbert and Sullivan's 'A Wand'ring Minstrel'; the family mobile. Joe walked over to the desk, where his five mobile phones were neatly placed side by side. The incoming number was blocked, so it wasn't his father. It was hard to remember which of his sisters might have blocked her number, as it was so long since any of them had called. They seemed to have at last accepted that as long as Joe kept in some kind of family contact by phoning his father regularly, they would not hassle him. He had spoken to his father no more than two hundred thousand seconds ago, so the sisters would have an up-to-date report. Why would one of them call now? Was there a crisis? He allowed the call to go to message. Joe had a vague memory that Babs blocked her number, but maybe he was just assuming she and Dick were the type to do that. If his mother was alive would she laugh or be shocked at the situation? Her boy with a hotline to his family, not to keep more in touch, but to keep them at bay. She would think it was insane at the very least. It wouldn't ever have reached this stage if she was still alive, would it? Joe was wary of his tendency to sentimentalize where his mother was concerned. They had disagreed on many things while she was alive: how he and Juliet had lived, for example; what she deemed to be the sinful extravagance of their lifestyle. She disapproved of their financial behaviour much more than the fact that they were living in sin, to use the old language. The idea of credit-card living, of spending to earn, of speculating to accumulate, was not just meaningless to his mother, she interpreted it as sly double talk, the language of swindlers and con-men. She could never accept that in the world of the late twentieth century, this was often the only way a young couple could get by. In one important respect, however, Joe knew she would approve of how he was living now. Even if owning five mobile phones was what she would call 'a bit simple', at least he was paying for them upfront, not living off loans. This was a good thing. What would she think of spending nearly a million euro in so short a time? On pleasure? Nothing put aside for a rainy day?

The phone tinkled. A message had been left. Even as he decided he had no choice but to listen to it, in case there was some terrible news, Joe smirked at a sudden thought. He would love to be able to write up a complete list of all his recent expenditure and summon his dead mother to read it and comment. Out of all that extravagance he would lay a large bet which item would immediately attract her attention and what her first bewildered question would be.

'A Polish cleaning woman! Twelve hundred euro! In the name of God and his blessed Mother, what for?'

'I really haggled with her, Mam. Fifteen euro a session I offered, and she laughed.'

'Of course she did. At you, throwing your money away.'

'No, because it was so little. I persuaded her to come and clean once, and if she thought fifteen euro was unfair then I would pay her more.'

'And what happened?'

'She said fifteen euro was fair.'

'Of course she did. Sure what work is there for her? Look at this flat, it's never used. It takes no cleaning. The fool and his money. No wonder she said yes. How often does she come?'

'Three times a week.'

As if she was standing at his side, Joe could hear the signature sigh of disbelief. The pure waste! There's no need for that woman at all. Explaining that need had nothing to do with it would be meaningless to his mother. How could he ever make her understand that he liked this strange woman coming to his apartment, moving about freely doing her job, making no demands, questioning nothing. She did not ask what the strange clock was, nor why there were no other clocks. She did not comment on his five mobile phones. She did not question why the wardrobe in the bedroom had a special lock. On one of her early visits, Joe heard her turn on the radio in the kitchen. He didn't recognize the song, nor did he wait to find out what it was.

'Turn it off!'

The radio was turned off immediately. There was a few seconds of silence.

'Sorry, Mr Power.'

She did not ask him why, and she never turned on the radio again.

Sometimes it was his pleasure to lounge on the sofa, in

silk pyjamas, sipping his favourite espresso, his eyes closed, just listening to her progress around the apartment. The bathroom sounds always reverberated a little more. The gurgle of water was a constant feature, as were wiry scouring noises. The kitchen produced cleaner, harder sounds of metal, ceramic, wood, plastic. A chair scraped on the oak floor or cooking implements clanked on hooks or clattered into drawers. When she reached the hall everything became softer, calmer. Cloth brushed wood. Her footsteps made so little noise on the carpet. She never spoke to him when she entered the living room. He didn't know if it was because she thought he was asleep on the sofa, and didn't want to disturb him, or she couldn't be bothered communicating. Sometimes she hummed as she worked, but always stopped suddenly, the tune unfinished. Joe assumed it was some consciousness or embarrassment at his presence. He imag-ined her alone humming more freely and concluding with sustained notes and perhaps an occasional flourish. The moment of greatest silence always seemed to be when she picked up the clock. Joe had to strain to hear the whisper of her cloth on hard white plastic. Once he opened his eyes slyly to confirm what he was hearing. He was a little disappointed to find that she appeared to have no interest in the clock. She was polishing it carefully, but staring out the window, her mind elsewhere. Just before she put it back down, she angled the face towards the light from the window, making sure it was spotless. Very often the apartment was cleaned in less than two thousand seconds. Only then would she speak. She never said much.

'I am finished now. See you next time.'

The usage 'next time' had been Joe's suggestion. He had asked her not to name days. She never questioned that either. Joe knew that his mother could never comprehend the perfection of this arrangement. It would still have pleased him to have her alive and present, even if it was just to fight with her about it.

Joe had no particular desire to find out which of his sisters had left a message, still less to listen to it, but he felt he had no choice. What if there was bad news of some kind, something he could not ignore? It really angered him that not only would he have to listen to the message, he would probably have to reply as well, because if he didn't then that would spawn more calls, his father would be drafted in, and a mini-crisis would develop. Where were you? Why didn't you get back to us? Why don't you keep in touch? The message was from Babs. Of course. Who else?

'Hi Joe. Sorry about the late call but I know you and your mad hours. I hear from Daddy you're planning some kind of holiday, he was a bit vague about the details, you know Daddy, but anyway, Marie Liston has asked me to come to Dublin with her on a shopping trip Saturday week, so I was thinking why don't we meet up for a bite if you're around. God only knows when you'll next honour Rochestown Road with your presence. Daddy says you're in flying form by the way, so I'm glad to hear that. Anyway I'm rambling, give us a call and we'll try and organize something. Dick says hello of course. Listen, I'm gone. Bye . . .'

Joe would be in Cuba at that time. So fuck you Babs, he thought. What was she up to, finding a stupid excuse like that to ring him? He kept his side of the deal, why couldn't she? He had bought a phone specifically for the family and given them the number. He phoned his father regularly, every five hundred thousand seconds or so. This should mean that there was no need for anyone else to be phoning anyone else. That was the tacit understanding. It had been fine. Joe couldn't even remember how long it had been since that phone had rung, although thinking about it now, he was fairly sure it had been that cunt Babs that time too. He regretted that, once dead, he could not witness her reaction in particular to the news that not only had Joe spent every last cent of his money, but by some extraordinary miracle his final spending had coincided exactly with his unexpected death. Tax investigators, accountants, Babs and the rest of them would marvel at this mystery. There would be bewilderment, perhaps a little awe, followed quickly by suspicion, acrimony and ultimately expensive litigation in the hope of discovering some fraudulent dealings. Joe certainly hoped to cause much pain and frustration.

He could text her back with the information about his absence from Dublin, but he decided to call. There was some other reason Babs had phoned him, he was sure, and though she was unlikely to come clean, listening to her talk might give him a clue. A brilliant and funny idea occurred to him. If he really had trouble spending all his money by zero time, he could simply give away what was left. He knew immediately who the perfect candidate would be: Polish cleaning woman. This idea was such a laugh that when Babs answered it was hard to focus on whatever she started to say. The thing would be so simple. He would not leave a will or anything like that. In his situation he wouldn't need to. Some time in the final fifty thousand seconds or so, when he had no more need to spend, he could go to his bank, withdraw whatever cash was left and send it to her, or leave it for her to find. Babs was expressing disappointment that he would not be around for her Dublin visit. As she talked on, Joe enjoyed imagining the fantastic shock it would be for this hard silent Polish woman – what age was she? forty-five? – if she suddenly got, say, five hundred thousand euro out of the blue, from this incommunicative, arrogant, rather mean, and now dead, Irishman. Mr Power would suddenly be transformed in her eyes: a saint. She might even try to acquire some photographic image of him, or an object associated with him – Joe couldn't remember the Catholic word for those things – and light candles before it. The sudden windfall would finance a triumphant return to the homeland, where the tale of the enigmatic Irish benefactor would become the stuff of family lore for generations. And fuck you Babs. Nothing left in the kitty for you and Dick and that child, whatever his name is. Joe suddenly wondered had he said any of that out loud. He forced himself to concentrate on Babs's voice:

'. . . If we all chipped in that much, it would cover everything no . problem. The only thing is of course we don't know how long for . . .'

What was she talking about? 'Chipped in' she had said, so it was something to do with money.

'. . . but I suppose we could review that down the line. I thought the best thing would be to set up an account for the purpose and we could all organize a standing order for it. Does that make sense?'

Unbelievably she actually paused to allow a reply. In the silence, Joe had no idea what to say. A familiar resentment was building. He wanted to get her off the line, out of his life. One thing he knew for certain now. As soon as he put the phone down, he was going out.

'Yes. Sorry, how much again?'

'A hundred a month each.'

Whatever it was for didn't matter. It was worth promising a lot more just to get rid of her right now.

'Fine, no problem. OK, I'll let you go so –'

'I mean he'll probably think it's next stop the home, but that's not it at all –'

'Yeah, sure, listen –'

'It's just to keep the place clean, and get a few messages done. He's not able for it any more . . .'

'Babs, is there anything else we need to sort out right now?'

'What . . . ah, not really. I can send you the bank details once I've set up the account . . .'

'OK.'

'. . . Oh and by the way, don't say anything to Daddy yet if you're talking to him. Wait until I've had a chance to go through it with him . . .'

'That's fine. Goodnight so, Babs. I have to go.'

'Oh, all right. Ahm –'

He clicked off before she recovered and launched another sentence. He had brought it to a reasonable conclusion. She had no excuse to ring back. He had put that part of his life back in its box for another while. What had she been on about? Organizing some kind of home-help for his father, was it? Interfering bitch.

Time to go out, definitely, if only for the relief of tension the night air might bring. Perhaps nothing more than that would happen. If so that would be OK. If he, Joe Power, took a walk wherever he pleased and returned safely without incident, that would not be time wasted. That was the deal he had made with himself. That was the basis. Joe decided to wear a Kris Van Assche jacket he had purchased recently. The collar was fur-lined, which might be provocative, but if so then let it be so. He had the right to dress as he pleased. It might get damaged or stained but he would take that chance. Joe slipped the clock into the jacket pocket and left the apartment. The girl in her early twenties with the stunning baby-doll face who lived across the hall was waiting when the lift opened at the entrance floor. She smiled at

Joe. Not for the first time he thought how unfortunate it was that she lived in the same building on the same floor; much too close to risk intimate involvement. She was clearly into him also, which made it more frustrating.

'Hi. Hey, great jacket.'

'Thanks. First time out, so it's nice to get the compliment.'

'Going out on the town?'

Joe nearly told the truth, or at least the simple surface truth that he was going for a walk, but suddenly realized she might suggest tagging along. If he lied and said he was going clubbing, she might notice him returning home shortly.

'I wish my life was that exciting . . .'

Popping out for milk? No, she would offer to give him some, which would be perfect if he was planning to fuck her, but unfortunately there was no way he could let that happen.

'I forgot to get petrol earlier.'

'Well, I admire a man who gets dressed up to fill his tank.'

Was that a little flirt or a little dig? Did she not believe him? Who the fuck did she think she was? Luckily she was already pressing the button for the top floor, and giving him a coy wave. Whatever subtle make-up she was wearing around her eyes made them look large and tantalizing. Joe was hugely tempted, but instead offered a casually friendly goodnight gesture and turned to the front door. He was really up for this walk now. If he was truly honest with himself, he knew that he would not be content if nothing happened. The roll-up entrance to the apartment building's underground car park clanked loudly. When it was halfway, Joe ducked under and walked quickly to the Merc, thinking about where to go. Not too far. He made his mind up quickly. Clare Hall on the Malahide road was only a few hundred seconds away at this time of night. Parking there would be simple. Joe pulled the clock from inside his jacket and placed it on the passenger seat before driving off, the red digits bright in the darkness of the car.

46255834 . . . 33 . . .

This was going to be time well spent.

9

Joe Power loved this time, driving alone in the night, building his sense of anticipation. At UCI cinemas on the Malahide road, the lights turned amber as he approached. Normally Joe would have enjoyed accelerating and running the lights, but he slowed and stopped. There was no traffic from the other side. It was as if the lights had changed purely to hold him there, so close to Clare Hall, intensifying pleasurable excitement. On the green light he eased forward. No rush. Almost there. He parked in a dark corner and sat for a moment, checking all around. Looking and listening. There were a few other parked cars, all empty. Joe heard voices. He inclined his head just enough to check. A couple was approaching from the all-night Tesco, with a twenty-four-box of bargain lager. Joe stayed still until they found their car and drove off. All was quiet again. Over to the right there were signs of life at the entrance to the Airport Hilton. Smokers in suits. What poor sad fucks stayed in hotels like that, stuck out on the edge of a dual carriageway? Joe hoped that clients were warned against going for a stroll in the area. Crossing the Malahide road for a late-night jaunt to Clare Hall might be safe enough, but what if some innocent ventured across the M32 and ended up in Darndale? Could be a bit of a shock to the system. Joe checked the clock:

46255418 . . . 17 . . .

He stepped out of the car and locked it. The smokers in suits were standing barely two steps from the hotel entrance. It was probably as far as any of these corporate slaves ever dared go into the real jungle: taxis brought them from their meetings to the hotel door, they ate and drank in the hotel, went to bed early, falling asleep to CNN, left in taxis at dawn. Oooh, the red-eye flight, so on the edge! Pussies. Joe decided he would walk for no more than three thousand seconds. Whatever happened, happened. If someone's number was up, so be it. Or not. He, Joe Power, was a free citizen going for a walk, nothing more. He crossed the road and entered Darndale. All worries and frustrations eased. The clack of his own footsteps set off a tingle up his back. The traffic noise from the Malahide road receded in a surprising way. Joe loved these night-walks more than anything in his new life. He was happy to accept whatever they might bring, knowing at least one thing for sure, that he would emerge alive, hopefully in a condition to return to his car and drive home. It was the comforting bottom line which made the uncertainty of all the rest so exciting. All was quiet so far. He stopped at the corner of Buttercup and Marigold. He could hear young voices male and female to his left. He walked towards them. A group of four boys and two girls were hanging out by a low wall. They seemed young but there was a drunken loudness, a slurring in their chatter. Joe hoped they wouldn't give him any trouble. Even though these walks were undertaken in a spirit of accepting whatever happened, that did not mean he wanted some puny fifteen-year-old to die. He continued towards the group at an unwavering pace. The best weapons Joe had at his disposal on these walks were his own total lack of fear, and the fact that he didn't really seem like someone who might be trouble. He passed the group. He didn't look directly at any of them. That would be provocative. One of the girls screeched to her friend in what she probably thought was a whisper.

'C'mere, I like that jacket, do you?'

'What jacket?'

'Your man's.'

Joe had passed. The calling began.

'Hey, mister, give's a lend a' your jacket, I'm freezing.'

'Come back, we're talking to you.'

'C'mere a minute.'

'What are you doin' around here?'

'Are you trying to find someone's house?'

'Tell us where. We'll show you for five euro.'

'Give us five euro anyway . . .'

The voices were tinny and harsh but not intentionally aggressive. Joe kept walking. He would turn again at the corner of Lilac to try his luck. When he heard footsteps behind he did not look back. He genuinely hoped that some misfortunate young skanger was not going to put himself into danger. On the other hand if his time was up, then neither was it for Joe to interfere with that inevitability. A hand fell on his shoulder. Joe wondered, was this it? He turned, prepared. It was one of the girls. She had a can in her hand and was chewing gum. She didn't seem that drunk. She was dressed and made up to look seventeen; probably fourteen.

'Where d'ja get the jacket?'

Joe was amused at how ladies from very different ends of the social and educational spectrum were equally drawn to his Kris Van Assche creation. He decided to be kinder to this poor slapper than he had been to baby-doll face earlier. Let her think that a jacket like this was somewhere in her buying range.

'You know Roches Stores?'

'Yeah.'

'One of the places there. Can't remember which.'

'Oh right. Zara, was it?'

'Yes, could be . . .'

One of the boys was now approaching. Joe needed to move on. He hoped that time was not up for this weed, any more than for the slapper, yet he had begun to sense that something was about to happen. Somewhere nearby he heard a gate close. He heard other footsteps approach from behind. Then he heard a shout, and he knew that as on other nights in some of Dublin's other dark places, the drama was under way.

'Lara, is that you, you little wagon?'

The Slapper looked to the Weed.

'It's me Da, come on, for fuck's sake.'

They ran, calling to their friends to get the fuck away. Joe turned towards the now fast approaching footsteps. A short muscled man of about thirty-five was running towards him. Joe knew that this was the one. This guy was clearly looking for trouble. He looked pumped up. He ran past, but that would not be the end of it. Realizing that his daughter was gone with her pals, out of reach for now, he stopped and turned back. His breathing was quick and very tense. This tension needed an outlet. Joe already recognized that this would be the source of the guy's downfall. If only he would say a quiet goodnight and walk on home, he would live. Simple. That was not going to happen.

'What are you up to with those kids? Who the fuck are you? I've never seen you before.'

Now he walked towards Joe, who didn't answer. Of course Joe knew he could turn and run. He would probably get away easily and the man would live. This mildly moral dilemma had crossed his mind on previous occasions too. He was surprised that it popped up again now, because of course, he had answered it a long time ago. He knew something that this man, advancing on him shouting angrily, did not know.

'Did you hear what I said?'

He was probably younger than Joe, and ostentatiously muscled, but it was clear that he was way too out of control. He was unarmed. It was all so inevitable.

'Are you dealin', are you? That's my daughter you were talking to. What the fuck are you doing hanging around here at this hour?'

His vocal cords constricted as his aggression increased. He grabbed hold of the fur-lined lapel of the Kris Van Assche. Joe could tell that this angry father was about to head-butt him. Still he did not speak. It was all up to Coolock dad now. This was the moment. If the guy chose, he could still release Joe and walk away alive. The grip on the fur collar tightened. The head tilted back, then came forward again, fast, aimed directly at Joe's nose and mouth. That was it. The choice had been made. There was no going back now. Joe wondered briefly how much pain he would have to endure in the fight, how badly injured before the man finally died. This one promised to be his most brutal encounter yet. This was not the addled drug addict trying a little thieving on what he thought was an unsuspecting passer-by, or the coward hiding behind darkness and a baseball bat. This was a raging pumped-up parent, a genuine working man, disturbed from his telly, sent out into the cold night by his wife because she was worried about their tearaway daughter. This father believed he had right on his side, even though in reality he was letting anger at his daughter spill over into an unprovoked assault on an innocent passing stranger. That was his only mistake. Joe did not fool himself that somehow this meant the man deserved to die. There was no moral judgement. His number was up and Joe's was not. That was all.

The man's forehead struck the hand that Joe had, just in time, raised. The back of his hand recoiled against his nose. The pain, though slight, performed its catalyst function. Joe instantly felt a blood-rush that made him clench his teeth tight so as not to bite his own tongue. This guy would pay. The strength of the hands that now grabbed and squeezed his throat told Joe that he would have to suffer this time before prevailing. This made his excitement and pleasure more intense. The saliva gathered in his mouth as Coolock dad pressed him back closer to the ground, his shouting now higher and hoarser. This not only wasted his strength, it was also probably the reason he didn't notice Joe's right fist swinging round. It struck somewhere between the left eyebrow and temple. If the pain Coolock dad felt was any-thing like the shock that went through Joe's fist, he should have ended up on the ground. He roared and staggered back. He released Joe's throat, but he didn't fall. The kick that followed missed his groin. Instead Joe felt hard stomach muscles against his shoe. He could have kicked the same spot ten times without much effect. Everything would have been so much easier if he had connected with his balls. Coolock dad was in trouble for sure, but nowhere near his end. Head low, he came on, fists swinging. No shouting now; the noises that came from his mouth had no words. The sheer weight of the attack could easily send Joe to the ground if he was not careful. Stay on your feet he warned himself, as the head gored his chest and flying fists hit a shoulder, a rib, then a neck, and scraped past his nose. Somehow he did stay upright, hearing himself whine at every blow. There seemed to be no other sounds in the world now but breaths, and grunts and whimpers. It was wild and fantastic. Spilt blood was the only missing ingredient, and Joe sensed that he would not escape this much longer, even if it was only spurts from a lip or a nose. He was determined, however, not to be the first to bleed. Coolock dad's hair was so short that grabbing it was almost impossible. Joe got hold of just enough to drive the head quickly at a gate pillar. No. 138. The sound of the cheekbone crunching off the concrete edge and the guy's roar should have woken the whole street. Joe pulled the head back to see. Blood was pouring from his cheek and mouth. Yes! Coolock dad buckled as Joe forced him face down to the ground. Pressing a knee between his shoulder blades, he couldn't get any kind of grip on the hair that would allow him smash the face again and again off the pavement. Instead he ground it down, pushing both hands as hard as he could against the back of the head. The blood in the dad's mouth was turning his moans into muffled gargling. Though he scraped his own face in doing so, somehow he twisted his head round and up, flinging blood-spit on to Joe's cheek. Suddenly he had wriggled completely on to his back. Joe was caught off balance. Raging eyes were the only visible feature on Coolock dad's face-mask of street dirt and blood. Even his mouth had disappeared and he seemed to have stopped breathing. Joe felt every part of the body beneath him writhe and press and surge to unseat him. A wild fist caught his left eye and blood trickled down, threatening to blind him on that side. Joe was heaving, bleeding and in sharp pain. Transcendent though it felt to be inside this moment, he knew it had to end now. This brave tormented bull of a man would have to be finished off. Joe had never performed the manoeuvre under such difficult conditions. If it wasn't quick and perfect then he might be in trouble. Coolock dad couldn't kill him, but he could yet do him serious, even permanent damage. It was in such delicate moments that the confidence bred of Joe's secret knowledge made all the difference; the difference between life and death. Coolock dad had no time to wonder why his opponent suddenly released the hold he had on his left upper arm. Before he could take any advantage, Joe's right elbow had smashed into his windpipe. This didn't kill him, but he blacked out, leaving him in no position to prevent his neck from being snapped a moment later.

Now Joe heard only his own huge relieved breathing in. He held it and inhaled the silence. Then out with a loud phooh! Then he closed his eyes and in a way that felt quite magical he began to hear the world returning from afar, heightened and yet precise. First there was a car in the distance, an individual car, not coming closer, just coasting along at a steady speed on the outer edge of his hearing. Then he heard a television. Someone near was watching a heart-warming American made-for-TV movie, judging by the noble swelling strings of the soundtrack. Of course there was a dog barking, why hadn't he heard that before? The traffic noise had become more general now, less interesting in a way. Still there were no human voices. Where had those kids got to? Had no one from the safety of their homes heard the roars of this great street battle? A door opened not too far away. Was someone coming to investigate? Was it the concerned wife and mother at last wondering not only about her daughter, but her missing husband? Joe opened his eyes and looked around. He could not see which door had opened. It was time to go. Standing up was painful. Walking was more so. Joe kept to the centre of the road. His eyes flicked left and right, alert for activity of any kind. It would be surprising if there was not something. It wouldn't really matter. Coolock dad's daughter and her friends would be the key eye-witnesses, and of course they would be hopeless. The fur-lined jacket would be their only contribution. Detectives would bring her to Roches Stores in search of the precise make and model.

The scream when it began had a husky wailing quality. There was nothing spine-chilling or tragic about it. It might almost have been male. Joe looked back. A woman was running towards the dead body, arms flung out, her cry a constant cigarette-stained note. She would certainly have seen him walking down the centre of the road. Joe turned right away from Marigold and reached the playing field. He really hoped that there would be no other encounters. He had never had to kill twice. It seemed highly unlikely that there could be two people in the same area on the same night, whose time was up. He did not care for that idea at all. The encounter had been truly awesome but now he was spent. He needed to rest and take it all in. Reaching the Malahide road quickly he paused in the shadow of the trees lining the centre island, letting the traffic noise fill his ears as he waited for a safe moment to cross. Joe imagined what an iconic figure he would make if he dashed across the road in front of an oncoming car, and turned a grimacing blood-stained face to the headlights. The eye-witness would be guaranteed a moment of tabloid glory. Instead Joe removed his jacket and held the inside lining to his eyebrow, pressing it gently until he felt reasonably sure that the stain had gone from his face. He folded the jacket under his arm. At a relatively quiet moment he stepped out from the trees and, face down, trotted across the road. A distant approaching car hooted a warning. He hopped over the low wall and walked quickly to his car. Sitting in, he tried breathing deeply and slowly to calm his near-delirious heart.

Joe felt terrific. He wanted to race the car now, duck in and out of traffic, run lights, brake hard and fast. He wanted to make lightning U-turns and screech off the other way.

He wanted to find a quiet winding dangerous country road and weave at ever-increasing speed, forcing oncoming drivers off the road. This was a superior car. He felt invulnerable inside it. If anyone approached now he could just take off and they'd never catch him. He looked at the clock.

46253479 . . . 78 . . .

Incredible. It had all happened in less than two thousand seconds. Why couldn't all time pass like this, so full and satisfying in itself, and with such positive consequences? Joe knew this would content him now for some time. His sleep would be long and deep. He would wake feeling calm. He would spend many thousands if not millions of future seconds in pleasurable recollection of this time. His bruises might not go away for a while yet, his flight tomorrow might be even more uncomfortable, but every little twinge and ache would also bring him back to this moment. Joe started the car. He was calm enough now to drive sensibly, discreetly. All along the Malahide road he listened for the sound of police sirens heading for Darndale. He was quite disappointed not to hear any. The entrance to the underground car park clanked down. Joe waited inside the car until there was silence. He wanted to be sure that there was no one else in the parking area. He stepped out, opened the boot and took out a large black plastic bag. He listened again. Satisfied that he was entirely alone, Joe took off all his clothes. He removed his wallet and keys from the pockets of his jeans. He searched for anything else that might have his name on it, and placed all the bits on top of the car, using his bunch of keys as a paperweight. It felt a little chilly now that he was naked. Listening for any sounds of cars or people approaching, he put all the clothes, apart from the Van Assche jacket, into the black plastic bag. He tied it up and buried it deep in the large communal waste bin. He did not expect any police investigation to lead to him, and this bin would hardly be the subject of a search before the next collection. Feeling quite cold now, Joe put the wallet, keys and bits of paper in the jacket pocket. He collected the clock from the car. He carried the jacket over his arm. A part of him was amused at the idea that one of his apartment neighbours might bump into him like this. He keyed in the code which allowed him into the residents' area and used the emergency stairs all the way to the top floor. The cement steps chilled his feet. Looking through the little circular window on the emergency stairs door, Joe could see that his lobby was, not unexpectedly, silent and empty. As he walked to his front door he couldn't help counting down from ten in his head. He reached his door at six. He was cool enough not let his hand shake or try to ram the key too forcefully. 5 . . . 4. It slid into the lock with its usual ease and turned. 2 . . . 1. He was inside and pushing the door shut at zero. Safe, he sank to his knees, let the jacket fall to the floor and placed the countdown clock next to it. Sprawling on his tummy, he stared at it.

46252765 . . . 64 . . . 63 . . . 62 . . .

How miraculous life is, how precious. These were Joe's thoughts, lost in the wondrous inevitability of time disappearing second by second. Nine hundred and eighty-four of them slipped by before he emerged out of his trance, feeling peaceful. It was time to check for visible signs. Despite the number of twinges and aches he felt, there was not a lot of evidence on his body. His knuckles were skinned, and of course the cut above the eyebrow would leave some kind of scar. Over the next few days bruises would appear here and there, but that was OK. He would be in Cuba. It wouldn't matter. Sex might be a little painful for a while. He might just have to lie there and let himself be sucked off.

The shower was both pain and pleasure. The heat of the water helped initiate an erection which Joe stroked gently as he watched all the blood and grime trickle away. He didn't bother to come, he just enjoyed the feel of his thickening cock in his hand, breathing in the scent of something expensive called Pomegranate Noir. Afterwards he bathed all his cuts and scrapes in a tea-tree solution, and bandaged them. He wrapped himself in his most comfortable robe, poured a large cognac and lay on the sofa to enjoy the silence. How different he felt now. All tension gone, despair averted. Once again his destiny had been re-affirmed. That was the most important thing.

Before going to bed, Joe picked up the Van Assche jacket with finger and thumb and carried it into the bedroom. With his free hand, he chose from a bunch of keys and unlocked the wardrobe door. There were just four items of clothing in the wardrobe, a heavy coat, a short-sleeved shirt and two jackets. Joe took one of the many spare wooden hangers and put the Van Assche on it. He hung it next to the others. They took up very little space in the wardrobe. There were at least twenty-five unused hangers left. It was, perhaps, because the stains were fresh and the damage was recent that the latest addition looked more battle-stained than the others. The very first item, a grey wool winter coat, didn't, at first glance, seem to have anything wrong with it. Joe knew that someone would have to look very closely to notice the hole in the left upper arm. He could have had it mended easily enough. There was no way he would do that. The coat in that condition was an important trophy for Joe. That memory seemed all so long ago, many millions of seconds ago. Even though it was getting harder to recall details in the right order, certain elements were definitely correct. It was still winter. Joe could not forget how cold that night had been. It must have been after he sold the Smithfield apartment and the studio, because otherwise why would he have been walking towards the North Strand looking for a taxi at that hour? Definitely he was returning to this apartment. It was also definitely before the first trip to Cuba, because he remembered checking the newspapers for news of the murder investigation at least a couple of times, and being amused when he read one report that said the Gardaí had information about the killer. He was about fifty, wearing a long black coat; almost certainly a trained assassin. On returning from Cuba he didn't read newspapers any more, so it must have been before. It was also clear in his head that he was still fat and depressed. This older woman he had pulled kept going on about how amazing it was to find a half-decent single man of his age who wasn't gay. He sneaked out as soon as she fell asleep. The sharpest memory, however, was of the moment he realized that his Mercedes had been clamped; how cold and dreary the night felt at that moment. He couldn't believe it when he read that it was 'Pay and Display 24 hours'. He had felt like going back to her apartment, kicking down the door, and dragging her by the hair from her bed all the way down to this sign; make her read the information out loud to him. Instead he had taken out his anger on the clamper guy and the mobile phone. He was very glad that he had his heavy coat on as he trudged across the river to Amiens Street. There were no free taxis. When he reached the Five Lamps, he suddenly stopped walking, his frustration at its height. Would everything subsequently have been different if a taxi had stopped for him at that moment? Joe was still surprised whenever he realized that these 'if' and 'but' questions never seemed to go away, despite his conviction about the inevitability of things. Joe couldn't remember how long he had stood in the cold, although he remembered it painfully. Neither could he say exactly when anger and impatience and frustration gave way to fear, but some time standing there it had. Poking a finger through the hole in the coat, Joe could smile now at how uncertain his reaction had been when the two young men stopped across the road from him and stared.

Out of the corner of his eye he sees one of them pull the other back and point. Joe continues to stare down Amiens Street, willing a taxi to appear. He hears the young men's footsteps cross to his side of the street, then feels something, a shoulder, brush against his back.

'Sorry about that.'

To answer or not to answer? Joe recognizes that either way lies danger. He speaks casually.

'You're grand.'

He still hasn't met their eyes, but now there is no way he can pretend not to notice their presence. That would be seen as cheeky. At this moment Joe's belief in his destiny is at breaking point. At the very least, he knows he will end up in hospital, perhaps only barely hanging on to life. It's two against one. They are in control.

'What are you hanging around here for? Are you one of them paedophiles?'

To speak, to explain to them what they know already, that he is looking for a taxi, would only play into their hands. To remain silent would be unquestionably provocative. It is at this moment that Joe begins to consider the odds on killing both of them. He looks at their faces. They are both around twenty, pale and thin, hard bony features, used to taking punishment. The idea seems unlikely. He can tell from the hand position of one of them – the angry one, as he now thinks of him – that there is a gun inside his jacket.

'Do you want my money?'

He tries to keep any hint of threat from his voice. It's not difficult. If giving them his wallet will sort it out, most of him wants to settle for that. Some of him is beginning to have other ideas.

'Show us.'

The angry one's voice is nasal and weak, almost camp. It diminishes his aura of menace, despite the hand on the gun. The other one lets his pal make all the running. Joe reaches carefully for his wallet. He takes it out and holds it up.

'If I give it to you, can I go?'

'Depends on what's in it, don't it? Throw it there.'

He is sounding more and more like a skanger drag queen. He points down between his feet. Joe holds on to the wallet.

'Come on, throw it down.'

The part of Joe that is confident he will not die tonight is winning out. It tells him to hold on to the wallet. That is the lure.

'Throw the fuckin' wallet!'

Joe wants to laugh as the pitch of angry guy's voice goes still higher.

'Come on, will you.'

It is the other one speaking. Quietly, as if warning Joe for his own good, not to be foolish. Just because his pal has a silly voice doesn't mean he's not dangerous. Joe says nothing, holding the wallet high, staring into the eyes of the angry one, who seems to decide that Joe is just frozen in fear. He loses patience too quickly, and makes his mistake. Pulling the gun from inside his jacket, he waves it about as he steps closer.

'You fuckin' spa! You want me to blow your fuckin' head off, do ya? Give it here!'

He holds out his free hand to take the wallet . . . and comes
too close. All Joe's controlled power goes into the sudden kick
that lands precisely between the angry one's legs. As he falls back
he pulls the trigger just too late. Joe hears rather than feels
something rip through the left upper arm. As the angry one lands
painfully, Joe takes a couple of steps forward and stands hard
on his wrist, forcing him to release the gun. Joe picks it up and
without hesitation fires three times into his face. The noise of the
shots and the dying howl from the angry one are terrifying. When
he looks up, the other one is already fifty yards away running
towards the North Circular Road.

Standing at the wardrobe, wiggling his finger through the
hole in the arm of the coat, Joe felt a little of the intensity
of his euphoria as he walked – danced might be a better
word – home that night, how casually he had dropped the
gun into the Royal Canal, how he had cleared out the
wardrobe as soon as he got back to the apartment, and hung
the winter coat on its own. Somehow he already understood
that it would be joined by others in the future. Such was the
importance of the moment, his brain had even fixed the
precise time on the clock: sixty-three million, two hundred
and ninety-four thousand, seven hundred and fifty-six
seconds. A curious fact had also struck him at that moment.
It was his birthday; thirty-eight in the old way of counting.
From that moment he had divined fully the nature and
breadth of his freedom.

Joe closed and locked the wardrobe door. It was time to
sleep. He had a plane to catch when light came. Sore, he
eased carefully into bed, his mind filling with images and
sounds from the Five Lamps, Blanchardstown, Wood Quay,
the Liffey boardwalk, and now Darndale too. The shapes of
buildings in the darkness, the weight of bodies above and

concrete beneath, the tense press of fingers, the rage of fists
and feet. He heard grunts and squeals, the crunch of a head
against some harder, colder surface, the soft tear of a knife
through skin. Drifting asleep, Joe saw some faces again.
Unforgettable expressions forever caught in their moment
of ecstatic pain.

8

Although with each successive journey Joe was hating air travel more and more, he wasn't particularly concerned at the chaos in Dublin airport this morning. This was partly because he was in such good mood from the night before, partly because, even in this crush and madness, the Aer Lingus self-check-in machines were not particularly crowded. He found a free one immediately, checked in quickly for the London flight, even managing to get himself a reasonably good aisle seat near the front. 5D. He went to security straight away. His bag was just about small enough to be acceptable as hand-luggage. He preferred to keep it with him, especially with a connecting flight. He did not like to let the clock out of his possession. The queue was long. That was inevitable. Joe had plenty of time. He had arranged for a wake-up call at 7 a.m. for a 10 a.m. flight. Air travel was one of the very few situations where Joe had to pay attention to traditional time. He didn't go to work, he rarely made appointments with anyone, he didn't watch television or listen to the radio. The movement of the sun and change of the seasons were obvious to him even if they were of little interest. The only time that mattered to him now was the disappearing seconds of the countdown. All the calculations of his life were based on that. He owned no other timepiece. This morning he marked the number on the clock as soon as the call woke him, estimating he had about ten thousand, six hundred seconds before the flight. When he got into the car, showered, moisturized, packed and dressed for the long journey, one thousand, eight hundred and sixty-eight seconds had passed. He checked again when he had found a space in the short-term car park. Three thousand, seven hundred and two seconds had passed. Plenty of time. The queue to go through security was moving very slowly. Joe dropped to one knee, opened his bag and felt for the clock, carefully wrapped in silk. He revealed the face without taking it out, and made the simple calculation: four thousand, six hundred and fifty seconds gone. Still OK, but it was becoming annoying. Why was it taking so much time? Attendants stood at both entrances, watching progress at the security machines on the other side. Joe began to notice how long the interval was between each person allowed through. He mentally counted. After ten people he was able to calculate that it was between forty-five and fifty-five seconds per person per entrance. What was going on? Had machines broken down? Were they short-staffed? Joe counted the number of people in the queue. It was difficult because of the arrangement of the barriers, forcing people to walk up and down half a dozen times, passing each other again and again, inching their way to entrances barely five paces away. There were at least sixty ahead of him. If they didn't speed things up that meant about three thousand, three hundred seconds before Joe reached the security area. He began to feel tense. Other travellers were impatient too. Behind him he heard an obvious sigh. The kind that invites neighbouring victims to join in a moaning session. Two voices to his right in the next channel of the queue were louder.

'Jesus, this is desperate isn't it?'

'Unbelievable.'

'It's not fuckin' moving at all.'

'Unbelievable.'

People had begun checking their watches, then looking around with frustrated expressions. A woman ahead of Joe pulled her small child closer and bent down to whisper angrily to her. The child sat on a bag and looked miserable. A man in a suit at the front of the queue was pleading with the attendant, who just shook his head and pointed to the security area beyond. An elderly lady leaned in quiet pain on her walking-stick. The general mood was uneasy. Cheery American voices from somewhere deep in the crowd made Joe even more tense.

'Hey, well, I gotta say it's good to see they're taking things seriously over here, huh?'

'You got it, buddy.'

'I sure don't mind a little extra time in line, if it means we all feel safer.'

Joe wished he could turn the volume down on that dialogue. The annoying fucks clearly had more than enough time to waste before their flight. They could stand there all morning talking shite, but if things kept moving at this pace then Joe would be in real danger of missing his flight. If anything, it had slowed even more. The man in the suit still hadn't passed through. When the attendant finally gave him the nod, Joe started counting in his head again. He reached seventy-eight seconds before the next passenger was allowed pass. This was serious. Behind him there were at least forty more people. Joe rounded the first barrier, which meant that no more than ten people had gone through since he had joined the queue. He could see the group of Americans now as well as hear them. They were smiling and relaxed. Nobody else was. Joe would have enjoyed killing at least one of them. Two attractive girls in what seemed to be uniform blouses appeared, and began moving quickly through the queue. They were passing out little plastic bags and sheets of paper.

Passengers began to open their hand-luggage and rummage. By the time one of the girls got to Joe he could see that the people ahead of him were transferring items to the plastic bags. She was smiling brightly. A bearer of glad tidings.

'Are you carrying any liquids, sir?'

What did she mean by that? Joe wondered.

'Check this list, sir. If you are carrying any of these items or any liquids, put them in the plastic bag and present them to someone at security.'

'What for?'

'It's just a precautionary measure, sir.'

Smiling, she moved on.

'I'm on the ten o'clock to Heathrow. I won't make it if it's going to take so long to . . .'

She turned back, her tone smilingly reassuring.

'There's no need to worry about that. All flights to Heathrow are delayed. There should be an announcement shortly.'

'Delayed? What's the problem?'

The girl's tone became soothing.

'A terrorist plot. But don't worry about it. They found out in time. There's the announcement now.'

She moved on again as the voice on the PA asked for attention from London passengers. All flights to Heathrow would be delayed indefinitely. There would be further announcements. Joe felt trapped, right in the middle of this queue which had grown to about a hundred people. He looked at the sheet of paper. There was a long list. Drinks, cologne, sun lotion, just about any liquid-like item a passenger might have, had to be put in the plastic bags. There was an apology for the inconvenience but they were sure that everyone would understand. The safety of all passengers was the priority. Joe didn't open his bag, even though he knew he had several of the newly offensive items. All he could think about now was his clock. With this heightened security they were bound to be suspicious about it. What would he say? Did it really matter what he said? They would take it from him. The queue moved forward two or three steps. Joe felt real panic now. Under no circumstances would he hand over the clock, but how could he stop them taking it? Even if he got it through security, the delay in the flight might mean that he would miss his connection. What then? How much time would he waste, and still end up stuck in Heathrow? Even the Americans seemed less happy-go-lucky now. Their voices had dropped below hearing range. On all sides Joe heard moaning and muttering.

'This perfume cost me eighty-five euro, are they going to take that?'

'Liquids. What the fuck is the problem with liquids?'

'What about the baby's bottle? Is that on the list?'

Joe tried to focus his mind on Havana. The *casa particular* on Calle Refugio. Even counting normal delays, he had figured he would arrive before the sun went down. OK, so now the journey would take longer. Surely it was still worth it. Moniquita, Valeira. He tried to calm himself. Maybe things wouldn't be so bad in Heathrow. What if it was worse? It was not knowing that was making him crazy. Ahead of him nothing seemed to be moving at all now. Around him people were bending over, hunkering down to rummage in their hand-luggage and transfer bottles into see-through plastic bags. The tension in the air was seeping into his brain and blood. He started counting in his head, watching the passengers at the head of the queue, promising himself that if someone was allowed through before he reached . . . what . . . how long . . . ? When he went over sixty and there was still no movement, he couldn't bear it any longer. He picked up his bag, pushed between two people, ducked under the barrier tape and walked away from the queue. He continued quickly to the entrance. Once he reached the fresh air Joe stopped and breathed in and out several times. What now? Go back in and find out exactly what the story was? Could anyone give him any straightforward information about his Havana connection? Unlikely. No. No chance. Surely someone might be able to fill him in on what exactly this whole thing was about, at least? Sky News was probably on screens all over the place; he could find out something that way. As he stepped into the doorway he heard confusion and uncertainty. The thought of looking at TV news for the first time in so long sickened him. He had promised himself long ago that he wouldn't engage any more. Until now it had not been difficult to keep that promise. He had successfully emptied his consciousness of events beyond the parameters he had chosen. The trip to Havana was intended as a further escape. Instead the attempt to get there seemed to be sucking him back into all the nonsense of the world. Joe was suddenly clear in his head. Fuck that. Fuck them all. Fuck Heathrow, and fuck Havana and fuck air travel. He was not going to waste another second of his time on this enterprise. He picked up his bag and walked quickly to the short-term car park. The simple act of making that decision made him feel better. As the barrier at the car park exit lifted and he drove through, Joe Power immediately felt free again. He didn't know what he was going to do next yet, but he had taken back control. That was the most important thing. One thing he did know. He would need to fuck someone tonight. Even as he turned down the slip road for the M1, he started thinking about who might be available. It would have to be someone he had been with before, there was no point in leaving anything to chance. Depending on the girl, he might even make an occasion of it, book a table somewhere nice, spend a lot of money on her, surprise her, make her feel special. Maybe that would only remind him of the lost pleasures of Havana. It was incredibly frustrating. He knew he would have to deal with a tiny corner of doubt about whether he had acted too hastily. That might take a little time. First things first: get home, relax, have a drink, sort out his options. Was he not better off already, sitting at the wheel of his beautiful car, in control, instead of crammed in that airport, a slave to PA announcements and screen information, his body rigid, his brain aggravated?

At the apartment block, as Joe waited for the electric gates to open, he noticed that a man standing at the pedestrian entrance appeared to be looking directly at him. Another man sitting in a parked car a few yards away seemed to be doing the same. Joe had no idea why it occurred to him that they were plainclothes policemen, but it possibly explained why, in the parking area a hundred seconds or so later, as he opened the boot to take out his bag, he was alert enough to notice a sound he did *not* hear: the clank of the roll-up entrance to the underground car park. Normally it closed down automatically twenty seconds after a car had gone through. Joe, certain that more than twenty seconds had passed, turned to see why it remained open. A man was standing in the entrance, a silhouette against the bright daylight outside. Joe was sure it was the same man he had noticed at the pedestrian gate.

'Is your name Joe Power by any chance?'

Joe was even more certain now that he was police, and felt the calm of someone who had been waiting a long time for such a moment.

'Yes. It is.'

The man walked forward. The car park lighting was murky but he looked familiar to Joe.

'Sorry if I startled you. It's just I recognized the number plates as you drove in. I had just called looking for you.'

He took out identification. Up close he was quite small-framed. His voice was quiet, with only a hint of country accent remaining. Joe couldn't figure why he seemed so familiar.

'Detective Inspector Drew.'

Joe pretended to be interested in looking at the ID. This was hardly about the night before already? How could his licence plates have been connected to the killing so quickly? Unless someone had followed him back to the car, and that had not happened, Joe was sure. Mr Drew's next sentence answered those questions.

'You're a hard man to track down.'

Not about last night then. Joe began to search his mind for details of other nights. He was growing quite excited, the disappointment of earlier disappearing.

'Are you just back from a trip?'

The truth? Of course. Joe explained what had happened at the airport. Something in Drew's intense listening expression clicked with Joe. The guy looked like Samuel Beckett, that particular photo he had noticed on display everywhere lately; the dark eyes sunk deep, the face crinkling with sad wisdom. This man was a younger version, more fifty than eighty, but the resemblance, once noticed, was startling. Mr Drew nodded, again, it seemed to Joe, wisely. This was a man worthy of respect.

'I heard about it earlier on the radio. Sounds chaotic. It's no fun travelling these days, is it?'

'No.'

'Well, I'm sure you're in no mood for questions from me after that experience. We can arrange another time?'

Joe answered immediately, sincerely.

'It's fine. What do you want to ask me about?'

Mr Drew looked around the dark spaces of the car park.

'Well . . . shall we sit in the car or –'

'Sorry, of course. Come up to the apartment.'

'Thanks. I won't keep you long. It's just we were asked to come and talk to you.'

'It's not . . . ah . . . a family thing is it?'

Joe was pleased he had thought of that line. It felt right.

'No. No. Nothing like that.'

'Good.'

Joe led him to the lift, thinking about Drew's curious choice of words. 'We were asked . . .' Who had asked? Whatever it was about, was it not Drew's investigation then?

'So will you get your money back for the trip?'

'Fat chance, I'd say.'

'Ryanair?'

'No, but still. None of them like handing back cash.'

'Been to Cuba before?'

Joe wondered if this question was less casual than it sounded. Visiting Cuba used to have a sinister resonance for the Gardaí, but surely not any more, and surely not for this wise old investigator.

'Yes, once. I love it. I'd recommend it to anyone.'

'So . . . do you think poor old Castro will recover?'

Joe wasn't sure what that meant. Politically? Economically? Was Castro ill? Had he been shot? Drew didn't appear to notice any hesitation. He smiled.

'Were you going to help him celebrate his eightieth?'

Joe hadn't a clue about Castro's birthday. A jokey response seemed the best way not to seem foolish. He tapped his bag.

'Oh, absolutely. Loaded with presents for the man himself.'

Drew smiled. Joe decided he had better take control of the conversation.

'Don't remind me of what I'm missing. It's a sore subject at the moment, as you can imagine.'

Drew nodded. He seemed very understanding. The lift door opened. Joe spoke about the chaos of air travel by way of a generalized lament as he led Drew to his apartment. As soon as he closed the door he decided to come straight to the point; much less suspicious than seeming too incurious.

'So. You can talk freely now, Inspector. What's it you want to ask me about? I'm dying to know?'

'I can imagine. Well, it's an odd one. I'm actually here at the request of the French police.'

Drew's face was turned away, walking ahead towards the living room. Joe wondered if they had been face to face as he spoke would he have noticed the flush that Joe felt spreading up from his neck. The physical reaction seemed to complement the mental jolt, as images long suppressed burst through to consciousness. There was no way Joe could stop them.

Sitting at the table in Roger Merriman's apartment, holding a glass of wine. Roger, sitting at the table also, picks up the clock. Something else he wants to say about it. By now Joe has had enough of his fake-sounding languid sneer. It's really getting on his wick.

'They gave me your name, among others.'

Drew was looking directly at him now. Joe created an expression of casual curiosity, as he tried to control the memories flooding his brain.

*Roger emphasizes some point, another sneering derogatory point
about the clock. As he does so he pats his hand on the back of
Joe's hand. Of course even though he knows there isn't a hope
in hell, he can't resist letting his middle finger linger, trail its
message of attraction creepily across Joe's skin. Roger is saying
something about the French company that had created the millennium clocks. After initial spectacular success, he claims there
were complaints from customers, suppliers. Stock was returned.
There was something wrong, the wretched things didn't work
properly, they were going haywire. Basically the technology of the
whole thing was fatally flawed. Or, to put it another way, just
plain bonkers. Roger seems to like that phrase. Cupped in his
palm, he holds the clock up as if it is a skull. The company, it
seemed, had gone bankrupt long before the end of the seventies.
Just. Plain. Bonkers.*

'. . . a murder investigation. It took place on December
sixteenth last year. The victim was an Irishman, living in
Paris. Roger Merriman.'

Joe hated remembering the uncontrolled rage of that
moment. It was shame at this coarse anger that had allowed
him never to think about it since. He should never have got
into that state, let things spin out of control like that. When
Joe had picked up the clock, that should have been it. He
could have left immediately. He had his coat on.

*The clock in his hand makes a large fist. He whips it across
Roger's chin. The knuckles connect with all the force of rage.
The old queen and his chair fall back. His head strikes the edge
of the white marble fireplace. The worst possible luck.*

'The French police asked us to talk to you because someone checking travel records noticed that you flew from

Dublin to Paris on the morning of the murder, and returned the same day.'

Joe nodded. He was confident that his face portrayed nothing more than surprised realization.

'Oh, I see. Yes, you're right. I went on a day trip to Paris not long before Christmas last year.'

'The sixteenth.'

'Sounds about right.'

Joe stands over Roger, poking him with his foot. Definitely dead. When he looks up again he notices that the gilt mirror is set so high over the fireplace that his head only just squeaks into the bottom of it. Roger himself was shorter. He could never have seen himself in it at all. It is puzzling. Joe pockets the clock and runs a hand through his hair. He wants to go immediately but knows that he will not be able to stop thinking that he left behind some vital clue. It is imperative that he take time and look around, try to remember everything he has touched since arriving at the apartment. Wash both glasses, clean every surface. For his peace of mind afterwards.

'That being unusual, although not as unusual as you might think, the French police would like to know why you were there that day, and what you did, as well as you can remember.'

The clatter of the lift as he opens the apartment door is the scariest moment. He closes the door again just in time. He listens to the lift pass and continue up two more floors. When the noise stops he leaves the apartment, closing the door quietly, and walks quickly downstairs. Now round the Panthéon, now down the hill to Maubert Mutualité. He briefly considers taking a métro. For some reason he feels safer on the street, so he walks on towards the Seine. Now through Île St Louis to the right bank

246

and up to the Marais at a fast pace. Somewhere on Rue du Roi de Sicile he sits down at a café. Only now does the shock of what he has done threaten to overcome him. Roger's death may not have been entirely intentional, but it is hard to accept where rage had taken Joe in that moment. It's less of a surprise that he feels no horror or guilt at the act itself. Joe takes the clock from his shoulder bag. One thousand, three hundred and forty-eight seconds since the last time he had noted it, the moment after he realized Roger was dead. He is now a healthy distance from the scene. Establish some kind of alibi.

'Well . . . God, this feels a bit strange, Inspector.'

He argues with a waiter. It is difficult to make it memorable. On its own this will never be enough. He becomes aware of the agitated sound of his foot tapping the ground, so he crosses his legs to keep still. He promises himself that he will never again lose control or act violently in anger.

He had kept that promise.

'Should I be calling a lawyer or something? Wow, a murder case?'

Listening to his own voice, Joe heard a nice balance between nervous jokiness and genuine worry; an innocent man suddenly on a collision course with the law; a classic Hitchcockian wrong place, wrong time scenario. Drew smiled again. Wise, fatherly.

'I wouldn't say so. Of course you're entitled to if you want, but look Mr Power, sorry if I've concerned you unnecessarily. You're not a suspect. To be honest with you, what seems to be happening is that the French police aren't getting anywhere on the case, so now they're chasing after every little thing. Clutching at straws, you might say. We just need to be able to tell them what you did that day; you know, was it business, or meeting friends, whatever. And that'll be that.'

Joe thought Mr Drew was a very clever man. Relax the suspect, then wrong-foot him. He was glad now that, sitting outside the café that day so long ago, inspiration had come to him after all.

He notices an immobilier *across the road. The frontage is newly painted blue. Immo-Marais. There are plenty of properties displayed for sale in the window. Joe selects one: elegant old 17th cent building, second story, 100 m2, just over a million euro, on Rue des Rosiers. A short walk away. He goes inside. The lady at the desk is talking on the phone. While he waits he finds a flier for the property and memorizes the details.*

When the lady finally gets off the phone, Joe smiles, offers his hand.

'Bonjour. Je suis Monsieur Power.'

The lady, smiling, shakes his hand and bonjours him. Joe adds, as if to jog her memory, that he is the man from Irelande. She says ah Irelande, then says something quickly. Joe guesses she is asking if she can be of assistance. This is his cue to perform. He looks puzzled as he explains in slow French that he is here for his 2 p.m. appointment, all the way from Ireland, to see the property on Rue des Rosiers as arranged. Now the lady looks puzzled. She checks her appointment book. Sorry, she has no record of this. Joe politely insists that indeed he spoke to someone over the phone. Was it a man or a woman? Joe decides it would be fun not to be entirely sure. What name had been given? It occurs to Joe that the poverty of his French is a real advantage in this situation. He struggles to remember. The lady offers several names. He seizes on Joubieux, yes, Joubieux. How curious, normally her colleague Joubieux would have noted an appointment in the book, and it has not been noted. Joe decides to turn up the heat. His voice rises and his French becomes increasingly garbled as he expresses frustration at this situation. He has flown all the way from Dublin specially, he is very enthusiastic about this property, he needs to purchase an apartment in the area quickly. He raises his arms in disbelief. He has finances already in place, and now to find that people cannot even keep a record of an appointment? How can he trust them to handle a sale? The situation is insupportable. He uses the word again and again.

'Right, Inspector. Well, that's fairly simple then. It was a property thing. I had a notion at the time to buy a place in Paris. There was some confusion over the appointment; the French can be very bureaucratic, especially when they are at fault.'

The lady picks up the phone. Whatever is said is too fast and whispered for Joe to make head or tail of, but he can tell that it's becoming a tense conversation. Finally she puts the phone down. She speaks quietly, carefully. Her colleague has no memory of a phone call either. There is no solution to this mystery, it seems, but under the circumstances, if Monsieur could promise to view the apartment quickly, she will take him there immediately. However, she must emphasize that she has another very important appointment in fifteen minutes and cannot be late. Joe shrugs, playing the client poorly treated but willing to make the best of it. The walk to Rue des Rosiers is quick and silent. He views the apartment at speed, making very positive noises. He thanks her and leaves.

'Eventually it was sorted out, and I viewed the apartment.' His friendly e-mail from Dublin regretted that the apartment, excellent though it was, was not for him. Her formal thank you was very short. He had saved both e-mails.

'What time was that?'

'The appointment was for two. I'm not likely to forget that after all the hoo-ha. I got to the Rue du Roi de Sicile maybe an hour earlier, so I had something to eat at a café across the road first.'

'Can you remember the name of the café?'

Joe could, but he thought that level of recall might make a man like Drew suspicious.

'Nah. Sorry. I mean you know, how many Parisian cafés? But it was directly across the street. Let me think is there anything I can remember about it . . .'

'Don't worry. They'll find it. So you didn't like the apartment.'

'I did, it was beautiful. But it was . . . well . . . I couldn't make up my mind what exactly I wanted. I still haven't.'

Joe sighed, hesitated, and dropped his head a little.

'Look, Inspector, you might know all this already if you've been trying to locate me, but well . . . my marriage ended last year, and . . . and since then our son died in a car crash. I was the driver . . . I've sold everything I owned. I'm renting this place. To be honest, I don't know what I'm doing with my life, you know. It's all a bit fucked up. Sorry about the language, but . . . well . . .'

Joe was pleased at the silence he had orchestrated. It felt respectful. He was fairly sure that someone like Drew would bring this to an end now. When he came to write his report he would probably indicate that in relation to Mr Joseph Power, he personally found nothing suspicious about his day trip to Paris on 16th of December 2005. It seemed to be on entirely legitimate business, and unrelated to the tragic death of Roger Merriman. He was confident that once his distinguished colleagues in Paris checked out the details, they would find this to be the case. Something along those lines. Drew resumed in the same tone of voice as before.

'Did you have any further communication with the agency?'

'Yes, I e-mailed them to say thanks, but no thanks.'

'Did they reply?'

'Yes.'

'So all that should be in their files?'

'Possibly. Actually I might have kept them myself.'

'From so long ago?'

A mistake perhaps? Drew seemed surprised.

'I tend to keep business stuff. Do you want me to check?'

'If you don't mind.'

Joe took his laptop from the bag. He brought it into the bedroom to connect broadband. Drew waited, perhaps too politely, in the living room. Joe called, 'Come in, Inspector.'

Drew walked into the bedroom and stopped directly in front of the locked wardrobe. Joe felt a shiver of pleasure at this image of the detective standing unknowingly next to damning evidence. He turned back to his laptop and typed 'Paris Property' into his e-mail search.

'Yes, here they are.'

Drew came closer and read both e-mails. He wrote down the address of the agency.

'Will I print them out for you?'

'Good idea.'

As the pages printed it occurred to Joe that he had not shown enough curiosity about the dead Irishman.

'So the man who was murdered was Irish?'

'Yes, apparently he moved to Paris about six years ago.'

'Where did he live?'

'Place du Panthéon. Near the Sorbonne, I'm told.'

'The left bank. Very nice area. Poor guy.'

Joe handed the printed pages to Drew. He was a little

sorry the encounter was coming to an end. How long had it been? The time had flown by.

'Thank you very much, Mr Power. I imagine you won't be hearing any more about this. Good luck.'

'Thanks, Inspector. I'm certainly having an eventful day, one way or another.'

Joe walked Drew to the door. He opened it. Drew stepped out and turned back. How much of his timing was deliberate Joe could not decide, but he knew as soon as Drew looked at him that what he was about to say was neither casual, nor unimportant.

'By the way. Nothing to do with this business at all, but just to satisfy my own curiosity. You had a car towed away a few months ago. An '06 Mercedes, only slightly older than the one you are driving now. Why have you not paid the fine and collected it?'

Joe was so impressed with Drew he decided to be as honest as he could be.

'If I could answer that simply, I would, Inspector, believe me. But I'm afraid the real answer would take me and a psychiatrist a long time to work out.'

Inspector Drew's wise eyes revealed nothing. His voice sounded perfectly satisfied.

'Fair enough. Goodbye, Mr Power.'

Joe closed the door. He had to be careful not to whoop and cheer out loud immediately in case the Inspector heard. He was certain now that he would hear from Mr Drew again. Surely a man of his depth would start to put things together and wonder about them. Had he noticed the five mobiles, the large lock on the wardrobe door? Would his mind shift from the Paris incident to these eccentricities and what they might mean? Surely. Paris might just have been a handy excuse for his visit anyway, the abandoned Merc being his real interest. Come on, Drew, Joe thought, what are you made of? Can you link the date and time it was clamped and towed away with the date and time of an unsolved murder at the Five Lamps? Come on Drew, you can do it. Maybe he had already. If so, then what a game was in prospect. Joe felt the time ahead might be more exciting than he had ever dared hope. Forget Cuba.

7

Almost two million seconds later, Joe began to sense he was under surveillance. Of course it was no surprise. In the absence of further direct contact from Inspector Drew, something like this was to be expected. The day was early but already warm. He was out on the balcony drinking coffee while making his now regular checks for anything strange or significant going on out there. In one of the parked cars across the road, a silver Ford Focus, a man sat behind the wheel. Not in itself suspicious, but it was something for Joe to keep an eye on. He finished his coffee and gave the mug to the Polish cleaning lady. He watched her take it into the kitchen, and listened to her rinse it out. There had seemed nothing different about her behaviour or demeanour in the last few visits. When he had phoned her to say that he had not gone to Cuba, she had sounded genuinely surprised, but asked no questions, which fitted exactly with the nature of their relationship. Had she done otherwise Joe would have thought it odd. Observing her since she resumed normal visits, Joe was reasonably confident that Drew had not got to her yet. That might only be a matter of time and, being an immigrant, she might feel her position was vulnerable, especially as she was almost certainly not paying tax on her earnings. Nor would she have any reason to feel loyalty towards Joe. He had intended to lunch in the sunshine on Howth Pier, but now found himself oddly reluctant to leave while the cleaning woman was still there. This seemed foolish, and he would have ignored the instinct, but on the other hand, delaying his departure might help confirm his new suspicion that he was being watched. He stepped out on the balcony again. The silver Ford was still there, the man still sitting inside. Would it be there, say, three thousand seconds from now? If so that would be very significant.

It seemed a good time to consider what all this might mean, and plan the perfect response. Joe lay on the sofa, his mind buzzing pleasurably. What did Drew actually know? No more than bits and scraps surely, signs of curious behaviour. Nothing that linked A to B to C. No evidence of anything other than what a privileged and free individual he was. What Drew suspected was the tantalizing unknown. What was his theory? What might he hope to discover by having his minions trail around after Joe? Even if he chose to take another night-walk and encountered a situation, his pursuers would merely witness a citizen defending himself against assault. They would probably feel they ought to intervene to protect him. That scenario amused Joe hugely. It might be fun to try and set that up. Of course it would be foolish to pretend that the contents of his wardrobe did not constitute a forensic treasure trove. Drew had stood right next to it. The fact that he had not yet arrived with a search warrant was reassuring. That situation could change. His investigation might turn up damaging CCTV footage from the Malahide road, or unexpected information from Paris. The lunch with Roger at l'Écurie, for example. Could he be identified? Or – Joe was shocked by this sudden thought – what about Trevor? If Drew discovered how Trevor and his ancient boyfriend had helped him to track down Roger, then a direct connection was established. As evidence, that was at least enough for a search warrant, in which case the contents of the wardrobe, perhaps even the wardrobe itself, ought to be destroyed. Not yet, of course.

He would resist that until he was left with absolutely no choice. Joe hated even thinking these words. No choice. Choice was everything. Choice was the very meaning of his freedom. He had abandoned a great deal in exchange for choice.

'I am going, Mr Power.'

Joe opened his eyes and smiled at the Polish cleaning woman, who was buttoning her coat. There was no harm in being nice to her. He made his voice sound warm.

'Thanks for everything. Goodbye. See you next time.'

'Yes, see you next time.'

'By the way, I want to talk to you about giving you more money.'

That certainly got a reaction. She didn't know what to say for a few seconds. Sensibly she kept it simple.

'. . . Thank you very much.'

'No problem. You deserve it.'

He gestured around the living room.

'Very good work. I must pay you better.'

She didn't exactly dance out the door, but then she wasn't that kind of woman. Joe figured he had brightened her day. He walked past his balcony windows, glancing slyly sideways. The silver Ford was still there. So. Well. He would soon find out more. He left the apartment immediately, eager for what was to come. While the electric gate did its noisy thing before slowly opening, he noticed a woman walk into view and start to cross the road. If he hadn't been on high alert this would have meant nothing, but he kept an eye on her as he pulled out and turned left. In his rear-view mirror he saw the woman get into the silver Ford Focus. Hardly had her door closed when the driver pulled out quickly, and followed in the same direction as Joe.

So. Game on.

Instinct told him to do nothing rash or strange, nothing that would indicate any suspicion. With luck this might be just the beginning of a complex battle of wits. As long as Drew and his people did not know that Joe knew he was under surveillance, then he had an advantage. It wasn't the only one. Time itself was on his side in a way that only he knew. If Joe Power had the patience to play the long game, frustrate and out-manoeuvre his pursuers until zero time, then victory would be his. Five hundred seconds down the road, the silver Ford was still there, staying three cars behind. Typical tactic. At Sutton Cross it disappeared right. Smart move. Now who would take over? Joe's vote went to a black Nissan which pulled out from Superquinn just a little too neatly as he passed. It was still following when Joe got to Howth village. Sure enough, once he turned to park on West Pier, the Nissan continued into the village. Who would take over now? By the time he parked and stepped out of the car there was no way of telling which of the hundred-odd strollers and shoppers on the pier might be his new tail. Not that it mattered right now. He was just going for a pleasant walk. Joe saw a little crowd gathered by the quayside and guessed that the fat old seal was around again. He joined the group. The voices were mostly East European. The only Irish-sounding person, a girl his mother would have described kindly as stout, had a tiny Indian boyfriend pinned in a romantic armlock. She used the squealing excitement of the occasion to press against him ecstatically, trapping one of his arms between them in the process. Was the tiny Indian regretting that the hot one-night stand he thought he had bagged was turning out to be far more complicated? It was obvious that stout colleen was a sticker. Poor fool. Snared. How lucky Joe felt when he saw stuff like that.

The seal's mottled head was well above the water, staring back at the starers. Its skin was not sheer glistening black but murkier greys and greens. The head was unexpectedly huge, and suggested an enormous body beneath the surface. Even though it hung around this part of the harbour all the time, unintentionally pleasing passers-by, there was nothing jovial about its manner. There was danger there. Having figured out that there was no food on offer from this ragbag of gawkers, it slid underwater. Joe always enjoyed trying to guess where the fat old seal would next appear. He chose a precise spot in the water and fixed his eye there. He began silently counting down from a hundred. The seal usually popped up within fifty seconds or so, but it might well stay under for a hundred and fifty, or more if it was in the mood. Joe couldn't ever work out any pattern or logic in the seal's movements and reappearances. They seemed entirely random. That was the pleasure of the game. Others seemed to think so too and waited, scanning the harbour. There would be a little 'Aaah!' when it was spotted again. Joe's guess turned out to be pretty good. When the fat old seal's head broke through the water again, it was close enough to be in his eyeline, slightly further out and only about twelve yards to the left of his chosen spot. Not bad at all. He had reached twenty-seven in his countdown, and also, in that short time, figured out his next move. One of Joe's mobile phones still had Trevor's number in its directory. When he returned to the safety of his apartment he would give him a call. But not before he had enjoyed his seafood lunch. He wasn't in that much of a hurry.

'Hello, yes.'
    Trevor spoke quietly. Joe could just about hear his voice

above the other sounds. A bar or a café? The clatter of plates buried deep in the mix made a café more likely.

'Hello?'

If anything his voice became slightly quieter, although a little more insistent. Joe remembered how Trevor hated raising his voice while talking on the phone in a public place. In the circumstances it was a surprise that he had answered at all.

'Trevor?'

'Yes. Trevor on Trevor's phone. Who's that?'

The impatient tone. Trevor used to sit on the leather sofa behind Joe during recording sessions, constantly on the phone to his drudges. 'And your point is?' It was not a tone he had ever used towards Joe. Until now.

'It's Joe.'

'Joe? . . . Joe? You'll have to help me here. I know quite a few Joes.'

The voice was even more coiled with tension now. He obviously regretted having picked up. He must have been expecting an urgent call back and just grabbed the phone without checking. Was he with someone? If so then he was probably doing a hand wave and throwing his eyes up. Joe heard the tiniest sigh.

'It's Joe Power, sweetheart. I know it's been a while but my voice hasn't changed that much, has it?'

The delay before the reply was not long enough to be significant. The shift in tone, however, was sharper than the Doppler Effect.

'Oh hi . . . hi . . . hi . . . wow, my God! Sorry . . . I hadn't a clue, where is my brain . . . well . . . hey, long time. How are you?'

He placed the emphasis on 'you' rather than 'are', which was always a sign of insincerity. Joe could sense fear as well, for some reason. He kept his answer very short. He wanted to listen.

'I'm fine.'

'Great, fantastic. Ahm . . .'

Joe let him flounder.

'. . . so I'm ah . . . I'm . . . right in the middle of something here, it's just a bad moment to ring . . . Listen, can I get back to you in a hour or so? We can have a proper chat. This is your number now, yeah?'

'Yes.'

'Brilliant! OK. Talk to you definitely before four. Listen, see you.'

He was gone. This was not unusual. Trevor was always very abrupt on the phone. Many times Joe had heard him click off without any form of goodbye. This would usually be followed by an exhalation of breath, the slap of the mobile tossed on leather, and a mutter.

'Fucking cunts.'

Followed immediately by a much cheerier, 'Sorry, Joe, where were we?'

They had created some shit-hot campaigns when they were both on the up together. Joe was not convinced that Trevor intended to ring him back. He checked the clock.

44212285 . . . 84 . . . 83 . . .

He would wait until 44205000. If Trevor hadn't called back by then, there was definitely a problem. Looking for something to distract him while waiting, Joe logged on to CamCandy and bought private time with Julyana. She had a Latin complexion and soft curling black hair. She wore a curiously elegant white top which covered her tits completely. Joe knew from previously that they were small, but when she brought them close to the camera, stroking the nipples to make them hard, it made him very hard. That moment would come later. He took out his dick and started to massage fairly casually as Julyana began with a dance that encouraged the punter to stare at her crotch. She fingered the tiny brown G-string as her hips swayed to a Latin pop song. Joe grew thick, semi-hard, but part of his brain was still occupied persuading himself that Trevor's reluctance to talk could mean just about anything. After all, this call had come to him out of the blue. It had been a long time. Before Paris? Julyana smiled just for him, then turned and bent over, stretching the skin of a very beautiful young ass to make it even smoother and bigger. Her finger slid along her crack and disappeared between her thighs. Joe couldn't help thinking that it shouldn't matter how sudden or inappropriate the call was – if Trevor had been pleased to hear from him, then the tone would have been different. In fact – and Joe was partly conscious that he wasn't getting any harder even though Julyana was now, with her back to camera, removing the white top – in fact the Trevor Joe used to know would have been at pains to indicate how anxious he was to talk now that contact was being established again after so long. And it was after Paris, not before. It had to be. Of course. It was because of Paris that Joe had deliberately arranged to bump into him accidentally on the street outside his office. Trevor was carrying two bags of Christmas presents and had insisted on walking quickly while searching for a cab. He had made a big deal out of not having time even for a quick coffee. His refusal had seemed hesitant and anguished, although as far as Joe was concerned the proposal had been quite casual. In the Christmas madness there was no chance of hailing a cab on the street, so Joe had stayed with him talking, as Trevor scanned up and down Baggot Street. Suddenly he had screamed, 'I should have fucking known it would have been faster to book,' and turning to Joe, smiled with embarrassment.

'Sorry, sorry, hey listen, let's have coffee, sorry, Joe.'

In Woods café he had phoned for a cab on the company account. The conversation that followed allowed Joe the opportunity to mention in a completely throwaway manner that as things turned out he hadn't needed to contact this Merriman guy after all. It was no longer relevant. He wove this information in with all sorts of stuff. At the time he had been confident that he had handled it perfectly, and saw no reason to change his mind about that now. There was one odd nagging recollection about the encounter. When the cab arrived, they both stood up to do a Christmas hug thing. Then Trevor suddenly pulled his face closer and kissed him on the cheek, whispering quite urgently, 'Come on, Joe, get yourself back to work. It'll be the best thing for you,' and more or less ran to the cab. At the time Joe had just thought it was the kind of sentimental queer stuff that Trevor was very occasionally prone to. Now he wondered had there been something else behind it? But what?

Julyana was now topless and so close to camera that her eyes dipped out of shot. She licked a finger and stroked one of her nipples, making it shiver and thicken. Even though his mind had been completely elsewhere, Joe's dick had got hard. What now? If he kept going he would come fairly soon. Or he could just stop now and stay focused on this other thing. He logged off. Had Trevor heard about Merriman's death? There might have been a mention in some Irish paper, or could it have trickled along the old gay grapevine? Would he have made a connection? That might explain his behaviour on the phone. If Trevor had some concerns or suspicions but had decided to do nothing about them, Joe's call might have scared him. This could begin some unfortunate train of events. How ironic that would be, if his own efforts to prevent something had instead caused it to happen. He needed to be so careful about that. Therefore, no jumping to conclusions or too-hasty actions. No point in killing Trevor unnecessarily. He must separate the facts from the conjectures.

Trevor was not happy to hear from him.

Even that was not strictly a fact, although Joe was content to call it so because of the disturbance he had heard in Trevor's voice. The possible reasons why he was not happy, however, were many. He must not choose any one of them until he had more facts. As for his instinct that Trevor would not ring back, there was nothing to be done about that until he had waited at least the length of time he had promised himself. Even then nothing was proven. What if he called Trevor at that point, and was told, 'Hey, I was just about to call you,' who could say that was not the case? On the other hand, if his most paranoid fears were true, then here he was hanging around doing nothing, wasting valuable time, while everything closed in on him. Joe checked the road outside, careful this time to peep from behind a curtain so as not to be seen. There was no silver Ford or black Nissan in sight. There was nothing in any way odd. No parked car with a watcher sitting inside. There was a bus stop just visible about a hundred yards down the road. Two women were waiting. One of them seemed to be constantly looking in the direction of the apartment building. Joe watched until eventually a bus came along. They both got on. Could it be that the surveillance was not constant? Unlikely. He looked at the clock.

44207947 . . . 46 . . . 45 . . .

One thing was sure, Trevor was in no hurry to call. Which, Joe quickly reminded himself, meant nothing. He lay down and did fifty sit-ups. He phoned Suppers Ready and ordered Potée Paysanne for delivery. He did fifty more sit-ups then made himself strong coffee. By the time the food arrived and he ate, darkness had fallen. The phone never rang.

6

The sun rose and fell five times before Joe gave up phoning
Trevor. Each call had made him more certain that there was
not going to be a reply. This did not stop him leaving the
same simple even-toned message over and over again; more
than twenty times. 'Hi Trevor, Joe Power here. Give me a
call, please. Ciao.' He enjoyed the thought that this routine
would become a little unnerving. It seemed so much smarter
and mentally stronger than whining or sighing, or making
impatient demands. It was a small pleasure, however, and
could not make up for the frustration of not knowing exactly
why his calls were not being returned. It wasn't just that he
needed to know, although that was becoming crucial. The
real significance was that this was the first time in many
millions of seconds that he had chosen to initiate contact
with anyone from his old life. If eventually he did sit down
and talk with Trevor, it would be the first meaningful verbal
interaction with anyone in a long time. Having decided to
do this, he was therefore not going to allow himself to be
ignored. So Joe stopped making calls only because he had
now chosen to initiate face-to-face confrontation. There
were dangers, of course. What if he ended up leading his
Garda pursuers to someone who could provide them with
important information, assuming Trevor had not already
gone to them? These 'ifs' were frustrating, along with Joe's
awareness that he had failed to gather clear evidence of
actual surveillance, which left him with no alternative but to
accept at least the possibility that he might be mistaken

about that, even though his gut continued to tell him otherwise. Drew was such a clever bastard. He would not make things easy. What Joe craved were more facts and certainties. Therefore it was worth pretty well any risk to meet with Trevor, as soon as possible, and find out exactly what was or was not going on. He thought for a long time about how, where and when to do this most effectively. It occurred to him that the Trevor he knew tended to become utterly docile if there was the slightest danger of any kind of public embarrassment. So their meeting should be somewhere crowded, and preferably with his partner present. Ideally it should not be easy for him to walk away, so a street would not be good, whereas a restaurant would be perfect. Surely Trevor and the ancient boyfriend ate out a lot?

Joe slept well and when he woke went to the gym. He had a strenuous workout and a long rest in the spa area. He drove into town. According to his parking slip it was Thursday. This was good news because it seemed logical that the traditional weekend was the best time for what he had in mind. He bought a new outfit, a muted grey slim-fit one-button suit, with complementary shirt and tie, and formal shoes. It was hard not to be impressed with the prime specimen gazing back at him in the full-length mirror. The suit emphasized just how fit he was. It made his cropped hair look even more masculine, his taut skin irresistible. But it was his eyes that were the revelation. They returned his gaze, clear, almond, and magnetically dangerous. Even the behaviour of the assistant towards him smacked less of the normal obsequiousness of such exchanges, and more of a kind of instinctive obeisance towards the superiority of his mere presence. After leaving the shop, Joe decided to stroll up Grafton Street, discovering himself curious about how the world was doing. It had been so long. He looked at people. Most were laden with purchases and dressed in hope of sunshine and heat. Was there a face that might excite any interest? Anyone even worth talking to? At the top of Grafton Street he crossed over to St Stephen's Green. There were lots more people to see there, lolling about. When he reached the little bridge over the stream he stopped, telling himself he might as well look at the ducks instead. In the last five hundred seconds he had passed by maybe a thousand people. He had had enough. Observing another thousand would not change the result. No one had interested him. Which was not the same as saying, he quickly told himself, that they were all unworthy of interest. What the experiment had proved, rather, was that he, Joe Power, had moved beyond any need or desire to engage. It was not unlikely that he might never again have what people liked to call a genuine conversation.

At that very moment he recognized a face in the crowd, moving in his direction. It was – it took him a few seconds to find the name – Rory. The last time he had heard from go-to guy was his voice on the answering machine in Smith-field. How harassed he seemed now. Just another dull, bald-ing man, looking mid-forties, pathetically swigging from a bottle of water as he walked. Then, like some kind of visual effect, Joe saw the face of his old friend re-emerge and the soft eyes seemed to pick him out from the crowd, holding his gaze as if struggling to recognize this apparition. Before it became too late, Joe turned behind some people and moved away quickly, listening carefully as he walked. To his relief he did not hear his name called above the dense soundscape of humans, ducks, trees and traffic. Perhaps Rory was still standing there, sucking on his water bottle, puzzling in his fat oppressed head just who those extraordi-nary eyes belonged to. He would tell Lisa tonight that he was sure he had spotted some celebrity in Stephen's Green, but couldn't put a name on him . . .

Joe had another very good night's sleep, and lounged around the apartment all through the day. Shortly before the sun set he showered, shaved, and put on his new clothes. He decided to bring the clock with him.

43702384 . . . 83 . . .

Hopefully he would discover in the next few thousand seconds or so if Trevor had spoken to the Gardaí. This time as he drove through the electric gates Joe noticed something he thought might be significant. A woman at the bus stop up the road took out her mobile and speed-dialled at the exact moment he appeared. Was she a scout for the rest of the surveillance team? Was she alerting the others? He turned left and drove towards her. She was still talking and seemed to turn away a little as he passed. He didn't get a good look at her face. Joe was now driving in the wrong direction, but that was fine for now. He had to be sure he was not being followed. If he was he knew it would not be the car immediately behind. It could be the next one, or more likely, the third or fourth. He slowed down just to see what would happen. The cars behind all came closer together. The silver Peugeot 206 directly behind started to overtake. The black BMW behind him came nearer. A BMW was an unlikely car to use for this kind of work, but the car behind it was a blue Ford and it didn't seem to be in any hurry, so that was a definite possibility. Joe was aware it would be dark soon and worried he might get to Trevor's house too late. He would have to do something decisive. The pedestrian lights up ahead went red. Joe, closing in on the stalled car in front, had less than five seconds to make his mind up, before he got too close. Because of the red light there was no oncoming traffic. He did a fast U-turn and took off, accelerating as quickly as possible. No other car followed. If there were pursuers then he had outsmarted them. Once back in the city centre, he took a few more sudden turns and detours, partly to set his mind at ease, partly because, he had to admit, he enjoyed the drama. He arrived outside Trevor's redbrick villa on St John's Road in Sandymount at dusk. There were cars in the drive and lights on inside, so it seemed that they were still at home. How long would he have to wait? Joe didn't mind, confident that this was not a couple who were likely to spend Friday night curled up in front of the TV. A nice formal restaurant would be ideal for his purpose. A bar or club might do. It was not long before it became clear that tonight would not be the night. It had been dark for around three thousand seconds when a car arrived and parked close by. Two men got out. They were both carrying something. They went to Trevor's house, and rang the doorbell. The ancient boyfriend opened. Joe heard squeals of greeting and saw hugs. They went inside. It seemed suspiciously like the beginning of a house-party. This was confirmed when hardly five hundred seconds later a young man came walking along the road. He stopped and looked at several entrances as if unsure which house was the right one. A passing car tooted its horn. The young man waved and followed the car to its parking spot. Two more men got out. There were embraces and laughing voices. All three went to Trevor's house. Again the ancient boyfriend did door duty. Again there were kisses and embraces and joyous shrieks as they all disappeared inside.

Joe drove away, feeling very pissed off. It did not seem like a good idea to go back to his apartment. Having evaded pursuit, he might as well stay undetected until he returned to Trevor's house at the next sunset. The Four Seasons was the nearest best option. They were very sorry but they had no rooms available. Seeing disappointment and frustration on Joe's face, the polite young man at the desk lowered his voice and, as if passing on some scandal or illegal information, suggested that if Joe wanted an excellent luxurious alternative in the area, he might try the Dylan Hotel which had just opened. Joe had never heard of it, but immediately liked the notion of holing up in a hotel so new that hardly anyone knew it existed. He got directions sotto voce from the polite young man. It was only a couple of hundred seconds' drive, hidden away off Baggot Street.

The huge candles burning in lanterns outside the main entrance, and the high camp drama of the foyer design, pleased Joe, as they increased his sense of an adventure unfolding. The belligerent newness of the hotel made him feel like it was a set created exclusively for him. The elegant girl at reception was delighted to be able to offer him the Dylan Experience Suite. She avoided showing any surprise that there was no luggage, but seemed a little put out that Joe did not want anyone to show him to his room and explain how everything worked. In the room Joe took the clock from his pocket and placed it beside the bed. He lay down, the disappointment of earlier now a little dissipated. Time would pass easily here. He would order room service shortly. He might even watch a film. Before sleeping he would shower. He lay for a long time quite still, his eyes closed. Idly, almost as an abstraction, he started to consider the idea of taking a night-walk. Would it be entirely uneventful to wander along Raglan Road, down Morehampton and back by Waterloo? Surely he would pass on his way unmolested in this part of Dublin 4, or in these times was anywhere entirely safe? It occurred to Joe that it was no more than a three-hundred-second walk from the hotel to Anabel's night club, where a bunch of rich kids had kicked another student to death not so long ago. People had been shocked at such savagery from privileged young men, although the assumption was always that their behaviour was drink-fuelled, out of character for these well-bred boys. Joe had always wondered if this was the real truth. Had even one among them known exactly what he was doing and desired it? Perhaps this incident had been the first occasion that something of the horror of his true nature had revealed itself to him? It amused Joe to imagine returning to the hotel in the small hours, after a little night-stroll, his new suit blood-soaked, the doorman bending his head politely as he entered, the smiling receptionist passing him his card-key and wishing him a peaceful night, drops of blood splashing lightly on the polished lobby floor as he waited for the lift.

His new suit would become crumpled if he remained lying on the bed fully clothed. Joe took it off and hung it carefully. Then he dialled room service and ordered seared tuna to start, fillet of beef, rare, and a bottle of Château Lynch-Bages 1995. Of course he would not go on a night-walk tonight. He had no need to. The images from Darndale still held their power and could be summoned at any time. Besides, he was holed up, lying low. He had to focus on the job in hand. He stared at his clock.

43690096 . . . 95 . . .

In about seventy-five thousand seconds.

5

The phone ringing was a surprise. It dragged Joe from a deep sleep. Not having requested a wake-up call, it was hard to think of a reason why anyone should phone. He was reluctant to pick it up. How long had it been ringing before it woke him? It stopped. His sleep had been so delicious. It was a pity it had been interrupted. Suddenly there was a hammering on the door, and anxious male calls.

'Hello, hello sir. Mr Power.'

Joe called back.

'Yes, yes.'

He got out of bed, pulled on the robe he had dropped on the floor some time last night and edged the door open. A young manager type was outside.

'I'm sorry, we were a little worried. We had phoned and there was no reply after quite a long time so we . . . well, were worried there had been . . . an accident.'

He picked up the complimentary newspaper from the carpet and offered it to Joe, who waved it away.

'No, I'm just a heavy sleeper. And your bed was so comfortable.'

'Yes . . . thank you. Well good, good –'

Joe closed the door and got back into bed. A few moments later the phone rang again. This was beginning to be annoying. He picked up.

'Mr Power?'

'Yes.'

'Good afternoon. I hope you had a pleasant night.'

'I did.'

'You may not have realized that checkout time is twelve o'clock. It is fifteen minutes after twelve now.'

So that was what all this was about. Joe didn't feel like moving.

'Oh, I'm sorry, I had no idea of the time. I'd like to book in for another night, please.'

'OK sir. But it is Saturday. I'm not sure if your suite is available. Hold on and I'll check . . . I'm sorry, sir, the suite is taken. We can offer you another room. It's smaller but with a king bed. You can leave your luggage and I'll have someone transfer it for you.'

Joe thought about this.

'Hello, sir . . . do you want to book another room?'

'When will it be ready?'

'Check-in is normally at three, sir.'

'Tell you what. I'll stay here until my new room is ready, then I'll go there. Otherwise let's just forget about it.'

'Oh. I'll ring you back in a moment, sir.'

Joe put down the phone. The calming effect of his lovely sleep and the pleasant anticipation of stalking Trevor and partner later were beginning to be spoilt. Maybe he should just check out and get some fresh air. The phone rang.

'Hello, Mr Power. Yes, we should have that room ready for you by one o'clock. If you want to stay in your room until then, that's fine.'

The disappointment of losing his special hideaway began to be offset with the prospect of another adventure waiting down the hall or up the stairs. Joe got dressed and sat by his window watching the rain. It struck him how curious it was that he could be more at ease hanging around like this for eighty thousand seconds, than stuck in an airport queue for less than three thousand seconds. Was it all about simple things like air, lighting, personal space, hating the oppressively close presence of other people? Or was it to do with lack of control, a horror of one's destiny shaped by smiling young folk distributing plastic bags?

Later, a young man came to show him to his new room. It was one flight up, smaller but just as spicily designed. Joe asked the young man to wait. He stripped off in front of him. The young man's eyes dropped to the carpet. Joe put on a complimentary bathrobe and gestured to the mound of clothes.

'Do you have an express cleaning service?'

'Yes, sir.'

'How fast?'

'Four hours, sir.'

'Very good. Is there a bag I can put them in?'

The young man found the laundry bag. A twenty euro tip was rewarded with a smile, but not, Joe noted, direct eye contact. Once alone, he phoned room service and ordered bouillabaisse, two bottles of wine, cheese, and coffee. He sat by a window again, enjoying a different view of the rain. He considered putting on some music but instead opened the window slightly so as to hear all the sounds from outside. Everything was dominated by the rain, the trickle along the gutter, the thump of drops on umbrellas, the constant swish of car wheels skimming slowly through puddles. There was no getting away from it, the power of water was very impressive. Shortly after his clothes had been returned in good time, the rain stopped and a low sun peeked out. Joe could see it from his window, which he knew meant his room faced south or south-west. The wine which he had been sipping slowly all afternoon had made him a little too mellow. He had enjoyed his waiting time almost too much.

He ordered two Singapore slings to give himself a jolt, took a quick shower, and dressed. He kept on the move while knocking back the cocktails, letting the bitter taste fill his mouth, awaken his buzz. He was ready now, even more ready than he had been the previous night. He put the clock in his jacket pocket and left. Joe flicked around music stations as he drove back to St John's Road, but nothing quite fitted his mood. It seemed like a good omen that he was able to park in more or less the same spot as before. The sun was still hanging on. Joe gave Phantom FM a go but only for a few minutes, preferring the relative silence of the late evening street. Waiting was harder now that he was so close to something happening and feeling so buzzed. At last it was night. Lights went on in Trevor's house again. Joe couldn't stop himself putting his clock on the passenger seat to watch the seconds of his life disappear, yet wishing it would go faster.

43615748 . . . 47 . . . 46 . . .

The clock read 43610367 when the taxi appeared. It slowed and stopped outside Trevor's house. The taxi-man phoned and within thirty seconds the door opened and the couple came out, looking casually elegant. This was good. If they were taking a taxi then they intended drinking. It was soon clear that they were headed for town along the coast road into Ringsend. The only real worry now was that they were going to some private do. Keeping a couple of cars between his prey and himself was easy enough because of the taxi roof sign, but it would have been much more difficult to follow an ordinary car. Joe wished he knew more about the tricks of the trade. The taxi continued up Pearse Street to Trinity College. When it swung on to Dame Street Joe figured the boys were headed for one of the gay bars on

Georges Street, but they passed that junction and continued for another hundred yards before pulling up at a Banklink machine. Joe had to think quickly. He would have to pass them. What if Trevor looked in his direction and recognized him? As he drove by he risked a little glance over. Trevor was already opening the door on the pavement side, while ancient boyfriend handed over cash. Joe quickly indicated left and swung into Palace Street. It was immediately obvious that there was nowhere to park, so he just stopped. It was a short cul-de-sac with gates into Dublin Castle at one end. He wouldn't be holding up any traffic here for the moment. In the rear-view he saw the taxi drive by. There was no sign of the couple. He would have to risk getting out to see where they had gone. Pretending to examine some problem at the rear of his car, Joe stepped out and walked backwards towards the corner, inclining his head as if trying to see underneath the boot. Dame Street was crowded; it wasn't immediately obvious where they had gone. It should be simple. They had either joined the Banklink queue, crossed the road or walked back up the way they had just come, which seemed least likely. Glancing around carefully, he spotted two shadowy figures entering the Mermaid Café on the corner across the road. They disappeared briefly then reappeared inside. They were far away but visible through the large glass frontage. The shape of the couple seemed right as they were shown to a table. This could be perfect.

It took Joe another eight hundred seconds to find parking in Christ Church car park and walk back to the restaurant. He felt intensely alive. He slowed as he passed along the front of the crowded restaurant, scanning for his boys. There they were at a window seat on the Sycamore Street side of the café. Joe was smiling as he turned back. He was going to have a little fun. He walked down Sycamore Street and stopped where the couple sat. They were too busy discussing the menu to notice him. He raised a fist and banged loudly on the glass. Both of them jolted and looked. Joe smiled and mimed a big 'Hi'. The ancient boyfriend just looked puzzled. Trevor didn't seem to recognize him immediately either, but then Joe saw something register on his face. Fear, shock, something dying inside, whatever inadequate words one might summon up, disquietude, perturbation, trepidation. Whatever it was, it was thrilling to see. Joe's glittering almond eyes met Trevor's nervous greys and he walked back round the corner. The couple would have about fifteen seconds to sort themselves. An explanatory finger pointing in their direction and a relaxed smile were enough to halt an approaching waiter. Joe's suit felt so right for the occasion. It was all working out perfectly. Trevor had turned towards him, smiling, but his forehead was already beginning to glisten. The ancient boyfriend just looked annoyed.

'Well, hello, you two.'

'Hello.'

'It's Joe. Joe Power.'

Trevor more or less howled with laughter.

'Of course we know it's you, Joe.'

'You didn't recognize me at first, though, did you? Flummoxed, right?'

'Well, yes. I mean it was just that you're looking . . . well, you're looking fabuloso.'

'Thanks. I'm glad you noticed. And let's face it, it has been a while.'

'Absolutely.'

'It must be nearly –'

Joe was so buzzed he almost said twenty million seconds, but stopped himself in time.

'– How long now? Although of course I was in touch with you lately, Trev.'

Joe chose that moment to release Trevor from his gaze. He saw a spare chair at another table and gestured to it. The people at the other table smiled and nodded. Joe took the spare chair and sat down, Trevor to his left, ancient boyfriend to his right.

'It's good here, isn't it? The fish particularly. Have you ordered yet?'

The boyfriend still hadn't spoken. He hadn't even looked at Joe. Unlike Trevor, his manner did not suggest fear, guilt or embarrassment. He spoke now.

'We were just about to. So ah . . .'

He gestured with his hands. A little upward motion as if ushering Joe out of his chair and sending him on his way. Joe focused on Trevor.

'Are you having starters? I don't have a huge amount of time but I might join you for a starter, as it's been so long and who knows when we might meet again. I'm guessing you're up to your eyes these days. Not a moment to spare.'

Joe turned away to catch the waiter's eye and allow the couple a moment to signal each other. The waiter approached.

'Am I in your way sitting here? I'd like to join my friends if that's OK.'

'I'm sure we'll manage, sir. I'll lay a place for you.'

He went to get the place settings. Joe turned back to the couple. Trevor had a nervous speech ready.

'Listen Joe, I'm – I'm – I'm sorry I hadn't a chance to get back to you, but why don't we meet up, say, Monday? After work. We'll have a pint, just you and me.'

'If you like. Sure, we'll see. Now what's good?'

Joe picked up the menu. The ancient boyfriend was clearly fit to be tied.

'What Trevor means is –'

'It's OK. Please. Let me.'

Trevor's voice was pleading. He turned squirming to Joe again.

'What I meant was, let's meet on Monday instead of you staying now. We were ah . . . hoping for . . . you know . . . a little time to ourselves tonight. You know yourself.'

'Oh, I see. Couples stuff.'

'Well, yeah. You understand.'

'That's really sweet. I mean considering you've been together for . . . well, forever it seems like.'

The waiter returned and began setting a place in front of Joe. The restaurant chatter all around sounded insanely happy pitched against the tiny thuds and clunks of glasses and cutlery being arranged at the silent table. The waiter asked if they were ready to order yet. The ancient boyfriend snapped.

'Give us another few moments.'

The waiter left. A laugh from the next table sounded coarse and aggressive. Joe figured it was time to get to the point.

'You see, I suppose this is a kind of a bird in the hand thing, Trev. You know I was puzzled and, I have to be honest now, even a little bit hurt that you never got back to me after saying you would, and then still didn't get back to me after I left twenty-three polite messages.'

Trevor blushed.

'So when I spotted you here as I was passing, it seemed like . . . well . . . a sign. You know, like it was meant to happen. That's Dublin for you. So I'm sure you under-stand that I'd be reluctant to let such a – I don't know, a serendipitous moment pass. I thought you'd feel the same. I mean OK, you guys are having a little romantic dinner for two, but come on, Jesus Christ, for fuck's sake, the pair of you have been up each other's arses for a very long time now. I mean it's not as if you have kids to distract you and you never get a second to yourselves you know. Whereas when did you and I last see each other?'

'I know, I know, Joe, and it's my fault –'

'No no no no no no. Let's not get into blame stuff, Trev. I don't believe in that. We're here now. The Gods have decreed it. Let's just go with it.'

As he poured himself some of their wine, Joe thought that ancient boyfriend's grey head might just explode. Deeply pleasurable though the feeling was, it was important not to push things any further, or he would not find out what he'd come to find out. Ancient boyfriend took charge.

'Look, I have to say I cannot understand why you are behaving like this. Isn't it obvious to you that Trevor does not want you here and I certainly don't want you here? So why are you imposing yourself? Now would you please leave?'

'Is that how you feel, Trevor?'

Trevor's head was sinking lower. His voice growing quieter.

'Ah, Joe, can't you see? What you're doing. It's just not . . . appropriate.'

'It's not really appropriate to promise to call a friend back and then ignore him. True?'

'OK, and I apologize.'

'That doesn't explain why you behaved that way.'

Silence. Joe turned to the ancient boyfriend. It was time to bring home the bacon.

'I don't suppose you know, do you?'

Trevor intervened.

'Look Joe, I've apologized. Things happen. People move

on. I appreciate that you're annoyed with me and again I'm sorry, but I mean I don't –'

'Tell you what, then. I'll leave right now if you tell me why you didn't return my calls.'

Trevor looked so terrified, Joe was suddenly convinced that he had spoken to the Gardaí. What exactly had he told them? How could he get him to admit it?

'That's fair enough, isn't it? Not only will I walk away now, you will never hear from me again, which I suspect is what you'd like. I'm just curious, Trevor. Why treat me this way?'

Trevor seemed incapable of replying. He was clearly aware that it was way past the time for faffing around, yet he could not seem to offer any form of words. Joe waited calmly, thinking, what have you told Drew, you cunt?

'Trevor doesn't like bullies. He has no time for men who hit women.'

Joe's eyes were on Trevor, so he only heard ancient boyfriend's icy words.

'Now you know why he didn't contact you. Will you go, please.'

Under Joe's stare, Trevor looked like he might have a heart attack.

'What is he talking about?'

'Trevor? Tell him, you might as well.'

'Oh, Jesus. Look, Joe. Can't you just please go?'

'He asked for it. So tell him. Or will I?'

Now Joe turned to ancient boyfriend. Asked for what? This was not what he'd come to find out. Trevor got in first.

'Will you let me handle this – Look, Joe, when I first heard about . . . what you did –'

What? Did what? Joe tried to regain control of his thoughts.

'I was shocked, but I tried not to judge. I mean . . . I knew you much better than I knew Juliet, and who ever knows what goes on in relationships anyway . . . So I suppose . . . I mean, I never commented because, well there was no point, you two were breaking up anyway . . . so whatever had happened, I mean it wasn't like it was going to happen again . . .'

Was this about the TV remote? Had Juliet told Trevor about that? Was she going round telling everyone her distorted version of what had actually taken place? Blowing it out of all proportion?

'. . . And with Eunice handling the studio end, I wasn't really seeing you anyway. Then the awful news about poor little Milo, and that was such a tragedy, and when I bumped into you Christmas Eve you looked so . . . you looked terrible, Joe . . . Anyway, I phoned Juliet and I told her about you and she said she was thinking of seeing you over the Christmas, and I said I thought that was a good idea. I encouraged her, Joe. So you know . . . like when I heard you went for her again I felt responsible. I mean for fuck's sake . . . Oh, Jesus, I can't bear this. Will you please go, Joe? Please.'

It ended as a dreary cowardly whimper and a head hung low. The ancient boyfriend, made of harder, colder stuff, continued to eyeball Joe. It was bullshit, this thing about hitting women. They hadn't been told the story properly. If he felt like it, Joe could tell them exactly what had happened. Trevor of all people should understand what it felt like to emerge into the air after an entire day in studio, spent with some actress recording an interactive talking timetable for Irish rail.

What day do you wish to travel . . . Did you say Monday

. . . Did you say Tuesday? . . . I'm sorry, I did not understand that. Could you repeat your answer please? . . . Do you wish to travel before noon or after noon? . . . Thursday, is that right? Say yes or no.

The session had recorded all the variations needed so that no customer would ever need to talk to a human being. The tone of voice had to be clean and neutral, free of impatience, anger, sarcasm, or, naturally, interest, warmth or concern. Joe had gone home that night numb. Bone-tired and brain-dead. But he certainly had not been looking for trouble. He was looking to chill. Sure, he and Juliet had been edgy for a while, but there was no way he could have guessed what was coming.

> *She is watching some French film on TV. Exactly not what he needs at this moment. He wants some late-night crap and a drink. He wants Juliet to organize him a big whiskey with a little ice, and rub his shoulders while he watches crap. So he picks up the remote and flicks to some American thing with beaches and bikinis.*
>
>   *'I was watching that. It's* Code Inconnu.*'*
>   *'Oh. Sorry, well sure you can get it out on DVD any time.'*
>   *She picks up the remote and clicks back to the film.*
>   *'Ah, Juliet come on, I'm not in the mood.'*
>   *'It just started, you might get into it.'*
>   *'I have no intention of getting into it. I just want to chill.'*
>   *He picks up the remote and changes channel again.*

Joe noticed the boys were both staring, waiting for something. They wanted him to go, but they had started this thing and now Joe couldn't stop himself thinking about what had actually happened. Most importantly, what Juliet had said. That was the really important thing. That was the bit he was prepared to bet no one had been told about in whatever twisted version of the story had got around.

After some childish tussling over the remote, Juliet takes hold of it again and says so dismissively, so spitefully:
'When exactly did you become so shallow?'
She points the remote at the TV as she speaks. Which is probably why Joe swings and knocks it out of her hand. That's all he does. Sure it makes a loud clatter on the wooden floor and the batteries fall out, but that is it.

How in that moment was he supposed to know what it would lead to, even as Juliet walked out of the room? Like was he supposed to foresee the future? He hadn't touched any part of her, he would swear that in front of a jury. He just flicked at the remote, tapped it out of her hand. Now he was having to listen to two queers, who weren't even there, tell him he hit women? It was laughable. Part of him wanted to explain his side of it, to nail whatever lie had been put about. Then he realized he didn't give a flying fuck what this pair thought, because they didn't matter any more, because now he had the real information he'd come for. It was clear from what Trevor had just told him that he had not spoken to the Gardaí about Roger Merriman. Poor old Roger had no significance for him whatsoever. The two of them looked pretty shell-shocked, waiting to see what Joe was going to do next. It was going to be tough for them to salvage any pleasure from the rest of their night.

Joe stood up.

'I'm disappointed in you, Trevor. But if that's the kind of person you think I am, then we have nothing more to say to each other.'

He liked the sound of himself saying that. He didn't glance back as he left, and once outside, he walked towards the car park, increasing speed until his walk became a trot. By the time he passed City Hall it was a dancing run. He was in the clear.

4

The clock will go below forty million today. This was Joe
Power's first thought when he woke. It had been on his mind
as he fell asleep. It was surprising how much significance this
moment was acquiring. He delayed opening his eyes for a
few moments to guess how much time was left: forty million,
five thousand and eight hundred seconds?

40008047 . . . 46 . . .

Two thousand . . . two thousand, two hundred and forty-
seven seconds out. That much less sleep. The sun was only
just rising. In the shower Joe liked how the early light
through the window turned the steam golden. The effect
lingered as he dried and buttered his body afterwards. Deliberately, he did not look at the clock on his way to the
kitchen, although he wanted to. He prepared coffee, particularly enjoying the first moment of aroma. He took it black
and stepped on to the balcony to watch the commuters inch
their way to work. The air was cold despite the sun. He
closed his eyes and listened with pleasure to the distinctive
revving and resting sounds, the frustrating stop and go of
rush hour traffic. Not for him. He stepped back in to check
the clock.

40006715 . . . 14 . . .

This heightened anticipation was puzzling. Joe did not
recall experiencing anything like it when the clock passed
sixty million or fifty million. Why now? About seventy-eight
thousand seconds ago, out of the blue it seemed, he'd had
a notion to buy a bottle of champagne so he could toast

this moment. The idea had amused him even as he dismissed it. Yet a short time later he had found himself driving into the city, to Mitchell's, and asking the gentleman there to recommend something.

'Is it for a very special occasion?'

'Of course.'

'Have you a price range in mind?'

'No. I'm entirely in your hands. I trust you completely.'

Joe smiled as he spoke, marvelling that he still had the knack of saying exactly the right thing at the appropriate moment, even though, in life, he scarcely spoke to anybody any more. Recently he had passed nearly five hundred thousand seconds without uttering a word aloud. He no longer bothered with even the most perfunctory nods to half-familiar neighbours. He managed to end pointless flirtations with baby-doll face across the hall by ignoring her attempts to get him to tell her his name, until finally she even gave up saying 'Hello.' Living without the aggravation of conversation was not difficult. Joe loved innovations like paying bills by touch-tone phone, without human interaction. Sometimes if there was an actor's voice involved instead of a computer-generated voice he would have a strange moment of recognition as he realized that he had recorded the material back in the Sounds Alive! days. Apart from the briefest flash of nostalgia, he never dwelt on the memory. Since the encounter with Trevor and friend he had sworn to focus entirely on the future, deciding not to track down Juliet and have it out with her about her insinuations. He had repeated to himself, 'Let it go. Let it go.' Even with things like old-fashioned face-to-face seduction, which still required some conversation, Joe was now practised enough to gauge within four or five exchanges if sex was on or not. Joe's recent experiences proved that even those women who

thought they wanted what they liked to call more meaningful encounters readily persuaded themselves that a fit man
who didn't say much was intriguing and probably deep.
Perhaps they foolishly thought that physical intimacy would
open the door to other kinds of intimacy. Perhaps they
didn't care.

The gentleman in Mitchell's, utterly seduced, smiled back
at Joe. He now felt responsible for making this special
occasion a success.

'Well, if you really want me to recommend . . . OK, we
recently acquired some bottles of Pommery Louise 1989. If
you like a dry champagne, how shall I put it, more yeasty
than fruity, then this really is one to savour. Especially for
a more intimate celebration.'

'Sounds perfect.'

'You sure? I think you'll be pleased.'

Joe just gestured his total faith. Delighted, the gentleman
presented the bottle. Joe nodded and smiled. This was irony.
His celebration was a parody. Joe told himself he was mock-
ing the vulgar obsession with champagne toasts on any
pretext, although forty million was quite a landmark. Why
not raise a glass to it? He thanked the man in Mitchell's in
a dignified tone that suggested he had done him a very great
service.

40006031 . . . 30 . . .

Joe wondered if the Polish cleaning woman would arrive
soon. It still puzzled him a little why he had not contacted
her to cancel her visit. It had occurred to him some time
before that it wouldn't really be appropriate if she was
present when the forty million second moment happened.
Did she always come at the same time? Joe had no idea. If
she did, was it early in the day or late? Early. Earlyish, he
thought. Then, suddenly, he had decided that this was not

worth bothering about. To phone her and cancel seemed like taking it all too seriously. What did it matter whether she was here or not? The strange thing was that now the moment was so near, he was half hoping she would arrive. Like so much about his mood since he woke up, he had no idea why he felt this way. Joe got dressed. He found himself choosing clothes he hadn't worn in a while. Autumnal shades. Comfy. Casually wealthy. Boyish. He felt like taking an energetic walk somewhere beautiful. Maybe he would head off in the car later. Drive out west in time to watch the sun go down on some wild headland. Stay overnight and then see what next. Popping open champagne now didn't seem quite enough. The moment needed some other thing to thrust him into what future remained. His mind danced about, and while no single thought seemed inspired enough, he felt confident that out of this miasma something amazing would crystallize.

40004674 . . . 73 . . .

Where was the cleaning woman? It was a little unsettling, not knowing if she was going to walk in the door or not. It occurred to Joe that he could ring her mobile and find out if she was on her way, or not coming until later, or whatever. This was tempting but felt just a bit hysterical. He had never phoned her about anything before, so that would seem a bit odd. He went out on to the roof garden and took a look down at the entrance. There was no sign of her. Joe cleared his table and wiped it down. He wished he had something attractive with which to cover it, but he owned no table linen. He found some coasters and tried to arrange them into a kind of centrepiece, but they didn't look right in any configuration. There was not enough time now to go and buy something. It was surely of no importance, yet he couldn't quell his frustration. He stared murderously at what seemed to him a bland white oak surface. Then something clicked. Fallen leaves. He laughed out loud but thought, what the hell. He would gather fallen leaves to sprinkle on the table. In the landscaped garden area at the back of the apartment building, he noticed not just leaves but flowers in bloom of remarkable range and colour. He hadn't a clue what any of them were, but they looked beautiful. His mad notion might be inspired after all. He darted about, plucking flowers until he had a large bunch. Then he gathered a little mound of red and golden leaves. Back in the apartment he dropped his loot on to the table and gave it a little shake-out. It worked, although perhaps a bit overloaded. Quite fussily now, he removed flowers and leaves, more or less one by one until the effect seemed just right. A deep green glass bowl seemed an amusing substitute for an ice bucket. He put it on one side of the table along with a cut-glass goblet. The clock was then placed right in the centre.

40002457 ... 56 ...

Joe knew that if he was being really picky he would have to concede that the sterility of white plastic and pulsing red digits did not sit well with the muted textures of autumnal flowers and leaves. It certainly wouldn't have been perfect enough for Juliet, so wasn't he the lucky one not to have to please her any more. It had gratified him hugely, when he drove past her new house one day, to see that she had painted her front door Sutcliffe green. His colour. Joe moved quickly from this line of thought. It was surely time to put the champagne on ice. He sat the bottle of Pommery Louise into the green bowl and emptied trays of ice around it. It was just deep enough to surround half the bottle. All was ready now. Should he put another glass on the table for luck? Perhaps she might arrive in time. Usually doing things like that ended up having the opposite effect. Leave it to chance. Now there was less than two thousand seconds to go. And then what? Then nothing. Forty million seconds, there it was – gone. Cheers. Mark the moment and move on into the thirties. Joe did not believe that was all. There was something going on inside him and it was not some blip. The more he thought about it the more he was sure that it was all tied up with his recent acceptance that the Gardaí were not on his trail and probably never had been. There had been no more contact from Inspector Drew, and no matter how closely Joe monitored, there was no evidence of anything going on that could be called surveillance. It was hard to accept that this might have all been in his head. How stupid would that make him feel? It was important to see the funny side too, of course. If he got to the stage where he couldn't have a laugh at his own expense, that would be pretty tragic. The important points now were that, one, the whole episode was behind him, and two, he was free to come up with better things to do with his time now.

40000999 . . . 98 . . .

Soon that number four would disappear forever. Nothing could change that. There were no buttons or switches or dials to pause or reverse. The exact figure on the night he first put the batteries in was sixty-eight million, nine hundred and forty-seven thousand, two hundred and forty-three. Now, so soon, it would be thirty-nine million. Nearly half-way there already. Joe heard a key in the door. He jumped up, smiling. The Polish cleaning woman came in.

'Hello, good to see you.'

The flicker of surprise on her face was fair enough. She had never been greeted like this before.

'I was wondering what time you were going to come.'

Now the woman looked worried.

'I'm sorry. I have no special time. I did not know that you –'

'No, no. I'm sorry. Of course you can come whenever you want. No, let me explain. I'm having a little celebration and I remembered you were coming today, so I was wondering if you were going to arrive in time for it. Look.'

The woman's eyes followed his gesture.

'Go on, take a look. You couldn't have timed it better.'

Joe went to the kitchen for another goblet. He was thrilled. When he came back the woman had taken her coat off and was standing at the table. He could tell she didn't know what to say.

'See the clock.'

She looked.

40000217 . . . 16 . . .

'It's about to reach forty million.'

'Oh.'

The woman nodded. Joe smiled and handed her the glass.

'You see what I meant about you coming just now. Another couple of hundred seconds and you would have missed it.'

'This is a special time?'

'Yes, very special. Well, you can see. It will be forty million for just one second and then it will be gone. That's why I thought it would be nice to have a little toast. You don't mind joining me?'

The woman shrugged.

'Not at all.'

Joe wished she would relax a bit, but he was aware that she had never seen him like this before.

'I know this looks a bit amateurish. But I only thought of it at the last minute.'

'No, it is nice. Like an altar.'

Joe laughed to make her feel that she had said something amusing.

'Yes, I suppose it is.'

40000165 . . . 64 . . .

'What do you think, should I wait and only pop the bottle when it reaches forty million, or should I open it now and have the drinks ready to toast?'

'I don't know. It is your celebration.'

'I'll open it. The toast is the thing.'

Joe twisted the cork carefully to avoid spillage. He motioned to the woman to raise her glass to be filled. She seemed to loosen up and allowed herself a little smile. Filling his own glass, Joe could scarcely believe how giddy was the pleasure he felt, but he went with it.

40000100 . . . 40000099 . . .

Now there was a hiatus. Both of them stared at the clock. Joe heard a tiny hesitancy in her voice.

'Always when you are waiting, time is the slowest.'

'Yes.'

'What does it mean?'

'Sorry?'

'This clock. For you. What does it mean?'

To his utter astonishment Joe felt an urge to tell her everything. He looked at her, unable to answer for a few seconds.

'It's . . . ah . . . it's a personal thing.'

'Oh. Of course, I am sorry.'

'No, no, it's OK.'

'So for the toast, do I say congratulations?'

'No. Just say "cheers". Say it in Polish.'

40000047 . . . 46 . . .

Joe wished he had left it later to pour the champagne. He should have known that took only a few seconds. This waiting might spoil the moment. He felt his face colour a little in the embarrassment and urgency of the search for the right thing to say. If the Polish cleaning woman was to put down her drink and walk away it would be all his fault. She seemed younger to him now. Not by much, more forty than forty-five say, just that bit less worn, softer. Joe wondered if she had children. She glanced from his face to the clock and back, and back again. Had she noticed his blush? If she had it seemed to make her even more relaxed. Her eyes were ice blue.

'Waiting is always pain and pleasure. We are so uncertain but we hope. You know I think this feeling is better than when the moment arrives.'

Had she really said those words or did Joe imagine it? She certainly said something. Her lips moved. Before he could formulate a reply he was distracted by the clock.

40000011 . . . 10 . . .

'Here we go, nine . . . eight . . . seven . . .'

Joe counted aloud and the woman, smiling, started to echo him quietly. They reached 'one' and stopped. In silence Joe contemplated, for that brief moment, the remarkable visual simplicity, the sense of order, the completeness of the number on the VDU.

40000000

He would never see it again, although it occurred to him that in the not so distant future he would see that image in reverse.

00000004

Literally seconds before his end. He turned to the cleaning woman and raised his glass. The ting! sounded mellow. It lingered. The sound of two people. The ting! still hung softly in the air as the cleaning woman said, '*Na zdrowie. Vivat.*' They drank. Joe grabbed the bottle and filled again and they drank again, by which time the clock was back to its jumble of diminishing numbers. The woman seemed to feel it was up to her to move things on. She put down her glass.

'OK. Thank you.'

She gestured around at the room.

'I must do my work.'

She went to the bathroom. It was as he heard water running that Joe had the big idea he had known would surface. He had wanted to mark this moment with more than just a toast. Maybe it was time for him to get away from Dublin and Ireland. Not just a holiday but for as long as he felt like it, perhaps forever, who knew? Of course there was still no way he could face the bullshit of flying, but this was the real inspiration. He would get in his car, drive to Rosslare, and ferry to France. After that, he could take himself where he liked, stay where he liked. Anywhere in Europe was his. He could go north to Scandinavia, east to Russia and on to Asia if he wanted. He could drive through Spain and take the night-boat from Algeciras to the African mainland. He could wallow in the most luxurious resorts, or court danger on a night-walk through the late streets of Marseilles or Rabat. It would all be his choice. He was grateful to his cleaning woman, who he could hear now scrubbing the toilet bowl. It flushed as he reached the bathroom door.

'I have to go out for a little while. Please do not leave until I return. OK? Do not leave.'

She looked at her watch.

'Please. I will be as fast as I can, I promise.'

It was important that she wait because the trip to the bank was especially for her. Joe intended to withdraw a thousand euro to give her as compensation for loss of wages while he was away. He would explain that he did not know exactly when he would be back, but he would contact her again as soon as he returned. This would be another surprise for her, he was full of surprises today, but hopefully she would be delighted with the free money. He wanted her to be happy, and to think well of him. Maybe he should give her more than a thousand. Yes. Why not. Maybe fifteen hundred.

3

The shaven-headed East European waved Joe into his parking spot. Passengers ahead were already opening boots and removing bags. A child consoled a mournful hound before his father closed the hatchback door. The father then consoled the child as they moved towards the lift to the upper decks. Joe sat for a little while, calm in his car, the clock beside him on the passenger seat. Everything had been very relaxed so far. This journey was going to be all right. He picked up the clock and stepped out. He opened the boot. No need to take all the luggage, but he wasn't leaving behind the bag that contained the contents of his wardrobe, each bloodied outfit in its own protective suit cover. This was so much freer than air travel. At the reception desk, standing in front of a large FÁILTE sign, a smiling pony-tailed blonde organized his cabin key. Her fluent English had the chirpy American intonation that so many East Europeans seemed to acquire. Joe liked his cabin. The bed seemed comfortable enough for a decent night's sleep and the window allowed him to hear sea and occasional bird sounds as well as the ship's hum. He lay down and placed the clock where he could gaze at his constant companion. It was soothing. When he felt the ship begin to move, he went up on deck. The sun was already very low. Ireland was not only receding into the distance, it was disappearing into darkness. Joe watched until there was nothing left to see. It was going to be a very cold night. Two crew members passed near, one of them waving a hand and doing all the talking in a low drawling cynical tone; not Polish, more like Russian. The other contributed only the occasional grunt. The mix of strange voice, sea and ship's engines blended rather beautifully. Joe was very glad that there were no yapping Irish around. His luck held even longer when he went down to the Molly Malone bar for a whiskey and soda. Both barmen were chatting to each other in what sounded like the same language as the crew members upstairs. It suited Joe perfectly. He could ignore other passengers and, so far, no one that he had to communicate with was Irish, so there had been no need for pointless banter or cheery questioning. It couldn't last of course, but so far so good. After three whiskeys Joe noticed that the ship had begun to roll more aggressively. He went back on deck to see and hear. The sky was quite starless black all round. White foam churning about far below was the only thing visible beyond the ship. The roll was slow but impressive. The wind had become biting cold. Joe closed his eyes to listen better. There was nothing gentle or soothing about this soundscape. Everything was pitched high and insistent. Tiny shards of sleet began to nip at Joe's face. The intensity of his loneliness suddenly overwhelmed him. He clutched the handrail for fear he might faint. He needed to sleep, that was all. Preferably a warm dreamless sleep, his body rolling in perfect synch with the sea.

The dream that Joe woke out of involved the smiling faces of his father and sisters. They came to him offering him drinks and food. Babs tried to take his coat for him but he held on to it. They all spoke to him, but he could not understand a word any of them was saying. As he tried to piece the whole dream together he noticed that there was no glow of red light. It was so dark in the cabin that he couldn't be sure of his position on the bed, so he squirmed round. Always at night, even when it was not directly in his eyeline, Joe was aware of the presence of the clock from the muted glow generated by the red digits. It was not anywhere he could see. Tense now, he located the outline of the cabin window so that he could orientate himself. His eyes began to pick things out. He looked to where he figured the clock should be, beside his bed. Maybe it had fallen to the ground? No, there seemed to be a circle of faintest white. All was dark besides. Joe felt around the wall above the bed for the light switch. When he flicked it on he discovered that he was already looking straight at the clock. It was where he had placed it by the bedside.

There were no numbers visible on the VDU.

Joe reached forward and grabbed it. He pulled it into the light. The VDU was as black as on the day he had first picked it up, as on the night he had removed the old batteries in order to put in his own. The clock was dead. Immediate panic made him shake it and tap the black face with his finger, knowing that would not change anything. Why had this happened while he slept? That was sickening. How long had he been asleep? When during that time had the clock died? He hadn't even looked at the clock when he came back to the cabin, so in fact, the last specific time he could remember was much earlier.

39798248 . . . 47 . . .

He had no idea how long ago that was. Joe was beginning to feel sick. Without the clock he did not know where he was in time. Part of his brain tried to assert some control over his hysteria. It had already occurred fleetingly to Joe that the explanation was probably very simple. Now the thought surfaced fully formed. The batteries had died, that was all. The simplicity of this had a calming effect immediately. It seemed the most likely solution. After all, the same batteries had been running for what? – twenty-nine million seconds. So. Yes. That seemed to be it. If that was what had happened, then was that such a problem? Those batteries could be bought anywhere once he got off the boat. That would be soon after daybreak. Joe opened the battery chamber and looked, as if expecting to see something to confirm his hope. He touched them delicately and turned them a little. This had to be the source of the problem. He closed the battery chamber again, put the clock away, and turned off the light. Panic had subsided, but it had not been replaced by calm. He would prefer if this . . . event had not happened. Hopefully he would have to endure the uncertainty for only a short while. Joe could feel something awake inside him. It was the beginning of a thought, tiny and barely breathing. He could refuse to let it surface or even name it, but he could not pretend that it was not there. Time dragged. Being alone was not good in this situation. He washed himself and dressed, keeping his eyes on the window for the first sign of light. It came as a streak glowing red along the line between sea and sky. He left the cabin straight away and went in search of breakfast and any kind of companionship. A series of broken English exchanges along with lots of eating and drinking helped him get through. Joe did not return to the cabin until the French coast came in sight. Soon it would be time to disembark. Opening the cabin door, it proved impossible not to make a wish that the clock would be all lit up and working as normal. It was not. Despite all efforts to distract himself, the tiny thought now had a name. Doubt.

When the instruction to begin disembarking came, an anxious puppy would not have pushed through to the car deck and reached his car with as much determination as Joe. The hurry was pointless, because he then had to sit waiting until his turn came to move. This seemed a hopelessly long time. Then the van in front moved off and he was waved along. The Mercedes slowly rolled out into the light, picking up speed as it went with the traffic. At the first roundabout vehicles began to disperse, and Joe found himself pulling into a lay-by. He had to stop. The plan now ought to be simple: before taking off across the continent to whatever destination took his fancy, he should sort out the clock. From where he sat he could clearly see, high in the air, the sign for a service station. It was no more than a couple of hundred yards away. He could buy the correct batteries there, and replace the dead ones. Joe sat thinking for a long long time, unable to move. All the vehicles from the ferry were long gone. The road was silent. Doubt had taken control and was paralysing him. He took out the clock and stared at it, unwilling to analyse his fear, but sure of one thing now. He would not be driving anywhere. There was nowhere he wanted to go.

Some time later cars began to pass in the other direction. They were arriving to catch the ferry back to Ireland. The sun, which had been facing Joe when he parked, was now almost behind him. He had to unstick himself somehow. The only way he could do this was to go back the way he came. Joe started the car, did a U-turn, and joined the traffic moving towards the ferry. He wasn't even sure if it would be possible to get a ticket back to Ireland so late in the day.

2

There was a large service station only a few hundred yards from the ferry port. Joe Power pulled in. Not having slept for the whole journey back, he felt bone weary. From the way he had sensed people staring at him as all the passengers had jostled down to the car deck, he figured he probably looked wretched. Pulling the rear-view mirror round, he saw an ageing man, unshaven, sweaty, red-eyed. In between vomiting and half-dozing, Joe's state of mind had tossed and rolled throughout the black slow journey to Rosslare. He had found himself incapable of leaving his windowless cabin, even though at times he'd yearned to go on deck, either to enjoy huge gulps of sea air, or to throw himself overboard. He had rewound every detail in his head over and over, always with the same result. Every piece of evidence based on his own direct experience since finding the clock, any logical analysis of the events, told him again and again that all he had to do was replace the batteries and the clock would resume as it had before. It was his destiny. If he believed in the clock before the batteries died, why suddenly stop believing? That made no sense. Joe noticed, as he got out of the Merc and moved towards the shop, that he was staggering a little. It was pretty embarrassing that a man such as he could deteriorate so rapidly. How long had it been since he ate or slept? Without the clock it was not possible to be exact, but it had been dark night when he woke to discover the dead clock, then a full day had passed, then a sleepless night on the ferry home, then it was day again. Now here he was. All in all it was probably no more than a hundred and twenty thousand seconds. If his mind was right and he hadn't put away a bottle of whiskey on the ferry in an effort to knock himself unconscious, he would not look or feel as bad as this. What depressed Joe most was how easily he had allowed himself to be consumed again with all the primitive bullshit: guilt, fear, pessimism, uncertainty. Doubt. He truly thought he had killed all that stuff stone dead long ago. It might have to be killed again. A harmless type coming out of the shop met his eye. 'What are you fucking looking at?' Joe heard himself say. The harmless type looked elsewhere and moved on quickly. Joe stared after him, hoping he would look back. It would be an excuse to go for him, prove his invincibility right here and now. The harmless type got into the car and muttered something to a tanned woman, his wife probably. She immediately glanced in Joe's direction and looked away quickly as her man hissed something at her. Joe turned and went into the shop. It didn't take long to find the correct batteries. There were two in each pack. He picked up one pack, but as he walked away, he thought, 'Think ahead, think ahead, don't be caught again in the middle of the night, don't go through this nightmare again, your time is short enough as it is.' He went back and grabbed more packs. The skinny Chinese with specs sounded slightly nervous.

'Thirty-two euro twenty cents.'

Joe picked up a pack of spearmint gum from a display case. At least he could do something about his breath. He dropped it on the counter next to the batteries. The skinny Chinese added the cost of the gum and told him the new total. Joe stared at the kid, smelling his fear, enjoying it. This felt much better already. Without explanation he turned away from the counter to the drinks fridge. He took out a bottle of chilled still water. That would be good for him too. He came back to the counter. He put the water with the other goods. The skinny Chinese added the cost of the water. His voice had lost its energy.

'Is that everything?'

Joe cocked his head slightly to one side, as if he had been lost in some other thought.

'Hmm?'

'Is that everything you want?'

Joe smiled and gestured at the goods as if to say, 'Does it look like I want anything more?' The skinny Chinese found it impossible to hold his voice at a normal pitch.

'Thirty-four euro and sixty-four cents.'

Joe gave him a fifty euro note, gathered up his purchases and walked away, ignoring calls about his change. In the car he unwrapped some gum. The taste of mint in his mouth was startling. It was soothing to sit chewing. Was his ordeal almost over? He could pop the new batteries in right now and end the uncertainty. If everything was OK, as surely it would be, it might even give him the impetus to turn around and take the ferry yet again. Why not? There would be spare time beforehand to check into some local hotel, have a wash, sleep a little, eat something and then roll back on, into the future. Was that what he really wanted to do? Why had he come back? Why hadn't he just bought the batteries in France and not put himself through all that pain? Joe acknowledged the answer: back there in that French lay-by, he had lost faith in his destiny. Now he felt like he was discovering it again, here in the forecourt of a service station in County Wexford. He could confirm that feeling in a matter of seconds. The skinny Chinese seemed to be squinting in his direction. Joe figured if he got out of his Merc and slammed the door a certain way, and walked towards the shop with a particular gait, and pushed the shop door open with a degree of force, he could make the kid shit himself. This was not the right place or mood to set the clock and his future in motion. The sea was near. The sun was shining. It would not take long to find a quiet and beautiful beach.

Joe found it comforting to listen to himself count the seconds as he drove. He whispered the numbers, one, two, three, four . . . thinking to himself that no life, not even one with his unique advantages, could avoid some lost time. Attempts at total control were fruitless. This particular hiatus had been harrowing, but it might teach him an important lesson for the future. The beach he found as he whispered seven hundred and forty-four did not seem to have a name. It stretched long and the sand was white and soft. Too soft to drive very far on to it. Joe turned off the engine and opened the window to listen. Apart from waves, wind and an occasional bird he could hear no other sound. The sun shone but it was chill. So peaceful. The perfect place. The clock was in a bag he had put on the back seat. He twisted round and took it out. Without the distraction of the bright red numbers, the object had an unsettling presence. The black rectangular face hinted at eyes behind, staring unblinkingly. It felt hard, unyielding in his hand, its smooth white roundness repelling any intimacy. Joe resisted a sudden desire to throw it away. Instead he picked up a pack of batteries. It was time. He felt a need to be more awake and alert for this. Even though the water looked choppy and black, Joe jumped from the car, stripped off, and ran full tilt into the sea. It was freezing. The splashes stung him as he pounded through low waves, and when he fell face down into the path of a breaking wave he couldn't stop himself crying out. The shock tactic worked. Back at the car he grabbed a shirt from one of his bags to dry himself. His head sizzled, his nipples became rock-hard and his dick shrivelled to a cigar butt. Joe rubbed convulsively, creating shock waves all over his body. Now had to be the time. No more delays. He reached in and grabbed the clock. He placed it on the roof of the car. He ripped open a battery pack. He turned the clock over, opened the battery chamber and removed the old batteries. He flung them towards the nearest dune. His naked body was still tingling. He would need to get some clothes on very soon. Get it over with. At the very moment he clicked the second battery into place, doubt washed over him again. Some heartsickness that wouldn't leave him erupted as, with a gambler's fatalism, he turned to see the red digits. In his head was an approximation of the number that he knew ought to be there. It was nothing like it.

5342784 . . . 83 . . . 82 . . .

He dropped the clock on the sand. What did these numbers mean? He grabbed another battery pack from the car, dropped to his knees and looked again at the clock.

5342773 . . . 72 . . .

He knocked the batteries out, and shoved in two new ones.

674590848 . . . 47 . . . 46 . . .

He took out one and replaced it with one from the first pair.

74382 . . . 81 . . .

He tried another variation.

473928809 . . . 08 . . .

And another.

573805 . . . 04 . . .

He pulled the pair of batteries out and immediately pushed the same ones back in. The numbers were entirely different.

9086723 ... 22 ... 21 ...

This frenzy lasted no more than twenty seconds. Then suddenly all Joe's energy collapsed. This fear which had been there since the clock had died ... no, not since then ... since always, really, admit it, Joe told himself, ever since he first heard the old man's story ... this fear was the case. The numbers had no meaning. Whatever function the clock had imperfectly performed in the last millennium, it had no purpose now at all. Its mechanism was basically fucked up, untrustworthy, out of its time.

The cold air was unbearable. Joe started to put some clothes on. What now? Uncertain time stretched before him. He could not recall how long it was since he last used the word he now heard himself whisper.

'Years.'

It could be so many. His father was seventy-two, or three, or four. He'd go another ten easily. His mother died at sixty-nine. Too young, but for Joe that was still thirty years away. Had he turned thirty-nine yet? He guessed not. Suddenly he needed to know exactly when it was in the world right now. He could look at his ferry ticket, that would have a date on it at least, but he had no energy left for calculations and guesswork. He just wanted to be told precisely. He switched on the radio. Someone was singing about wanting to freewheel. He didn't recognize the singer or the song.

Joe gave in to the rage. He jumped out of the car and, standing over the clock, he raised his foot and stamped on it. Again and again and again he pounded, trying to make the obdurate plastic yield, crack, lose its shape. Instead it just pushed further into the soft sand, until nothing was visible except a shiny white crown. Joe dropped to his knees and dug it up again with his hands. How might he destroy this thing? It crossed his mind to drive to Longford, hunt down the old bastard, take the clock and stuff it down his throat until it choked him. Joe heard the station break followed by the time beeps for news.

'It's one o'clock on Thursday the second of November. On the news today . . .'

He would have guessed November: the temperature, the length of days and nights, Christmas stuff he had noticed appearing in the shops. He would not go to Longford. The old man had told him a true story. Everything that followed had been his own doing; his free choice. Joe's brain registered the date. November 2nd. Milo.

The news reader was saying that analysts were predicting yet another interest rate hike before Christmas. One year ago. Today. Milo. Joe could not bear it any more. Did this mean something? That he should be here at this moment and turn on the radio at this time? Now suddenly he was thinking about his son. Now he felt the need to do something. Begin all over again? Surely not possible. Joe opened the boot, took out the bag containing the bloody contents of his wardrobe, stuffed the clock into the bag and carried it down to the water's edge. He threw it as far as he could into the sea. It sank immediately. Let someone find it, he thought, let them work out what it means. Joe returned to the car and reversed towards the road. At least he had somewhere to go. In the circumstances it seemed there was no choice.

I

Not long after three o'clock Joe parked on the road outside the cemetery. Once inside he approached cautiously. On this day there could be someone at the graveside. Juliet might be there, keeping a vigil. From the shelter of the yews he saw a new headstone, small, grey. There was no one around. He stepped into the open and came closer. A fresh spray of white flowers had been placed recently. Lilies and daisies and carnations and others Joe could not name. Juliet without question. She had such good taste. The headstone was a simple granite rectangle. He read the inscription.

OUR BEAUTIFUL BOY

MILO POWER

OCTOBER 2000–NOVEMBER 2005

Our. It was hard for Joe to believe he had been quietly included. How could that be? He didn't deserve it. Beautiful boy.

> *He is opening the front gate in Ballyphehane for Juliet. The new baby is in her arms. He sees two huge smiles at the window, but it is his mother who is first to the front door, cantering towards them, arms outstretched, breasts bobbing, her voice broad with happiness.*
>
> *'Is it him, is he here at last?'*
>
> *Juliet and Joe smile at each other as tiny Milo is seized and enfolded.*

'Isn't he beeuutiful, beeuutiful, our beeuutiful boy. And not a sound out of him. As good as gold. Well, I'll tell you one thing, Juliet, you'll have an easier time of it with this little angel than I had with that screamer there. He used to raise the roof, the scamp.'

Remembering her laughing words as he gazed at the headstone, Joe finally could resist no longer. The levees in his brain gave way and the awful sounds he had held at bay so long flooded his mind. Now he heard Juliet's cry as his fist came towards her. She raised both hands to her face and he heard the crack of his knuckles on hard plastic. The remote control flew high and he heard it clatter on the wooden floor, the batteries roll. He heard the living-room door slam and footsteps on the stairs. He heard Milo's voice and, more quietly, Juliet's. He heard his own savage breathing. He heard one set of footsteps squeak warily back down the stairs, and he knew that Milo was heavy in her arms. He heard the front door open. He heard the car door open and slam. He heard the engine start and the car drive away. He had not moved throughout it all. So the end began. The long long end with still no end in sight.

Joe turned from the grave, hearing at last the silence in the living room that had carried the whisper of a terrible truth. Many times since that night, he had made all the right sounds of apologies and begging, and fervent promises to Juliet that it would never happen again, but sitting there alone, in that moment, all he had wanted was to smash her face in. There had been no guilt or grief in Joe and never would be. It seemed he had no choice in the matter.

Tears tickled his cheeks as he sat into the Mercedes. He opened his mouth and howled and blubbed. His body heaved uncontrollably. Forlorn at last. He could not tell if this dreadful sound told of grief for his dead son and mother, or sorrow for his severed love, or self-pity for who he was and the future he could not bear to face. He slumped at the wheel, staring at the road before him. Where to go now? Anywhere he wanted, apparently. Joe Power was a free individual.